CHASING ATHENS

ATHENS

MARISSA TEJADA

ACKNOWLEDGMENTS

I would like to thank my editor, Marci Clark, line editor, Michele Hamner Moore, and book cover and book designer, Kelly Shorten. Much gratitude goes to the talented bestselling author, teacher, mentor, and friend, Kristin Harmel for all of her support, guidance, editorial skills, and advice from day one. Many thanks to author, Pauline Wiles, for her advice and excellent beta reading skills. Cole Louison for being a supportive friend along the way and way before we even knew we'd be real writers. Much thanks to Jennifer Missas McCarthy for her love of women's fiction, encouragement, friendship, and coffee talks. I'm grateful to my little sister, Melissa Tejada, for understanding me and making me laugh. I'd like to thank my parents, Gonzalo and Tripina, for their love and support. I'd also like to thank Amina Khan, Andriani Makri, Christine Umayam, Theresa Evangelista, Christine Tejada Minch, and Eva Lorane Ward for their individual support along my journey. Finally, a special thank you to Jenny Kasimatis for always caring, always listening, and for always believing in me.

ACKNOWLEDGEMENTS

CHAPTER ONE

"I AM not a criminal." With my pulse pounding and my cheeks flaming, I repeated myself slowly. Clearly, no one around me spoke English. "I swear, I'm not a criminal," I blurted out with the hope a more desperate tone would project all kinds of truth telling. I had proof. Well, sort of. "I'm really sorry."

The officer checked my ticket for a time stamp that I *would've* had if I had remembered to stick it into one of the validation machines on the bus. I hoped that the ticket at least counted for something.

"I just forgot. Don't know what I was thinking."

He tapped both sides of the clean baby blue stub which didn't have the imprint he was looking for. "No." The little word rung thick with a heavy Greek accent.

I opened my mouth in an attempt to form a sentence in his language, but not a single word of the basic Greek I had learned in the last seven months came to mind. So there I was, I couldn't speak Greek to save myself and he could only say *one* special word in English.

"No. No. No," he repeated in tune to the beat of his tapping foot.

My heart sunk. The passengers around me started to talk amongst themselves, and one even seemed to be speaking out in my defense at the relentless ticket officer. But then again, he could've been rehashing last night's soccer match as far as I knew. I made a mental note to rededicate myself to Greek class.

A woman stuffed in her window seat leaned toward me. "The crowd say that *he* should let *you*, the little foreign girl, go. They understand mistake, but..." She paused. Her blue eyes, highlighted by the bright morning sun, softened with sympathy then darted toward the direction of the ticket officer. "He say you broke law. No exception. You pay seventy euros now or give your passport so they give ticket. Your name?"

"Ava," I said in a small voice. "Ava Martin." *Ava Martin, who brainlessly walked out of her Athens apartment this morning without her wallet.* My stomach tightened in a knot at the thought of possibly going to jail for being so careless. *Ava Martin, who should've known better.*

"Miss Martin, if you cannot do what he say then go to police station."

My mind raced as fast as my pulse. I could never handle two things at once, even the little things. I just didn't realize that here in Greece, something as little as forgetting to validate a bus ticket could be considered anything other than a stupid mistake. Instead, I half expected the Greek equivalent of a SWAT team to rush in and pin me to the ground at any moment.

I perked up my shoulders and tried to smile. "I'm rushing to Greek class which already started. You know, to learn your language. Tell him how much I love Greece!"

She translated to the officer. He offered me a gaze that easily translated to, *If you know what's good for you, you'll follow me.* I sighed. *That* I understood.

My translator pursed her lips. "He says police to decide. That is his job."

I gave up and frowned as the bus sped through Athenian streets I didn't recognize. My translator tapped my arm gently. "In future you must remember. It is hard time in Greece. They make example of anyone—for anything. *Kali tichi.* Good luck."

The bus jerked to a stop, almost knocking me down. I tripped over my feet as I followed the officer down the street. I glanced around, thinking for a split second that I could run for it. The thought almost made me laugh out loud. The way things were going for me lately, I couldn't trust myself to do anything right. The bus sped off and Greeks shuffled past me, continuing on with their morning, acting like it was a normal day. Didn't they know I was being taken into custody at a Greek police station? The only police activity I had ever encountered was that first grade field trip to a New York State Highway Patrol office to record my fingerprints. I supposed my university campus safety lost and found didn't count. My stomach tightened even more thinking of the consequences. I forced myself to concentrate on the present. I couldn't think fast enough about what I should do next.

The ticket officer mumbled something to himself as I followed the loud and abrasive sound of his baggy, brown corduroy jeans brushing together as he kept his pace ahead of me. Greek ticket control officers, I had heard, didn't wear uniforms so they could surprise any offenders who attempted to ride public transport for free. He turned around to throw me a shifty look and I rolled my eyes in the other direction. He apparently thought that I was one such culprit.

I pulled out my cell phone and discretely sent a text to Eleni, one of my best—and only—friends in Athens.

HELP. I tapped the keyboard hoping not to fall over myself and hoping that the block letters would speak for themselves. As we approached the police station, sandwiched between two apartment buildings, I glanced up to check the station number on the door. I tapped out a second text that said, *POLICE STATION 85.* I had hit send just as he swung the station door open to let me in first.

Within a minute, I found myself face-to-face with the Greek police. I raised an eyebrow noticing that they also happened to be three handsome twenty-something rookies, each sporting the typical young Greek masculine look: short, dark brown hair, and scruffy, day-old facial hair. Dressed alike in crisp, navy blue uniforms and black combat boots, they stood up at the sight of us. Two had stopped swinging their *kombolois,* a string of rosary-like beads that Greek men carry around, oftentimes clicking and petting out of habit. The third police officer put down his iced coffee, which Greeks called a *frappé.*

The officers eyed me up and down as the ticket officer caught them up on the story of my transgressions. I yearned to catch some meaning, but the Greek sounded like Greek to me and too fast.

"Mr. Panos say you left your wallet at home," one officer said in perfectly clear English. Finally, there was someone who spoke my language well. Perhaps, there was hope. "You walk in Greece with no *diavatirio.*" He cleared his throat before he corrected himself. "Passport?"

"All of my ID cards were in my wallet and I was in a rush," I said, wide-eyed. "Besides, I've been living here for seven months now."

He looked unimpressed. "Name?"

"Ava Martin."

"Age?"

"Um, thirty." I bit my lip wondering why that mattered.

"Really?" He narrowed his eyes at me. In my rush out the door, I threw on a pair of baggy jeans, a green T-shirt, and my blue Converse. I looked like a college student; adults my age usually dressed to impress. But I hadn't been feeling very adult lately, to be honest. It was clear that this officer thought I was a complete liar. My hopes sank.

"Thirty, yes," I confirmed.

The officer glanced at his two co-workers who gave him a look I didn't understand. He composed himself to return his attention to me.

"Married?" he asked quite professionally.

Silly question but it was a common inquiry even among Greek strangers, so why not from a police officer?

"Yes, my husband isn't in Athens this week." I resisted the urge to add something about the fact that Greg was *never* home lately. But I had enough sense to realize that airing my marriage's dirty laundry probably wasn't going to make the situation any better.

The officer lifted his dark brows with interest. "He is a Greek?"

"No, we're both American. I'm from New York and I'm here with Greg Brown, my husband."

The officer shot me a glance, his lips pressed flat. Did he not believe me?

Then it came to me. "Oh, I never changed my last name. He's Brown and I'm Martin, but we're together... together forever," I heard myself say in a singsongy voice.

He looked at the bus officer then back at me, his face emotionless. I cupped my hands together in front of me. "He's in Rome, I think." My voice began to crack. Why did I have to say his name? Why did I have to talk about *us*? Maybe, I just gave up too much information. I talked too much sometimes. In any case, Greg and I had hardly talked, Skyped, Facebooked, Vibered, Whatsapped, or even e-mailed for the past two weeks. I wished he could've helped me but he wouldn't have even answered his phone if I had called.

"How we know you say the truth?" The officer's blunt question jolted me back to reality.

"I promise," I said, realizing that it sounded entirely lame. "I swear. I'm American, and lately, I'm behaving like a total moron." As if promising and swearing to be an American moron could be a legitimate argument. I flinched. Gosh, I'd put me in jail.

"You don't look *Amerikanida*," he said in a friendly way.

"I know." I didn't take it as an insult. Many Greeks I had met seemed to be confused with the argument that not all American women were supposed to be California blondes. My European-American mother, who didn't even know her roots, and my father of Mexican and Chinese descent made me a little bit of everything, including olive skin, dark hair, brown eyes, and Asian-Spanish characteristics. No one could ever tell what my heritage was, or everyone guessed I was one of them.

In any case, I liked to think my mix made me the real example of a modern American woman and my little own melting pot. Not like that explanation could've gotten me out of police custody.

"Please, I won't do it again." I begged, and then

managed a smile.

They seemed to soften and my hopes rose again. The rhythmic click of the marble *komboloi* beads filled the silence. All three nodded their heads. The English speaker picked up his iced coffee for a quick sip before he pointed to the other end of the room. "My lady, he decide, not we."

The bus officer nodded his head sideways with a little smirk on his face. What hopes? I had just lost.

"No," he said curtly, just like I expected he would.

Then the door swung open. I recognized the dense clicks of her heels before she rounded the corner of the room.

Eleni.

My savior.

My hopes rose again.

She walked straight past me with determination in her dark brown eyes. All four men stood up straighter as she approached. It was the way men acted around Eleni and I didn't blame them. Three words described my best girlfriend in Greece: sexy, confident, and aggressive. Even first thing in the morning. I'd hate her if I didn't love her. She was the total opposite of me.

With her chest held high, she stuck her nose up higher, gently placed her red Gucci purse on a nearby table, and turned to face the officers. Her high, stylish ponytail swished to one side as she straightened her right leg out. Her clenched fists landed on each side of her waist. She began with a firm, *"Geia sas. Endaksi, alla."*

Since I had calmed down a notch, I understood that she greeted them hello in a formal, polite manner then went on to say, "Okay, but."

I completely lost her when she began talking a mile

a minute. As their voices sliced sharply between each other, each one added their own hand movement: pinched fingers in the air, a stretched out arm, two stretched out arms, and the classic upward chin movement. I'd seen them all before. The once strange gestures were becoming quite normal to me. They made the most normal of conversations strangely interesting.

I caught something about *paidia*, or children. I narrowed my eyes. Who had kids? Then I heard her say Greg's name, followed by *haos*: Greek for *chaos*.

Suddenly, they turned back at me in unison. I shifted my gaze around the room and back at them. I had no idea what Eleni said, but their expressions had all miraculously transformed from annoyance to doe-eyed pity.

Their conversation continued, and then it became lighthearted, super friendly, almost jolly.

Eleni grabbed my hand. "Okay, Ava *mou*," she said using the characteristic possessive ending, *mou*. *Mou* meant *my*, and Greeks tacked it on as a term of endearment, a gesture of the language I always liked.

"We're free?" I whispered, but I already knew the answer.

"We wish you luck in Greece." The English-speaking police officer offered a smile.

"Yes," the ticket officer said in my direction, and then he continued in Greek addressing Eleni.

Eleni translated. "Mr. Panos said you must remember to validate your ticket and that he's only doing his job."

I flashed him a smile through gritted teeth to assure him that I would remember to do that.

Before we left, Eleni spoke to the ticket officer one last time, in English. "Why you pick on the foreigners?

Make an example of the Greeks at least."

She probably didn't want him to understand that. Thank God, I thought, I didn't need him to change his mind. He didn't. Instead, Mr. Panos's eyes lit up and a loose smile formed on his lips. Eleni had already won him over. She took my arm and we marched out together.

"Thank you, Eleni!" I collapsed into her and pulled her into a hug.

"I know, Ava *mou*. What would you do without me?" She batted her mile-long eyelashes. "I got your text and took a cab over. You can always count on me."

A bus pulled up and we hopped on. I validated my ticket. Eleni nodded with approval, a little smile playing on the corner of her lips, and we grabbed seats beside each other.

"Crazy stuff," she said rolling her eyes once the bus started moving.

I gave her a double take. Hearing her Americanisms always impressed me. Eleni's English was one the best of all the Greeks I had met. For someone who had never lived abroad, she made few mistakes and spoke with incredible ease. As a lover of second languages, I admired her for that.

"You look like a decent, nice citizen," she continued. "Plus you are a girl and obviously a foreigner. I am surprised they would take you to the police like that. I think it is a very not Greek thing to do."

"I'm dying to know what you said. I only caught a few words like children and chaos and Greg."

She leaned in closer to me. "I told them how your friends think your Greg is a cheat. You are too nice, so you cannot see the truth. Your life is a big mess so, of course, you can forget to validate your ticket." She folded her arms with satisfaction. "*Fisika*, they felt sorry for your life."

Gosh, at that moment Eleni convinced me that I should feel sorry for my life. "You told them about my marriage problems?" I wasn't surprised. It had been a hot topic of discussion between Eleni, Nikos, and me. Nikos was my other best friend in Greece, and for the last few months, we had been three peas in a pod. I used to make a lot of excuses about their conclusions, but with Greg's frequent absences and other signs, I was beginning to think my friends had stable arguments.

Not that I appreciated the police being looped in.

"I had to," she said sharply. "Oh, I also told them that it's hard because you have two baby boys and now you might be with a third child."

"Eleni!" I didn't know whether to laugh or cry.

She laughed. "It is a good story, no? Or you had to pay seventy euros. *Panagia mou.* Better to use the money for good cocktails we like!"

"Thank God that's not true," I muttered. Things had changed so much since I moved to Greece. My mind clouded over as I thought about my pathetic marriage.

"I guess I'll head home." I avoided her eyes. I looked out the window and thought of Greg again. "I missed Greek class anyway."

"I have a better idea." Eleni unzipped her purse to pull out her phone. "We can go to Nikos. I know he has a photo shoot now which will make you feel good. I will call *mana* to tell her to stay at the shop."

She speed-dialed her mom and I understood enough to know she was describing how she saved me from the *astynomia*, or police. Her relationship with her mom was much like my relationship with my mom, tight and strong. As Eleni chatted away, I calculated that it was exactly five in the morning on the east coast of the United States, too early to call my mom.

I speed-dialed Greg instead. I held my breath with the thought that he might answer; instead it went right to voice mail. I exhaled slowly and tapped the touch screen to end the call, but I found myself continuing to stare at the screen, as if it might be able to provide me with some answers.

CHAPTER TWO

"**N**IKOS did not tell me any details." Eleni's voice echoed through the marble stairwell as we made our way up one floor to Nikos's apartment. "*Mono*, we should come." As she turned to glance at me, I caught her forehead crinkling with concern.

She wanted to cheer me up with her enthusiasm, as she always tried to do. Eleni hated it when I worried about Greg. Maybe it was because she only ever heard my side of the story, which, ever since Greg and I moved for his job, hadn't been good. He never answered his phone, texted me instead of calling me back, and threw the same excuses for not coming home from his European business trips.

Seven months ago I looked forward to discovering Greece with my husband. But that wasn't how things had worked out. He traveled all the time, which left me alone and very lonely in a city I didn't know at all yet.

And then I met Eleni and Nikos. We'd only known each other for half a year, but I felt like I'd known them for my whole life. They grew up on the same block in Athens and had been inseparable since. They folded me into their little group, and I felt more at home than I ever did with Greg. I adored Nikos's sympathetic nature and admired Eleni's gusto. Add that with their senses of humor, and I had some of the best times of my life with them.

Nikos leaned against the frame of his door, smiling wide as he cradled his camera under a skinny arm. He adjusted his big blue eyeglass frames—one set from his collection—on his nose, a habit I'd gotten used to. He leaned in to offer us the typical Greek hello with cheek kisses, brushing each of our cheeks. The kisses, I learned early on, were as romantic to Europeans as sweeping the floor. I glanced at his T-shirt emblazoned with a silkscreen of Moby, which on him, looked like he was walking around wearing a T-shirt with himself on it. The famous DJ and Nikos could be long lost twin brothers. They were small-framed, bald, and wore trendy glasses. Nikos argued that Moby actually looked like *him* and that they were both "uniquely creative artists." He confessed he had gotten a date or two that way.

"Tsk-tsk. You missed it, girls." He playfully scolded us as he followed us in.

"But there are many cars parked outside." Eleni scanned the room. Several television trucks were parked outside, so we'd assumed that we would walk into some sort of action in progress. Nikos was always at the center of some sort of adventure.

He placed his camera down carefully on a table. "Some journalists are still here." He waved toward the other end of the flat. "It was last minute; I thought it wasn't going to happen."

"What was the commotion about?" I asked. Nikos specialized in model shoots but recent business included some of Greece's famous actors. After studying and working in London, he returned to Athens. His reputation had climbed high since and he hadn't even turned thirty.

He whispered loudly, *"Greek Idol."* He left his mouth open and spread out his arms waiting for Eleni and me to react with a roar.

"Ahhh!" We screamed in unison, clasped our hands together, and then jumped up and down. We may have been born on different continents but we both grew up to love cheesy reality singing shows.

Eleni fanned herself with one hand; two of her bangles clinked. "Marcos Giannetos?" She waved her other hand in a small circle at her side, a Greek hand gesture that indicated something was either really good or really bad. In this case, the gesture was something really good because she was in love with the *Idol* finalist.

Nikos waved us over to his Mac. "Take a look."

A bustle of people walked through the room. The makeup artist he worked with, Penelope, led the remaining journalists out. Her leather flats shuffled on the tile as she headed toward us.

"It was super, *telia.*" She planted two-cheek kisses on me and Eleni. Her bleached blonde hair was cut stylishly close to her neck and spiked as if she had just gotten out of bed. "I cannot believe you did not come. Let's order lunch and discuss!"

An hour later, we finished our delivery order of *souvlakia,* my favorite Greek fast food of grilled meat and toasted pita bread while Penelope and Nikos spilled the details about the shoot. Eleni and I hung on every description, including what the contestants wore.

That was when Eleni dove into the wardrobe rack left behind by the stylist. She dug through it, examining each designer piece with her keen eye. If a piece of clothing met her approval, she held it up against her body or mine.

"Here she starts." Nikos practically grew up around Eleni's obsession with designer labels.

Penelope turned to me. "You sew, don't you?"

I nodded, flattered that she remembered. "A bit."

"You make something good lately?"

"I'm thinking about it." I sewed clothing for fun. I never considered myself a designer. Instead, I followed patterns I found simple and beautiful, and then added my touch with unique buttons or fabric.

"Not my style." Eleni plunked a hanger with a pink mini skirt back on the rod. She grew up around haute couture since her family shop sold clothing by high-end Greek designers including Michalis Aslanis, Makis Tselios, and Sophia Kokosalaki. That kind of upbringing had made her picky.

"*Dokimase afto*, try it, try it." She held up a black Versace dress in front of me.

I look down at my T-shirt. "Oh, yeah, I can definitely fill that out," I said sarcastically.

Eleni rolled her eyes. "You make nice clothes, but you don't know anything about them sometimes. All the women have the breasts to show."

I giggled as she stuck out her chest. She pushed the dress toward me again. I grabbed the hanger, knowing I'd prove her wrong.

"Go on, Ava," Penelope coaxed. "Try it!"

I slipped behind the wardrobe rack and pulled the dress over my head. She was *right*. It felt right. I looked in the mirror to confirm it. I then slid on a pair of Manolo Blahnik platform leopard heels that had been discarded near the door and teetered out from behind the rack. The shoes were a size too large and about four inches higher than anything I usually wore, but I straightened my posture and jokingly pursed my lips in an attempt to be more model-like.

"So, ladies and gentleman. What do you think?"

"*Koukla*," exclaimed Eleni, a high compliment from her which meant *doll*. She clasped her hands together. Meanwhile, Eleni had put on a dark green, low-cut, Prada catsuit which suited her curvy body. She changed into super high, black, open toe booties.

"It makes you feel good, no?" She adjusted her cleavage, taking in her reflection. She pulled down her ponytail to shake out her long, brown hair.

"Now the most important accessory," Penelope said. She grabbed her makeup case and started to touch up Eleni's face—not that she needed much help. Eleni rarely left the confines of her apartment without applying her full makeup routine. I would need much more attention. I tried to put makeup on every day, but I was always unsure if it really made a big improvement. As Penelope thoughtfully looked over my face, she seemed to map out a well-thought out beauty plan.

"You have nice features. Exotic." She sponged some creamy beige foundation on my forehead.

"Really?" Exotic, to me, was the nice way of saying *you stick out*, which wasn't necessarily a good thing. Growing up no one could tell what ethnicity I was, and at one time or another during my childhood, I'd been called every ethnic slur in the book. I wished at one point I could look just like my mother who looked "normal," like the other kids in my hometown in Upstate New York. But as I got older, I came to like my differences.

Penelope took a step back and shook her head. "Of course. Your cheeks and your eyes. Where are you from again?"

That was the question I got almost every time I met someone. Living in Greece and "not looking Greek" meant I got a lot more attention. I found that Greeks, from taxi drivers to the little old lady sitting next to me at the bus station, loved to know personal details. If I replied with the truth, that I was from New York, I got weird looks. Nikos explained the questions were because Greece was pretty much still a place where foreigners stuck out combined with the fact Greek people had a natural curiosity. Eleni explained it was because her people were too nosy, and where I came from was nobody's damn business—unless it was a good-looking guy asking. For me, getting questioned by Athenians was always a good opportunity to practice my Greek.

"I have a white-American mom and aChinese-Mexican dad but I was born in New York." I managed in Greek, *"O babas mou einai misos kinezos ke misos meksikanos ke e mama mou einai amerikanida. Yennethika stin Nea Yorki."*

"Your Greek is good." Penelope sounded impressed as she brushed blush onto my cheeks. "I am from Athens, not interesting." She tucked a strand of my long, brown hair behind my ear. But I disagreed. Like many beautiful Greek girls, she had a strongly defined facial structure and big, expressive eyes.

"Look up." She dabbed a mascara wand on my skimpy lashes. "I finish."

I blinked my sticky lashes together to find Nikos snapping photos. I turned to the mirror to check. I *did* look good.

"Ava *mou*," breathed Eleni. "The colors are perfect."

"Greg will see you and be very happy." Penelope admired her work.

With the mention of Greg, the corners of my mouth dropped to form an instantly painful frown.

Nikos looked up from his camera, pushing his eyeglasses back on his nose. "He's not coming back from Rome is he?"

Eleni shooed Nikos's comment by waving her hand. "She's had a rough morning, Niko. Eleni said Nikos's name in the Greek vocative tense. "*Asto*...leave it." Penelope glanced between the three of us. She realized she had said something wrong, but she didn't know what.

"We're just having issues now." I managed a weak smile but I felt my cheeks warm up as my eyes started to moisten. Maybe it was the gobs of mascara, but maybe it was all of my emotions pent up inside of me that needed to be released for once. "Things will get better," I said in a small voice, realizing how unconvincing I sounded.

"I remember you were married before you came here?" Penelope asked with concern. "Greg is from the same place like you?"

I shook my head, wondering why it mattered. Then again, maybe she wanted to try to cheer me up by getting me to talk about things. "Greg's from outside New York City. I'm from a town called Ithaca, in Upstate New York, about a six-hour drive north of New York City."

"Ithaca, ahh, where Odysseus is from. It is my favorite story and," her voice brightened, "where my name is coming from. But I think you know the story since you are from a place called Ithaca."

"My Ithaca isn't a charming little island like the Greek Ithaca is, but it's nice in its own way. It's a simple college town. It was all I knew before I came to Athens."

Greg and I had been happy there. He was busy finishing his MBA, and I had my marketing job at Ithaca State University and my mom nearby anytime I needed her. I focused my view on the oversized Manolos dangling off my feet which were about to drop to the floor.

"Things suddenly changed when we came," I said softly.

"*Den einai efkolo.* Marriage can be hard, Ava *mou.* I had a divorce last year," Penelope admitted nonchalantly.

"Oh." I squeaked with surprise at how causally she mentioned the *d-word.* She was twenty-eight, just a year younger than Nikos and Eleni. My opinion was that divorce was a very big deal because it totally changed lives. Just like my parents' divorce changed my family. It definitely changed me.

"I didn't know. I'm sorry,"

"*Ohi.* No. I'm better off." She placed her hand on my shoulder. "I do not think anyone gets married with the belief it will go bad. If you try to save it, that is enough."

"I don't know. Eleni and Nikos think he's a cheater. Maybe I didn't know him long enough before we got married." My mother had said this more than once, but I had always ignored her.

"Maybe. Maybe not," Eleni chimed in. "We can find out what is wrong. Hopefully, it is just a *malaka* stage."

Malaka was one of the first words I learned because I heard it so often. Two close guy friends can casually address each other, *malaka,* but it was also an insult tossed around by both men and women with passion. Loosely, it meant *jerk.* In fact, with how often Eleni used the word in reference to Greg, it was like Eleni didn't know his real name.

"You know we met him only once so we can't really judge him properly," Nikos said. Sadly, Nikos was right; my husband had met my Greek friends just once in all this time. "If he stands you up this time, what are you going to do?"

I slouched down in my seat. "I'll have a talk with him soon."

"We came to forget about the *malaka*. We want Ava to relax, right?" Eleni urged, and then nudged Nikos on the shoulder.

Nikos's face softened. "Of course. You know what you mean to me, Ava *mou*."

"Yeah? What do I mean?" I raised an eyebrow at him shooting him a playful glance.

"Just like Eleni, you're like my little sister. You both need someone to watch after you in this crazy ancient city, so it might as well be me."

My heart softened. As an only child, that meant a lot to me. I never knew what it was like to have a brother, but Nikos was my idea of a great one. A caring, sincere, and fun person I could trust.

And to think that the reason I met him and Eleni was because he spotted me in a bar, assumed I was Brazilian, and tried to flirt a bit with the only Portuguese phrase he knew, which, oddly, turned out to mean, *How's it going, baby kitten?* By the time Eleni and I had finished laughing at him, the three of us had already become friends. There had never been a spark between Nikos and either of us, which I was grateful for. Chemistry, I'd realized, only made things more complicated.

"Oh, Niko *mou*." Eleni grinned. "You must promise you will always tell us about your funny pickup lines which never work."

"Funny!" He feigned a look of shock. "Well, they worked to bring Ava into our life, didn't they?"

Eleni winked at me. "We cannot argue with that."

Eleni and I left Nikos's flat together as the sun set.

"Don't forget about your bus ticket now, Ava *mou*." She gave me a wink before she cheek kissed me goodbye, and hopped on her bus.

The crisp evening air caressed my skin as the bus pulled away. Another fresh Mediterranean spring night was sweeping over the city and I decided it would do me good to walk home and enjoy it. Although I changed back into my jeans and my T-shirt after our little impromptu fashion show, my makeup was still fresh on my face. I felt prettier and more confident, which gave me a little bounce in my step. As I walked, my mind trailed off to what Penelope said about her divorce.

Even if Greg and I had problems, I simply couldn't imagine getting a divorce. Greg and I loved each other. I followed him to Greece and committed to follow him wherever his career would take him. I quit a job I loved at Ithaca State. I left my only family in this world—my mother. I gave up everything. There I was in the middle of Athens, wondering if I should have come in the first place.

But divorce? Never. Greg would return the next day as he promised, and we would have a serious talk. We had to find each other again.

I turned onto my street, Ploutarhou Street, and glanced up at the sign in Greek, understanding how to read it. I walked slowly pass the little Kolonaki Café, named after the upmarket district. I glanced at a couple sipping their Greek coffees that filled tiny round coffee cups. I peeked inside the Despina Bakery window, which had changed the display since I remembered last. A set of almond pastries and chocolate tarts caught my attention. I resisted the urge to go in and headed farther up the sidewalk past a few rows of apartments, which, like my own, offered a sweeping view of Greece's capital, a sprawling metropolis.

To get to my flat I needed to dodge the orange trees planted right in the center of each sidewalk tile. I used to wonder why some idiot planted them there after I almost crash-landed my face into them several times. But as I breathed in the delicious scent of the orange blossoms, I thought maybe their placement was part of a good plan. I closed my eyes. The strong essence of the orange trees melded with the faint smell of melted milk chocolate and bitter coffee from the shops I had just passed. A mix of voices speaking Greek danced around me as people took their evening strolls. The din of traffic on the main city road, Vasilissis Sofias Avenue, continued beating its nightly rhythm even farther off in the distance behind me.

When I opened my eyes, I truly believed everything would be fine. I smiled. After all, I was living in a great city, I was learning a new language, and I was lucky to make some great Athenian friends. I convinced myself that my husband would come around. He was just in a bad place. These kinds of things would come and go in a marriage.

As I unlocked my door, still awash in the magic of the orange blossoms, I found the lights were on.

"Greg?" I called out.

He sat on the couch with his back to me, home a whole day early. My heart leapt for a second, thinking he must have come home to apologize, to try to make things right with me, to start over.

But then he got up at the sound of my voice and walked toward the window without turning around. The sun had set and the city's streetlights twinkled brightly in soft brilliant shades of orange and yellow. He clutched the beige curtain with one hand, the other hidden in the pocket of his gray trousers.

"Ava." He stared out the window. A strange nervousness laced in his voice stood out and made my skin prickle in the most uncomfortable way. "I have something to tell you."

CHAPTER THREE

I STEPPED toward Greg, every inch of my body tensing up. "What are you doing home?" The urge to kiss him on the lips struck me, like nothing was ever wrong with us in the first place. But there was always this invisible field around him, and I couldn't bring myself to step any closer.

He turned to face me, his eyes searched mine. He ran his right hand through his thick, wavy brown hair a few times.

I stepped forward, stretched out my hand, and reached for him. "Greg."

He pulled away from my small advance and turned to look out the window.

"Ava, I need..."

"Yes?"

"You have to know something." He bent his head down.

"Look at me," I said softly.

Our gazes met again but he squinted and looked off to the side a moment after. The freckles on his face were more noticeable, his cheeks flushed. His lips turned down. Even upset, he looked so handsome.

"I'm glad you're home," I confessed. "I missed you."

I expected him to tell me that he missed me too, but instead, he blurted out, "It's over."

"What's over?" I asked in a stiff whisper.

"We are. I want a divorce." He said it so fast. Too sure.

My legs buckled beneath me. In one moment, my body took on a new sense of weight propelling me to drop down onto the soft leather of our couch.

"Divorce," I repeated the awful word meekly—if I were to have said it louder that would have made it true.

"It's just that," he hesitated. "Obviously, we're both unhappy."

A tear slid down my face. He exposed the truth, a truth I couldn't come to terms with but was being forced to face. I wanted to wail and scream and hit the wall, but like any other frustrations I have had in my life, I funneled it back down inside me.

"I don't think I'm cut out for marriage," he said flatly.

I swallowed the words. "What did I do wrong?"

"Nothing." He sat next to me. The city lights blurred behind my watery vision.

"I thought you would make me a good man, a husband, even a father. I love you for what you brought out in me. But you need to realize that my life runs on traveling and being away."

"But I followed you here. I left my family, my home, my country, my job." My voice trembled and I hated how pathetic I sounded. I left big things, the things that matter to someone, things that some women might never have given up for a man. I looked up at him. "I left everything."

"I love you for that." His voice was soft. "This has nothing to do with you."

"What do you mean?"

He got up and stood to face the wall. He ran his hand through his hair again. "I cheated on you. There, I said it."

My throat closed up. I squeezed my eyes shut, the way I used to when I was a little girl and wanted bad things to disappear, but like then nothing felt better right away. I wondered if it was worse that I had the idea he had cheated on me and denied it, or that he just admitted it.

"Something clicked in me the day we got married," he explained. "I had more second thoughts when we came here, but I didn't want to hurt you. I thought I would shake it off. I know that being married isn't what I want. At least I know that now."

"So everything you promised me was a lie," I said flatly.

"No, it wasn't a lie. I wanted us to be happy together. But you know my past. You know that being on the road is what drives me."

I fell in love with Greg in my hometown where he was living during his one-year break to earn his MBA at Ithaca State. I fell in love with his stories about being abroad, his confidence, and his intelligence. He had backpacked all the way across both South America and Asia, and he yearned for more. I told myself that he'd settle down one day, and when he surprised me by proposing, I thought that day had come.

I still couldn't look at him. "I thought you'd changed."

"I did change. But I'm changing again."

"You don't even want to talk about it?"

"There's nothing to talk about, Ava. I made up my mind months ago."

Months ago? I gulped. My hands clenched up. I met his gaze again. "Do you know how many times in the last few months I've tried to call you? You didn't even bother to call back most of the time. We could have talked, Greg."

"It wouldn't have helped."

With those words I couldn't help but think that everyone but me expected this day would come. My mother expressed her fears just after Greg and I started dating. Eleni and Nikos always thought he couldn't possibly be faithful.

"You can go back to your mother in Ithaca. It's where you belong, with her. Not me. I shouldn't have brought you here, but we can fix that."

My heart felt disposable. I was easy to get rid of. I was a total failure.

"But you *did* bring me here," I said in a small voice.

As if he didn't hear me he said, "I have to leave tonight for London. They've been meaning to move me there. The market isn't what they thought it would be with this damned economic crisis. But that'll make it easier, Ava, because I'll be gone, and you'll have all the time you need to move out." He paced in front of the bookcase and paused to pick up our honeymoon photo taken in Mykonos. In the photo we looked so happy, both tanned and smiling.

Greg had arranged the surprise honeymoon trip. Instead of heading to our Athens flat, which was where I thought we were going, we transferred planes to land in the famous Cycladic Island. The ten-hour flight from New York City to Athens was long enough for me since I had never flown internationally, but when Greg told me about his plan upon our arrival at the Athens airport, I was immediately renewed with energy. I had never heard of Mykonos before, but it was a place Greg, who was so well traveled, always wanted to go.

As soon as we got there, I understood why. Greg loved the crazy nightlife, bars, and all the international tourists that loved it too. I loved the gorgeous sunsets, charming whitewashed architecture, and perfect pristine beaches. We ate fried calamari and fresh grilled fish right by the sea, our toes just feet away from the clean, clear blue water. It was my first taste of Greece, and in the process of discovering it I'd fallen in love with Greg even more. Apparently, the experience didn't do the same for him.

"I'll pay for the divorce." He placed the frame back on the bookcase. "You won't have to worry about any of it. Tony, my buddy from grad school, can help us. There's not much for us to split anyhow, so it will be easy." He stood there with both hands in his pockets.

I couldn't think about his buddy, Tony the lawyer, and making things easy.

"I'll be in touch with details," he continued when I didn't respond. "I want to just make this separation as easy as possible. My company will pay for all of the moving expenses. Since we're still technically married, you're allowed to stay in Athens on my account. You should take your time moving out. I know this is tough, but we should both just move on."

It was like he was having a normal conversation, not like he was dumping me. *How cruel.* I clenched my teeth.

"So Intraspec knew you wanted a divorce from me before I did?" I tried to wrap my head around his confession. "And you knew you were moving to London for months and never told me?" I shook my head realizing I had absolutely no say in anything.

"I had your best intentions in mind. I've known for a while that our marriage would be over. I just wanted to make it as easy on you as I could." As I opened my mouth to respond, he disappeared from the room and returned rolling in his carry-on and a suitcase.

"Wait, you're leaving *now*?"

He was literally walking out on me after a twenty-minute conversation that completely shattered everything I believed in.

"My flight is at ten." He appeared anxious, like he needed to leave—fast. "I think the sooner we both get on with our lives, the better. Denise from human resources will call you." He pulled aside the luggage to step toward me. He bent down and grabbed my arms, forcing me to look at him face-to-face. "You are a beautiful person, and I always wanted the best for you. I still do. I don't want you to hate me forever." It sounded like something from a how-to-leave-your-wife script.

He gripped me tight. I tried to pull away, but couldn't leave his hold. "Just leave. Please."

"I don't regret our marriage, only that I hurt you. I'm sorry for this. Know that, please." He loosened his hold on me and finally let go.

I slipped off my Converse and gathered my knees to my chest to hug them tight. I lowered my head onto my knees and my hair fell around me. The luggage wheels scraped the hardwood floors, then the door closed.

Like that, he was out of my life.

I uncurled my body and stared out the window. My heart pounded faster and my skin burned. The tears poured out as I realized I was a step behind catching my breath. I needed to cool down. Fast.

I ran to the bathroom, swiped the faucet handle hastily and splashed cold water on my face. It wasn't enough.

I stepped into the shower, fully clothed, turned on the cold water, aching to feel it run down my body. My tears continued to spill under the strong spray. I backed myself up against the white tiled wall, closed my eyes, and held my hands to my aching chest. It was so simple for him to tell me he didn't want me, to walk out on me. It was so easy for him to not love me.

Why couldn't I see it? Why couldn't I see what everyone else could?

Then again, I had seen it, hadn't I?

I don't know how much time passed when I finally felt the need to peel off my jeans and T-shirt. I cocooned myself into my oversized, terry cloth robe. I headed straight for the fridge and uncorked a bottle of wine. I landed back onto the sofa, bottle in hand, and took gulp after gulp. The cool bitter taste of the Greek white wine felt like nectar from the gods.

I picked up the cordless phone and began to dial my mom's cell phone, but I hung up before I hit the last number. I didn't want to break the news to her right away, not when I knew I'd burst into tears before I got a word out. She'd worry too much, and I couldn't handle her pain and disappointment along with mine. So, I called Eleni instead.

"Ava *mou*." She sounded occupied but her voice rang with her usual enthusiasm. "I just got off the phone with Nikos and we're invited somewhere fun!"

I croaked out, "I need you guys."

"Ava, are you crying?" Her tone was suddenly warm, concerned.

"Greg left me." It sounded so wrong.

"We are coming now." She hung up.

CHAPTER FOUR

I OPENED the door and found two sets of familiar brown eyes, wide open with unfamiliar disbelief.

"What happened?" Nikos pushed his glasses and shook his head.

"I—I don't know. He was here when I got home. His suitcase was already packed. And he just..." I couldn't finish my sentence.

"I'm so sorry." Eleni's eyes drooped in pity.

Nikos took me by my right shoulder in a hug. Eleni embraced my other side as they both guided me back into the living room.

As we passed the hall mirror, I glimpsed at my reflection and understood their shocked expressions. My hair was soaked and tangled from my fully clothed shower, and huge black and blue makeup smudges streaked like war paint under my eyes made me look like a character out of a weird horror movie.

Nikos settled on the couch next to me. "Tell us everything."

Eleni stomped out of my bathroom with cosmetic wipes and an angry scowl. "Where is the *malaka* now?" She jabbed a wipe on my cheek.

"He's been transferred to London and he's gone for good. It happened so fast. You were both right all along."

Nikos placed his hand on my shoulder. "I'm sorry, I wish I wasn't."

Eleni seethed, "I want to kick him in the nuts." She hastily pulled out another wipe from the box. "Kick *ta archidia tou* hard with my steel toe boots. He would not have been able to crawl out of this flat!"

I sniffled. "He said he wasn't ready for a commitment. He says he won't change and he knows he won't because..." I stopped. "Because he cheated on me."

"*Malaka*," Eleni spit out. She flipped up her hand in disgust and dropped a dirty makeup wipe. She sped walked around the couch and muttered a variety of Greek curses waving her hands about.

Nikos let out a big sigh. "It doesn't feel like it now, but it is better he's gone."

"Well, Greg would agree with you." I said with a sarcastic ring to my voice. "He says I deserve to be home with my mother instead."

After I described the rest of my brief encounter with Greg, we sat in silence as my tears started to subside. A long talk was what I needed to feel human again.

Nikos broke the lull first. "You know you can count on us."

"This means you will return back?" Eleni asked. "To America?" Her eyes shone with concern.

"I suppose." I shrugged my shoulders. "What else would I do?"

Nikos patted my knee lightly. "You have time to think about what you want."

"I feel like my world has been turned upside down. He just left me here in the middle of Athens...alone." I cried out again. I collapsed my head forward into my hands.

"You are not alone," Eleni said. She rubbed my back slowly. "You have us."

That was true. "You know what I mean." I looked up at them again. "I don't even want to stay in this apartment but I have to pack and..." I shook my head, my heart was pounding. "I don't want to think about it. Tell me something else to keep my mind off this," I pleaded.

Eleni and Nikos looked at each other then back at me. At that moment, I wanted to be anywhere else but the apartment I shared with Greg.

"Although we think you tend to ignore your problems," Nikos began with a glance at Eleni, "we understand why."

"Here is my idea. We can go to *bouzoukia*," Eleni suggested. "When you called, I was about to call you to get dressed. Maybe it will make you feel better."

I certainly didn't want to dwell on Greg. Plus, we had been talking about going to a *bouzoukia*, a type of live Greek music club, for weeks. They were dressed for it. Eleni wore a black miniskirt, tight blue tank top, and pearls. Nikos wore gray striped Diesel jeans and a white, long-sleeved button up shirt.

"But we don't have to go there," Eleni continued. "We want to do what makes you feel better." Her voice perked up. "Maybe you want to eat some pizzas? Your favorite?"

I immediately calculated that pizza would make me cry more. It was Greg's favorite too. I slouched back down on the couch.

"A *bouzoukia* might keep your mind off things, at least until tomorrow," Nikos said.

"We're definitely going out." I made my decision. "But I can't even think of getting dressed and you guys look so nice."

Eleni pulled me up. "*Ela,*" she commanded. We headed to my closet and she pulled out a black sleeveless dress and black heels. She brushed the knots out of my slightly damp hair and clipped it into a loose bun.

"I think I had enough makeup for today," I told her. "It will probably run anyway."

She looked me over then gave me a kiss on the cheek. "You are a doll no matter what."

A half hour later, we arrived in front of a *bouzoukia* in the southern part of the city. It was about half past midnight, around the time when Greeks started to head out to clubs. It was our friend Alexandra's name day. Name days, or saint days, could often be impromptu last-minute get togethers. In Greece, it was the one day a year all the people with the same name celebrate. It was like having another birthday and not uncommon for the celebrant to pay for a night out on the town with friends.

We wished Alexandra *xronia polla*. Relief washed over me since she didn't seem to notice anything was wrong with me.

Eleni linked her arm to my arm. "How are you?" She nudged me and raised her brows. "Do you prefer a double *tzeese*, bacon pizza? It is not too late." Her Greek accent actually stood out, pronouncing her ch's like a tz which I thought was adorable and made me smile.

"Definitely not." I wrinkled my nose at her.

Nikos linked my other arm to his. "Do you want to stay?"

I breathed in the cool night air. "Let's go in. I need a drink." Alcohol would help me forget everything as it had in the past.

Music pulsated from the central stage of the large, dark, arena like club which was lined with long tables that extended out from a raised stage. Each chair was occupied. Cigarette smoke, laughter, and loud Greek beats swirled around the *bouzoukia*. A singer with a tight black bodysuit crooned into her microphone in front of a live band. She stamped her stiletto pumps in time to the music, crushing a bright carpet of red and pink flowers that covered the stage floor.

I followed our group to our reserved table. Friends of friends I didn't know laughed openly and glasses clinked. A tall woman dressed in a tight black mini-dress passed by me, she had a bored smile on her face as she held up a pancake-like stack of trays filled with bright pink and orange carnations. There were several sexy flower sellers circling the room.

"Men buy loads of trays at ten euros each to impress girls," Eleni explained to me. "The flowers are thrown over her head while she dances by her table. People buy the flowers to throw them on stage or to throw at each other. It's also what we do instead of throwing plates on the floor. It's a sign of appreciation, like clapping." She winked at me.

I laughed at the charming insanity of it. Colorful bullets of petals landed on the stage from all directions. Some even knocked the musicians smack on the head, but they didn't seem to mind. Several groups linked arms and danced around their table in a large circle. Two women from the next table climbed up on the tabletop. Avoiding the bottles and drinks at their heels, they swung their hips and raised their arms in seductive yet traditional movements to the oriental beat of the music.

In a quick moment, someone placed a shot in front of me and broke my concentration, tapping my glass and saying *xronia polla* for Alexandra. I swallowed the alcohol fast.

My toes numbed as the whiskey took hold. When I drank, my problems seemed to melt away. I hated that I liked the feeling because it reminded me of my father, the alcoholic. When I started drinking in college, my mom had a long talk with me about how I could turn out like him. I usually managed to control myself with that in mind, but some moments called for desperate measures. Nothing ever beat a glass of wine, a beer—or two—or four. I'd already decided that I deserved to get drunk.

Instead of helping me feel better, the alcohol made me think about my family and my past. My father left my mother and me twenty years ago, and I hadn't heard from him since. Not a single letter. Not a single phone call. I should have been over it, but a lifetime had gone by, and the same thing was happening to me again. A man I loved—Greg this time—walked right out of my life like I didn't matter.

I had considered looking up my dad up when I visited college friends from downstate. He had cousins on Long Island and I had always wondered if he'd moved there, but I brushed it off each time. The simple fact that he didn't want me and he had walked away so easily made me sure I didn't want to see him. My mother had always told me it wasn't my fault. Greg brought everything back to the surface.

"*Geia*. Hi." Someone yelled close to my ear and the blurry memory of my father disappeared once again. A tall, dark-haired man took the seat next to me, attempting to be heard above the noise. "I am Konstantinos, friend of Alexandra. You are the American, no?" His day-old facial stubble framed a big smile. "You can call me Gus. More?" He lifted the bottle of whiskey.

I politely offered a weak grin. "Sure." I reached out my glass.

"You are from the Big Apple?" he asked with a handsome grin.

"My husband just left me," I blurted out instead of answering the question. I clapped my hand over my mouth, surprised at myself.

Gus's genuine smile disappeared. "Oh. I am sorry."

"I trusted him," I continued, raising my voice, feeling the liquor kick in more. I liked talking to Gus. "He's the only man I ever trusted after my father left me. But you know what? I was right! You can't trust anyone. Men, anyways!"

"Oh." His brown eyes darted to the left, then right.

"Where's *your* dad?" I turned my chair closer to him.

"He stay in Sparta."

I narrowed my eyes at him. "Never abandoned you, huh, Gus, has he?"

Gus's gaze continued to shift around the room at my questioning. "Um, no."

"My father left me. I thought I was a good kid. But then I thought I was a good wife too. Guess not!" I punched him in the arm feeling my body shake from letting loose and laughing out loud. I took a big gulp of my whiskey.

My attention turned across the table where Eleni

had migrated to greet more friends. She caught my gaze, glanced at Gus, then looked back at me to give me a thumbs up. It was a classic Eleni sign to show her approval that Gus was handsome. She had no idea I was being a dating kamikaze.

"So, um, you did not say your name?" Gus asked.

He was still trying. That was cute.

"Ava."

"*Harika poly*, nice to meet you. Um, I am sorry about your dad and your husband. I really am."

I grabbed the whiskey bottle and poured myself another shot. I tilted my head back and swallowed, loving the way it burned my throat. It was nice to feel something that didn't have to do with betrayal. Whiskey never pulled any tricks; its burn was always upfront and immediate. I looked around, feeling woozy, wobbly, and lightheaded. I turned to say something else to my new friend, Gus, but he'd left me. "Who needs you?" I mumbled to the air. "Gus is a dumb name."

I quietly soaked in all the energy and commotion that surrounded me. A few trays of flowers tumbled in a pile in front of me. My friends reached in to grab flowers to throw somewhere in the club. The familiarity and unfamiliarity of the Greek language traveled in one ear and out the other, the colored lights glared in all directions, and the loud beat to the music meshed in a strange mosaic that filled a new emptiness inside of me.

I was all alone. My husband left me. He didn't want me. Just like my dad didn't want me. It was happening again.

I took another shot. I felt deeply lost, my body becoming more and more numb without any more strength to cry.

CHAPTER FIVE

"**B**EYONCÉ loves my apples!"

Beyoncé? I turned over in my bed. Something was wrong with that statement. Maybe it was because it rang out from a deep, gruff voice laced with a thick Greek accent. I opened one eye slowly, and then promptly snapped it shut again as the morning sunlight caught my vision.

"*Freska prasina ahladia!*" hollered another man.

Fresh green pears.

Fresh air might have been nice for a hangover but my wide-open bedroom window also invited the distinctive bustle of the local farmer's market on the street below, right into my flat. Every week, dozens of vendors lined up on a designated street in each district of Athens to sell the freshest in-season fruits and vegetables straight from the countryside. Sometimes, the sellers came up with what they thought were clever lines to coax someone to their stall. Since Kolonaki had a fair share of foreigners, it was no surprise Beyoncé made the cut. I'd heard that Madonna and even Prince William and Kate Middleton had invested in village honey, fresh calamari, and Kalamata olives. I was understandably skeptical of all these claims.

"*Aggourakia!*" whelped another brusque voice.

Little cucumbers.

It was way too early for any of that. In one swift

motion, I hurled myself up with the intention of shutting the window, but the full effects of the night before hit me the second my feet touched the floor.

"Ahh," I moaned. The back of my head pounded and pulsated. I looked down to see my strapless black dress. I reeked of cigarette smoke and whiskey. The room spun around me. Everything began to flood back.

End of marriage. Impromptu *bouzoukia* night. Greg. Gone.

"Kales times! Pantzaria!"

Cheap beets.

With all my strength, I rose up and managed to drag my body five steps more to shut the window properly once and for all. The street noises of steel shopping carts scraping the sidewalk, the bargaining between vendors and shoppers, and the continuous whooping sounded like it all had been swiped into an empty tin can. I swiftly slid the blackout curtains shut. I desperately wanted to sleep off the headache and the slimy, disgusting feeling I had.

I drew back under my covers, nestled myself in my sheets, and closed my eyes.

I had almost fallen back asleep when the phone, located conveniently next to my head, rang. Was it ever that loud? *"No,"* I moaned.

It rang yet again, jarring my head. I picked it up, anything to make it stop.

"Hello." I winced at the awful sound of my voice.

"Ms. Ava Martin?" a woman with a strong British accent asked.

I swallowed hard to try to sound more presentable. "Yes. Who is this please?"

"It's Denise Williams from Intraspec's human

resources department in London. I'm sorry if I woke you. Shall I ring back?"

Denise from human resources. Someone who knew about my divorce before I did. I hated her immediately.

I cleared my throat as much as possible. "No, I'm fine. Go on," I answered but clearing my voice only made it more scratchy and dense.

"Greg asked me to call you as soon as possible to help you arrange your move back to Ithaca, New York. He says you'll want to leave in the next few days."

"I guess so," I said. Why was Greg telling Denise Williams what I want? The incessant panging in my head made me want to get off the phone, but I imagined how that would play out: Denise Williams calling Greg to report on how rude his soon-to-be-ex-wife was. I was determined to be polite.

"The good news is that you need to vacate the company flat by the end of the month anyway. Our moving company can take care of all the packing, so you don't have to worry about a thing."

They were giving me less than two weeks to leave Athens.

"Right," I mumbled as I tried to register it all.

"I have two flight options for April thirtieth. Just tell me your preference. This is all in an e-mail so you can be assured the wheels are in motion," Denise said ever-so pleasantly.

Maybe Denise worked on the same floor as Greg. Maybe Greg was standing nearby. Maybe she knew Greg dumped me and left me here all alone in the middle of Greece or maybe she was the other woman. What did Denise look like anyway?

"Thank you," was all I could muster.

"Call me if you need anything. My direct line is in that e-mail. Have a great day!" The line went dead.

As if on cue, my head pulsated with even more pressure. I dropped the phone. The muffled noises from farmer's market hung in the background.

Everything was going so fast. I just wanted to lie in bed and not deal with any of it. I pulled the covers over my head and cocooned the stale stink of the club smoke around me. Even with my pounding headache, I somehow managed to doze off.

Late in the afternoon, I woke up a bit more sober facing the fact that I needed to break the news to my mom. After I drank a gallon of water and took a long shower, I sat in the living room with the phone in hand. I looked down at it then locked it back in its cradle. I needed to distract myself first.

I opened my closet doors to think about my packing plan. I shuffled through my hangers and pulled out my favorite outfits, the ones I'd made.

My sewing started when I couldn't find anything I liked at the local mall in my home town. My bottom and thighs were my two worst enemies. If only I'd inherited my mom's slender shape, my whole body would be in proportion. As a teenager I used to envy how she never had to squeeze into her pants or skirts or hide in them. Lopsided weight issues were never an issue for her.

When I was sixteen, my mom had had enough of my crying fits about my body. She suggested I try to make some of my own clothes. She only knew the basics of how to sew and hem, but I caught on quickly to what she taught me and liked the challenge. We found an old dress form and from then on, I took it a step further and started to actually make clothes.

My creations weren't anything couture but they fit me, and once in a while I got compliments on them. I usually found fun or sophisticated buttons or gorgeous fabrics. When I would finally complete something that fit properly, especially after I had toiled over it for so long, slipping it on was a wonderful high. Over the past few years, I managed to finish a handful of dresses and skirts. Each one had taken me anywhere from a few weeks to a few months to complete after making mistakes on the seam or cut. Each piece had one thing in common; it was finished during a milestone in my life.

I held up my full-skirted yellow dress in the sunlight, then the simple black v-neck dress I wore to my college graduation, followed by the red-collared dress I made to celebrate earning my master's. I tugged one of my favorite scarves off my scarf hanger. I sewed it together out of a series of leftover material so it would complement many of my dresses. My bright white cotton sleeveless dress was my latest piece, one I finished before I moved to Greece. I wore it for the first time during my honeymoon in Mykonos. It made the cut as one of my favorites because it magically shed five pounds off all the right parts of my body. I hoped it wasn't just a fluke, but rather evidence that I was getting more skilled with my designs.

I grouped all of my creations together at one end in my closet. I closed the doors then patted my old dress form which sat next to it. Since moving to Greece, I hadn't used her to help me create anything exceptional. I had only made a few scarves, which I had given away as presents. I opened the cloth-lined wicker box next to the dress form and pulled out a few pieces of patterned linen and paper-thin cotton fabrics I had planned to make into unique scarves. Clearly, I had been on a creative dry spell.

I would have to start my next piece in Ithaca. I would be back on New York State soil in two weeks. Exactly where my mom was, whom I needed to call, I reminded myself.

I jumped up and down a few times feeling my stomach turn. "Just do it," I said out loud. I pressed number two to speed-dial her. The number tones raced in my ear with the notion that I would feel like even more of a failure saying what I had to say, but I had no choice.

"Hello, honey!" As usual, Mom answered the phone brightly.

My heart ached for her. I missed her. Plates clanked in the background, and I imagined she was standing at the kitchen sink, washing the dishes. A morning talk show blared in the background.

"Mom, hi." My voice trembled. I couldn't control myself.

I heard the tap stop. "What's wrong?"

I managed, "I'm coming home in a week."

"That's great, honey. I'm glad Greg finally got his crazy schedule in order." She sounded relieved.

"It's not *we*. Actually, I'm going home for good. Greg." I stopped at his name.

"Oh, dear." Her breath blew loudly into the receiver. I pictured her placing her hand over her mouth.

I exhaled. "He wants a divorce."

"Ava," she gasped.

To my surprise, Mom didn't interrupt me at all during my hour long vent.

"It's good you're coming back." She sounded positive. "The college will hire you back. You can move in with me and you'll have your old life back. It's the only solution."

"I guess so." I shrugged. Something in me felt like I was taking a giant step backwards.

"I'll take good care of you. We both know Ithaca is where you belong."

"I was a bit worried to tell you all this."

"Honestly, you know how I feel about Greg, so I'm not surprised. I just didn't think he would do this so suddenly and leave you all alone in a foreign country. I know I've always told you that Greg isn't right for you, but for your happiness, I always hoped I was wrong."

"I had no say. It's like he didn't love me." I gulped as a hot wave of disappointment burned inside of me.

"He did in his own way," my mother assured me. "Remember, he cheated on you. That's a hard thing to forgive someone for. The positive thing is that he can't control your future." Her voice was firm. "You'll be back here soon and realize you just weren't suited for each other. You'll see that in time."

"Will I?" I thought Greg and I suited each other just fine. Even after what happened, I still believed we did in many ways—sadly enough.

"You're like me, too hopeful and too trusting. People like Greg take and don't give back."

"Maybe it was all the stress from work," I countered. "Maybe I could've been there more."

"How could you say that? You couldn't have done

anything more. We'll let him have his life back. You are young, beautiful, and have everything going for you."

I wanted to say that I didn't feel young and beautiful, and I totally felt like I had wasted the last year of my life. That coupled with the fact I was an unwanted woman who also happened to be unemployed in a foreign country. Instead I said, "I miss you." I held back tears thinking of my new standing in life.

"I can't wait to see you, honey," she said reassuringly. "You'll move on once you are back where you belong."

After we had said our goodbyes, I looked around the living room. The next step was the move and separating everything, my stuff and Greg's stuff. Our boxes would go to two different cities to be unpacked. Their contents would be the stuff of two different lives once again.

I scanned the bookshelf and my stack of my Greek language workbooks. I flipped open my grammar text and began to read and make out words that months earlier were complete gibberish.

Inspired by my mixed heritage, I took Spanish and Chinese in college and loved every minute of it. But speaking Greek proved more fun for me since because I actually practiced with native Greek speakers. I frowned thinking that part of my life would be over soon.

Greg's impressive collection of travel books sat neatly on the next few shelves. I ran my finger horizontally down their spines. He had about a hundred packed with every travel detail about exotic places like Hong Kong, Kenya, Puerto Rico, and Venezuela. Then, on the next shelf sat the only three travel books I ever bought in my life: Athens, Greece, and The Greek Islands. I thumbed through my Greek Islands book and randomly opened to a page brightly printed in the colors of some Greek turquoise sea. I never imagined I would ever visit Greece. I would soon return to New York and I could tell everyone that I had lived in Greece. I liked that.

I closed the book and placed it carefully back on the shelf, back where it belonged. I then picked up our honeymoon photo that Greg glanced at last night. His big smile in the photo made my stomach turn. I placed it face down on the shelf as a deep, hollow feeling washed over me.

CHAPTER SIX

"*K*amaki," I said in Greek. "Going fishing for girls."

My Greek teacher, Mr. Stavros, nodded. "Yes, this is the meaning of *kamaki*." He drew a trident on the plastic white board, tapping the speared fork he just drew. With other colored board markers he drew a comical looking fisherman, waves, and a few fish.

"That man is fisherman and girls are fish?" Anna, a student from Romania, asked with a laugh.

"Remember *kamaki* is for foreign girls like us," Jessica, a Canadian, said in a cautious tone. She stressed the "like us" part by pointing her finger out at the females in the room. "Don't be fooled, single ladies. That's how I met my husband."

A small ripple of laughter echoed through the room. Besides the intricacies of pronunciation and verb tenses, my Greek class always found the more important words to know as foreigners.

"We are finished, *kyries ke kyrie*, or ladies and a gentleman." Mr. Stavros glanced at the only other man in the room. Giovanni, a thirty-something dark haired Italian, moved to Greece for his Greek girlfriend.

Most of the class consisted of foreigners from all over the world who, like me, had followed their husbands or boyfriends to Greece. A lot of our conversational topics had to do with family and relationships, so we learned a lot about each other's personal lives.

I approached Mr. Stavros after class. I had told him earlier in the week my last day was coming up sooner than I would've liked. When he asked why, I said my husband and I missed America. It wasn't so easy to admit my marriage was over, it seemed. I didn't need Mr. Stavros or anyone else to feel sorry for me.

I offered my hand. "I learned a lot. *Harika poly.*"

"*Harika.* It was a pleasure. *Kali tyhi ke elpizo va sinehiseis ta ellinika sou. Eisai poly kali,*" he said slowly.

"You're telling me good luck and to continue because I'm good!" I bounced in place out of self-satisfaction.

"*Bravo!*" he responded with a smile.

I walked out with my books in tow and was immediately greeted by the warm Mediterranean midday sun. I turned down the cramped city sidewalk and just as I pulled out my cell phone to check for messages, two familiar voices called my name.

I turned and saw Nikos and Eleni. A moment later, they were greeting me with the standard two-cheek kisses. I expected to see them later for dinner. As part of our plan to help me get through the week, the three of us had figured out a full schedule to keep me distracted. A lot of it had to do with coffee by day and cocktails by night. The schedule helped me to create final memories of my Athenian life and to forget that I would be leaving—alone. I hadn't spoken to Greg at all. He hadn't reached out, and there was no way I was going to make the first move.

"Since it's your last day, we plan to spend as much of it as we can with you," Nikos explained.

"Best idea ever. Where are we off to?" I asked.

"Monastiraki," Eleni said. "I am hungry."

We filed behind each other as we walked through Kolonaki's streets, unable to fit shoulder to shoulder on the uneven and narrow sidewalks. At some points we had to step down in the street to let others pass. We neared the butter-colored exterior of the neoclassical building, the University of Athens Law School, which appeared anew with more graffiti from the last time I passed it. On the entrance gates, a fresh colorful layer of political posters were plastered over several layers of older ones. The courtyard in front enabled us to have a normal walking talking conversation. Just as we delved into the details of last night's jazz performance, Nikos pulled my arm as he broke into a run across the street—a street that usually bustled with traffic.

"Faster," he ordered.

He quickened his step, which quickened my pulse. Panic rose up in my chest.

I hurried to catch up, Eleni close behind. I couldn't understand what the panic was about but I trusted Nikos who didn't reply after I asked what happened. He had his camera out instead.

When we made it to the other side of the road, I took in the sight of an organized sea of protesters lined in the distance, forming a tight barrier of bodies that blocked the street. The front row clutched a white cloth banner that fluttered in time with the slow motion of their march. Bright red, capital-lettered Greek words, beyond my vocabulary, scrawled across it spoke for any gaps in silence. A booming voice coming from a megaphone made up for the rest.

"What's going on?" I asked watching other pedestrians rush across the street.

"I forgot, today is the *apergia*. Strike day," Eleni

moaned as she shuffled carefully in her espadrilles.

I had discovered that employee strikes were a part of European, especially Greek, life. In general, Athenians were usually informed about strike days in advance, since many times the striking employees worked for major infrastructure. In an effort to show displeasure with the current system, public transportation stopped, airports had delays, and public hospitals worked with skeleton staffing. Eleni and Nikos told me, even with all of the efforts, nothing changed. Politicians and rich Greeks got away with white-collar crimes and tax evasion continued. Even small businesses and taxi drivers avoided giving receipts since that would lead to more taxes on their part.

With Nikos and Eleni next to me, I wasn't concerned at all until a strange, painful sting burned my eyes.

Eleni blinked her eyes rapidly. "Tear gas. Do not touch them, Ava," she warned.

I had seen the effects of tear gas on television and from photos Nikos took in the past. When police threw a tear gas bomb to disperse a crowd, the protestors were usually forced to calm down although many came prepared with gas masks. I pulled up the collar to my T-shirt to try to cover my face as the invisible attack on my senses continued to hit me with strange, painful stings.

Nikos looked over his shoulder as we hurried around a corner. "That's the worst of it." He unzipped his backpack and secured his camera inside.

"We can relax now," Eleni confirmed.

I lowered my T-shirt collar, almost afraid to breathe in again. My eyes were still stinging. "I never thought I'd find myself in that."

"*Gamoto*," Eleni swore. "I need to join one."

"Really?" I asked. She didn't seem to be the protest-marching type. Her designer jeans would not fare well in what I had been witnessing on the news. I would be too worried knowing she'd put herself in the middle of it all on purpose. "That's kind of not your style."

"I feel desperate sometimes. Athens is *hamos*. How you say? A mess." Eleni threw her outstretched fingers in the air, a Greek hand gesture to emphasize a point being made. "My family business is not what it was."

"I didn't know it was so bad."

"I never said to you but, yes." She turned to me. "I am mad like many Greeks. That is why I want to be there too," she said wryly. "I must borrow clothes from Nikos. He has the riot gear."

"Really?" I asked, my voice ringing with disbelief.

"We all have to do our part," Nikos answered. "Half of our friends are unemployed or not getting paid their wages. We're a country of educated people with no work. Things need to change."

"I hope they do," I said. I didn't know how to comfort them. It was true. Some of our friends who lost their jobs had been on the hunt for employment for months even years.

Nikos asked with a ring of sarcasm, "Aren't you going to miss Athens?

"It's never boring." I grinned.

"You are right. It is sad some days, but I think that is why you cannot leave," Eleni added. "It doesn't mean the world will stop moving or friends will stop caring."

We ducked into Monastiraki, one of my favorite areas of the city. Along with Thesseion, Plaka, and Psiri, it is considered Old Athens. In Old Athens, neoclassical buildings crumbled next to a few that continued to stand grandly. Especially on its residential streets, small balconies protected by intricate, iron wrought designs surrounded classic French doors. Clay, burnt-orange roof tiles contrasted smoothly against the chipped white or yellow painted exteriors. Exploring this part of town guaranteed a run-in with tiny historical Byzantine churches as well as two-thousand-year-old archeological ruins. Worn and polished, off-white and dignified marble stands grandly at the Theatre of Dionysus, Ancient Agora, and the Tower of the Winds. They were just a few remnants of a glorious ancient past as modern Athens continued to transform around them.

Within a short distance, perched on its central hill and higher than anything built in Athens since, remained the Acropolis. The ancient citadel sat on high rocks and at the center of it, the symmetrically picturesque columns of the grand Parthenon stood—a gorgeous marble temple. It was the first archeological site I ever visited and it impressed me more than I imagined. Something about the ancient nature of the site, to know great people with great minds once stood there, intrigued me. The complete three-hundred-sixty-degree view of one of the world's oldest cities, a sea of ancient marble juxtaposed among modern concrete stretched out to the sea in its own haphazard pattern.

The name *Monastiraki* referred to the little monastery in the neighborhood's main square, but it was also known for a maze of small pedestrian streets full of small mom and pop shops known as the Athens Flea Market. The shops were filled with a variety of items: heirloom jewelry, Greek military clothing, handmade leather sandals, trendy clothes, religious items, cheap souvenirs, and antiques of every kind. Tourists and Greeks weaved in and out of them. Meanwhile, shop workers stood by the pedestrian path trying to woo foreigners with several foreign languages. It was hard to believe business as usual continued on, when just less a mile away, tear gas bombs were being thrown at Greek workers.

As I passed the window of an antiques shop, something caught my attention in front of an old sewing machine—a set of cream-colored oversized buttons. All six of them created a unique set, something I envisioned to add to my next sewing project. I checked them out immediately and waved to Nikos and Eleni to join. Instead, they both headed to another corner of the shop just as a man approached me with a thick black mustache, his hands held behind his back. A *koumbouloi* clicked out of sight as he asked, "Can I help you?" in a thick Greek accent.

"I would like to see those buttons, please."

He picked them up carefully and handed them to me. "Ah, yes, beautiful and very old. Very old. You are *frrrom*, Miss?" He asked rolling his r's.

"New York," I mumbled as I continued to admire them piled up in my open palm.

"I love New York," he said.

Based on how smooth they were I imagined they must be ivory. My smile widened a mile; what a surge of good fortune.

"How much?" I asked.

"Forrr you...a New Yorrrker..." He paused and raised a brow. "Special prrrice...five euros each piece."

"Thirty euros for six buttons?" The price was too

high, I thought, but I was in love with them, proved by my stomach fluttering slightly. That rare feeling made me think they might be worth it.

"What is thirty euros?" Eleni asked from behind me, breaking my train of thought.

"These gorgeous buttons." I held them out in my open palm to show her. "He said they're antique."

Eleni picked one up and then looked at the shopkeeper with a sweet smile. She started to speak in Greek. I knew the motions for *pazaria* or bargaining. *Pazaria* was another one of Eleni's many Greek talents. As an American, bargaining was a big mystery to me. I promised myself I'd learn a few tricks from Eleni and even Nikos. They both looked at it as a fun game, as well as a simple survival skill one must learn to avoid getting cheated in Greece.

After a few minutes of raised voices and a little back and forth, Eleni turned to me. "He will give to you for ten euros. They are ivory, by the way."

I dug in my purse to hand over the cash before the man had a chance to change his mind. As we left the store, Nikos checked out my prized purchase. "I can't wait to see what you do with these."

"That *malaka* shopkeeper tried to cheat our Ava," Eleni huffed. "One good thing is that you will be far away from these cheater, stealer shopkeepers and taxi drivers. I cannot even start with the taxi drivers!"

Eleni despised all kinds of social and political injustice. Nikos and I exchanged glances as we listened to her ramble on, her hands waving about as she spoke. I smiled thinking how Nikos and Eleni had looked after me from day one. I wondered if I would ever find friends like them again. I wondered how much I'd miss them and if they'd remember me.

They took the lead down Monastiraki's cobbled streets. I couldn't help but think that the next day, I would be on a plane back to New York. No more cobbled streets, Greek lessons, long coffee talks, or tear gas attacks. No more cheating shopkeepers and taxi drivers or being asked incessantly where I was from or where I was *really* from.

I thought I'd be ready to go, but it just felt like my heart was continuing to prepare for something I didn't want to do.

My memories of Athens hardly had to do with Greg because he was never home. I shook my head at the thought of him and how he was already moving on with his life without any real feelings for me, or for the devastation he'd caused. I managed to escape my thoughts of self-pity hearing Eleni tell me to watch my feet as we headed up narrow cobblestone steps.

Just as we turned, a wide concrete staircase spread out before us. On each broad step, little wooden tables were situated on each side of the pedestrian walkway. They belonged to six different cafés and traditional informal Greek restaurants called *tavernas*.

Eleni swung around before I made it through the door.

"*Perimene*. Wait," she commanded in Greek and English.

Suddenly, Nikos covered my eyes with his hands. A tingle ran through me. I adored surprises. With my vision blocked, I couldn't help but think about Greg and for one foolish second I imagined that he had flown back from London to give me a romantic apology in a little Greek café. I wasn't going on the next plane back to New York. Nikos and Eleni were in on it too. Just as quickly, I decided I was mildly insane.

"*Prosekse!* Careful where you step," Nikos warned behind me.

"*Tora!*" Eleni exclaimed.

Nikos released his hands just as a chorus of voices sang in unison.

"Surprise!" Three dozen different faces familiar from various parts of my Greek life surrounded me. Greek friends, ex-pat friends, and American friends milled around a few tables where helium balloons floated.

I had come to know so many people from so many countries, all of different ages, professions and backgrounds, and all of whom had a special tie to Greece. Suddenly, I was struggling not to cry.

Eleni squeezed my arm. "We hope you like it."

"So much," I responded, furiously blinking back tears.

"We wanted to give you an special send off and let you know how much we all love you," Nikos said, adjusting his big, black frames.

A warm feeling ran through me as I beamed at my friends, "*Efharisto poly!* Thank you!"

Two hours later Nikos, Eleni, and I sat in the café's back corner after our guests had all gone back to their day. Eleni sorted through my pile of gifts. She flipped through a hardcover picture book of the Greek islands. "I want a party too," she pouted.

I placed a few presents in a large bag. "It was weird telling people about Greg. Now everyone knows the story. You know, I think I'm getting more comfortable saying I'm getting divorced."

"Everyone knows you will be okay," Eleni said.

"I think I heard *malaka* in fifteen different accents," I recalled with a small smile. It felt nice to be vindicated by everyone's horrified expressions.

Nikos unzipped his backpack and fumbled inside to pull out a little blue bag.

"This is from us," Eleni said proudly, straightening up in her chair.

"Really?" I took the little bag and pulled out a tiny white box. Inside a shining, silver necklace with a pendant sat inside, a small but twinkling blue circle. I had seen it before: a *mati* or the evil eye. My gift was a fancier version, studded with an array of dark blue crystals, light blue crystals, and what appeared to be a black onyx stone in the center. I found it absolutely beautiful and, more importantly, meaningful.

According to Greek tradition, people hung the *mati* around the home, office, or in the car. It was usually made of blue glass or plastic, with a light blue eye in it. Women wore tiny *mati* charms on jewelry, especially on bracelets and necklaces. Babies were given little trinkets with them attached. It was also found on key chains or as ornaments in every tourist shop. The idea of the evil eye was to fend off bad karma or jealousy from people because it watched over its wearer. Eleni was a firm believer and usually wore a stylish black leather cuff bracelet with a tiny silver eye strung onto one of its braids. I immediately tried to hook it around my neck. "I've always wanted one. I love it. Even more so because it's from you guys."

Eleni clasped it. "You could not leave without a *mati*."

"This will watch over you in America," Nikos chimed in, "since we won't be there."

Eleni reached into her tote bag. "There's one more thing."

"Wait, this is enough," I protested as I patted the *mati* pendant hanging from my neck. "It's amazing."

"No, we just found it in the antiques shop. You did not see how Nikos did *pazaria*." She handed me a small plastic bag.

"We both saw it at the same time and, well, for some reason it reminded us of you," Nikos added.

I pulled out a small copper colored box half the size of my palm. Across the top were a few tiny *mati* eyes and in the center, a carved design of a monarch butterfly. My eyes watered, but not because it was so pretty.

Eleni reached over to take a closer look. "You like? To put the necklace inside!"

"Oh, Ava, are you okay?" Nikos interrupted.

"How did you guys know? You can't know." I looked at Eleni then Nikos, searching for an answer.

"What do you mean? It's an old, beautiful box." Eleni smiled. "It's so pretty inside, orange."

I swallowed hard. "It's about my father."

They glanced at each other and then at me after I mentioned my father. I took the box from Eleni and held it tight. They knew he was a sore subject that I didn't bring up easily.

Eleni started softly, "We know your father left when you were—"

"—ten," finished Nikos.

I nodded. "My dad's father, my grandfather, José Martin, was from this town, Patzcuaro. I've never been, but my dad said his favorite memory as a kid was taking time off from school to see the butterflies. He doesn't believe in much, but, well," I paused. "It was a big deal because Patzcuaro is known for the millions of butterflies that migrate from America to Mexico every winter. They kind of did the opposite of what my grandfather did when he immigrated to New York. " I managed to smile a bit thinking of the old photos. "Dad used to show me all of these pictures of him and his grandfather surrounded by all of these Monarch butterflies."

"Neat," Nikos breathed out.

"Yeah." I pursed my lips. I rubbed the monarch engraving on the tiny box. "I never met my grandfather, but he taught my dad that butterflies are good luck, and my dad taught me. So when I was a little girl I loved to try to catch them, but I never could. It made me feel like I was failing him." I drifted off. "Gosh, sorry guys, I didn't mean to bring up a depressing memory."

"No, that is nice what you said," Eleni said. "Butterflies are beautiful. I'll look out for them now for a little luck."

I realized I hadn't seen a butterfly in Greece. Not even once. Maybe there was no luck here for me after all if Greek butterflies couldn't find me. "Even though I associate them with Dad, they will always be a lucky sign to me. It's a part of my history." I looked down at the box. "Thanks for this. I'm lucky to have this, to have met you both, to have lived here, despite all that happened." I sighed deeply.

"See, this box was meant to be for you," Eleni said. "Imagine it's a Greek-Mexican trinket box with *matakia* and a butterfly."

"Actually, Ancient Greeks loved the butterfly too," Nikos informed me, raising one finger in the air. "The word for butterfly is *psyche,* which also referred to the human soul. Well," he continued, quite matter-of-factly, "I don't have to give you the whole 'English comes from Greek' lesson now." Nikos reached for the box then held it up to examine it with more interest. "So maybe the designer of this box knew what he was doing."

I smiled at that thought. Then the reality hit me. At that moment, as I wore my own evil eye and analyzed the coincidence of a parting gift emblazoned with a butterfly from my two best friends, a heaviness weighed on my chest, like a rush of sadness had hit me. I was about to part with a life I didn't expect to make. I was supposed to be in Greece with a husband, but found myself among the company of amazing friends. As the hours wound down, a new start waited in a familiar place on the other side of the world.

Nikos filled my glass tumbler, and then Eleni's, with white wine. "No more tears. Let's toast."

"This is not the end, it is the beginning. We will go to visit New York City." Eleni winked at me and leaned back into her chair.

"You mean Ithaca," I responded wryly. All week she had been telling me to go find a job in Manhattan, where she was certain quality shopping existed.

Eleni laughed. "You know we will go find you anywhere."

"You'll be back here every summer," Nikos said with a strong nod. "*Oposdipote.*"

"*Stin ygeia mas.*" I proposed the Greek expression for cheers, as cheerfully as I could.

"And new beginnings full of luck," Nikos added.

"And a friendship like ours," Eleni added.

Our glasses clinked in unison.

CHAPTER SEVEN

I GLANCED down at my leather watch. The dials hadn't moved since one o'clock in the morning, around the time Eleni, Nikos, and I hugged goodbye. We all agreed that we wouldn't be able to bear a depressing airport farewell, so our tapas bar excursion was it for us. At one a.m., we were all pretty down, and apparently, my watch had felt our pain.

My cell phone displayed the correct time. Nine a.m. My luggage sat in the hallway. The pocket of my purse held my passport. Everything was as planned.

The moving company had already taken our belongings. I stood there looking at the empty spaces of the flat thinking how everything changed so fast. Two weeks ago, I thought it would be my home for a few more years. Two weeks ago, I had a marriage. Two weeks ago, I thought I knew who I was and where I was going in life. Once again, Ithaca, New York would be home. Exactly where I started. Where I hoped I'd get over my disappointment and go on with my life.

I opened the window and folded my arms as I gazed out at the view before me—the baby blue sky streaked with wispy clouds framed the grand symmetrical pillars of Acropolis' ancient temples. There it was, the Parthenon, a revered monument remaining high above the modern city—a city that had changed in so many ways over the last two thousand years. There it was sitting on its plateau where it had always belonged and always would.

"But why can't I stay?" I asked myself out loud, just to hear the pipe dream sounds of the words. I wondered if Athens could be my home even without Greg as my anchor. I pushed aside the thought. Greg supported me and made all of the money. "But what if I can?" I asked myself. Nikos and Eleni both offered to let me live with either of them if I wanted to stay on longer. I had savings to get by for at least a few months and *maybe* I could find a job like many of my ex-pat friends had. They may not have had the exact careers they would have in their home countries but they got by, and in return they loved living in Greece. Some of my friends even stayed illegally, while I had a permit to live and work in Europe. My Greek wasn't perfect but I was a fast learner and I'd continue to make the effort with pleasure. My cell phone rang and startled me out of my fantasy.

"*Kuria*, Ava Martin," inquired a man in a heavy Greek accent. "Your taxi is outside."

"*Efharisto*. I'll be outside in a minute." My dream of living in Athens turned back to the reality of leaving Athens at that moment. There was no other choice. The movers and the flight were paid for. Everything was decided. The plan was set. I just needed *to go.*

The pit of my stomach churned with the thought that I just needed *to go.* Thoughts exploded within me. Was I crazy to consider staying on my own? My heritage didn't connect me, I wasn't fluent in the language, and I didn't even have a job. There was an economic crisis. The headlines made that clear each day. Greeks were begging for jobs around me. I then thought of my mom waiting for me. My old job—waiting for me. My old life—waiting for me. The way things were before Greg, before Greece. I needed to accept that old life and forget about Greg, like he never even happened.

Except that he did. He happened, and he changed my world. My heart swelled brimming full of disappointment. I shut my eyes; the pain of my emotions ran down every part of my body to the tips of my fingers. I had changed too much. I had become someone else. I had become a woman I wouldn't have recognized seven months ago. I pulled my suitcase behind me and out into the hallway. I turned the key in the lock slowly, three times to the left. I leaned my head against the door. My heart thudded, feeling defeat. I dropped my keys inside our mailbox that had our names printed side by side, Greg Brown and Ava Martin.

Two names I had once believed belonged together.

From the lobby I spotted the taxi double-parked on the one-way street. I wanted time. I wanted to walk up to Lycabettus Hill, buy a Greek fashion magazine and study new Greek words, drink coffee, and just think. I needed to think. I wanted to grab the next tram to the south and waste my day walking by the sea.

I inched closer to the window when suddenly something colorful flapped against it. Right there, in front of my face.

A butterfly. The first one I had ever seen in Greece.

I placed my hand up to the pane, expecting her to go but she didn't.

"You're stuck aren't you," I said. She frantically flapped her wings. Maybe she wanted to break through the glass.

"That's the wrong way," I said, smiling. I made out the details of her black insect body and the dark patterns swirling in a delicate form on her golden wings. She squirmed. She didn't know better. I could've caught her if nothing stood between us, the way I always wanted to catch butterflies for my dad.

But butterflies aren't meant to be caged. I decided at that moment, I wasn't meant to be either.

That was the sign I needed. I couldn't change my life again feeling this way. I may not be sure of most things lately, but I was sure I wasn't going to go backwards again.

I walked out the door, stood on the stoop, and breathed out as I faced the yellow butterfly. She was still there. I reached out to her and, softly, she landed on the ridge of my index finger. Her delicate wings brushed gently against my skin, and then she flew off again, but away from me. She flew above a small olive tree and disappeared into the distance.

I hurried out of the front gate, pulling my huge suitcase behind me. As the taxi driver opened his door to come and help me, I turned sharply the opposite way.

"Ms. Ava?" The driver yelled toward me.

I quickened my step. I wanted so badly to break into a run, but the fifty-pound oversized plastic box on tiny wheels stopped me, or would keep my arm in the process. I pulled it, expertly avoiding the sidewalk's orange trees. I dodged a little old Greek lady dressed all in black, almost running her over.

"*Signome*," I yelled back. While apologizing to the *yiayia*, I somehow managed to roll my suitcase over a businessman's foot as he jabbered on his cell. I even winced feeling my luggage slow down behind me right over his shoe.

"*Po! Po!*" he moaned loudly in Greek—their version

of *ouch*.

Oops. Couldn't stop or look back again. Each step away from the taxi filled me with more assurance somehow.

The thing was assurance didn't give me any direction as to where I really should be going. Out of breath and panting, I glanced back to see the driver blocking the morning sun with his hands to see where I had gone. *What kind of a lunatic pays for a full cab fare then bolts?*

I turned the corner and ducked into a playground taking a seat at a bench. No kids had arrived yet, no noise. All at once, I felt alone.

"What the hell am I doing?" I asked no one.

I wasn't ready to leave and I didn't want to come to terms with it. The outings, the bars, the restaurants, the movies, and quality time with my Greek friends were all special to me and I wasn't ready to say goodbye. The country, the city, my favorite places, the language, the food—it was all still a part of me. The weirdness and the familiarity that surprised me each day I continued to live in Greece wasn't something I wanted to give up. The butterfly showed me where I belonged.

I don't know how long I sat there as the park began to fill up with foreign nannies and mothers with Greek children in tow. Toddlers screamed and laughed as they ran toward the swings. I was supposed to be at the airport. I looked down at my watch which continued to tell me it was one o'clock. It really didn't matter what time it was. I took a big breath, got up and tugged at my suitcase. I hailed a cab on the street.

The driver rolled down his window. "Airport?"

"No," I said. "Massalias Street."

I swung the door open to Eleni's family-owned clothing shop on the other side of Kolonaki, dragging my suitcase behind me. At that moment, Eleni's legs topped by a bundle of clothes walked out of the back room. She peeped from behind the pile in her arms to check who came in. Her eyes lit up, and she dropped the bundle gently on a nearby table to hurry over to me.

"What are you doing here?" Her eyes danced with confusion as she glanced up at the clock. "You will miss your flight!"

I gave her a small smile. "I'm not leaving."

She gave me a double take. "*Alitheia?*" She clapped her hands together.

"I can't do it." I sat down on the white leather couch across from the cashier desk. "I just couldn't get in the cab, so I took another one here."

"You did the right thing. It is what you feel." She sat next to me and folded her hands over mine. "Stay with me until you decide what you will do. You are confused. It is natural."

"I was thinking how much I like it here and maybe I can just see what it's like to live here for a little while longer. Maybe," I said hesitantly. "I can be on my own. I practically was anyway."

"We tell you that you don't need Greg or anyone else," Eleni said firmly.

"I don't know what I'll tell my mom," I said.

I heard the door swing open and the essence of Chanel No. 5 wafted through the room. I didn't have to turn around to know it was Vera, Eleni's mom.

"Ava?" she asked with the same confused expression Eleni got. "What are you doing here, *agapi mou*? *Min mou peis*, did you lose your flight?"

With a little more assurance from just a moment earlier I replied, "I think I'm staying,"

She clapped her hands together. Her perfectly lined red lips spread into a smile. "You can stay with Eleni, of course." She patted me on my shoulder. "Stay longer. Whatever you want to do, you have us. You are family, but you know this."

Eleni and Vera began conversing in Greek and headed toward the back of the store.

"Excuse us, *agapi mou*," said Vera.

I nodded. Their conversation was getting pretty involved. I heard my name a few times and then I heard Danae, Eleni's cousin, mentioned. The rest, as usual, was too fast for me to comprehend. A few customers walked in the door, and Eleni motioned for me to stay seated before she approached them.

"No, I need some fresh air," I protested. Eleni and Vera needed to get to work and I didn't want to be in the way. "It's better if I take a walk."

"Be back in time for when we close for the afternoon," Eleni said.

It took me a minute to remember which day it was. In Greece, small mom and pop stores closed in the middle of the day for a siesta break and then they re-opened at around five p.m. and remained open until nine p.m. It wasn't consistent though. When I first came, I'd go to the neighborhood pharmacy or book store, for example, and it would be closed when it was open the day before at the same exact time.

"Nikos will come here later, so don't call him yet. We

can tell him together and then we can take the suitcase to my flat," she whispered loudly.

As I turned to leave, Eleni called me back.

"Ava *mou*." She blinked, and I could've sworn I saw tears glittering. "I am happy you will stay."

"Me too." I stepped back out into Athens.

My favorite corner table awaited.

Just then someone said, "Your table is ready, Ava."

I turned to see the only person who could possibly know that. George, the morning waiter at the Rose Café stood there holding a pitcher of water. He nodded his head offering me his familiar friendly smile.

"*Kalimera*, George," I greeted him good morning.

I took my seat closest to the open window. A few minutes later, George arrived with my usual order, a double Greek coffee.

It was five in the morning in New York but I needed to call my mother. I pulled out my cell phone and Skyped her.

"It's so funny you called. I couldn't sleep and I was just thinking of you," my mom answered.

I hesitated.

"Ava, did I lose you?"

I answered right away. "Something's happened."

Her voice perked up. "Did your flight get cancelled? I heard there are storms in Europe," she said.

I cut her off. "No. Mom, I'm going to stay."

"Sorry?"

"I'm going to stay with Eleni. I couldn't get in the taxi. I can't explain it." I looked out of the window to see a couple stroll by holding hands.

"The tickets were paid for and set. I thought you *wanted* to be back in New York." Confusion rang in her voice.

"I know, Mom, but something came over me. I'm not ready to move."

"How long do you think you'll stay there?"

"I don't know." I didn't mention the lucky Greek butterfly.

"I'm just worried about you." She paused and then added, "You're all alone there."

"I'm not alone," I protested. "I may not have Greg, but I have Eleni, Nikos, their families, and so many good friends." I bit my lower lip. She had every right to be concerned. I was her only child. "I'll be okay, Mom. I might stay a few more weeks. I couldn't leave on Greg's company's timetable. I have a life here that I made without him."

"I just don't understand."

She sounded so disappointed. I sighed. I hated disappointing her but my mind was made up. It was a temporary solution anyway.

"I'm sorry," I apologized. My chest tightened up.

"I can't imagine why you'd want to stay there. I think you're really confused, which worries me even more," she said. "Call me as much as you can. Let me know what you're doing and when you're going to come home. I know you'll be back soon. Your life is here."

I hung up after promising to call the next day. I turned the wedding ring on my finger and looked down at the white gold band. I pulled it off and examined it in the sunshine that was streaming in the cafe.

"*Theleis kati allo?*" George asked if I wanted something

else.

I pulled down my hand and slipped the ring in my pocket. "No, not today." I smiled. "Just coffee."

"It is nice, this day." He pointed outside. "Athens is the top, the best in May. It is best time for city, you will see it."

His words, "best in May," lingered with me as I sat there alone. I didn't know what to expect or whom to believe anymore.

CHAPTER EIGHT

I APPROACHED Eleni's shop as Nikos just finished parking his little red Peugeot. He caught my gaze and quickly ran to me and took me by the shoulders. "Did you miss your flight?"

"I'm moving in with Eleni, for now. I couldn't get in the cab this morning."

He rubbed the back of my head gently. "You know we had this feeling you'd do that. I wasn't sure if it was the sangria last night, but it just didn't seem like you were ready to go."

"Is there twenty kilos of olive oil in here? How did you take this with you?" Eleni huffed as she pulled my suitcase out of the door. Nikos rushed over to help.

"She told you? Ava will stay!"

"Guys, I was just thinking I don't really know how long," I said.

"As long as you want," Eleni said. "Nikos, we will take her luggage to my flat." She winked at him.

"Great idea," he said.

I helped Nikos maneuver my suitcase into the back seat and then climbed in next to it.

"It'd be a shame for you to go now in the spring anyhow," he said. "Next thing you know it's summer. Why not stay for the summer? That's what life is about here, spring in Athens and summer in the islands." The motor started to hum, and as he maneuvered his car off the sidewalk he said, "Live a little, you deserve it."

Ten minutes later Nikos parked in front of Eleni's apartment in a part of Athens called Pangrati, where her family members owned an apartment building with eight different flats. Her flat was on the second floor and her older sister rented one next to it. Her cousins rented out the rest. I found that many Greeks have similar living situations, sometimes a whole family can live in separate apartments within one building, if they didn't rent them out for income.

We walked into the lobby, where one of my favorite photos hung, a big black-and-white picture of what the building looked like before it was razed, a gorgeous two-floor neoclassical which matched the rest of Athens prior to the 1960s. Eleni's grandmother had lived in this neoclassical with her mom and their family, but that changed after the Second World War, when Greece went through major political and economic change. As a result, all over the city, many neoclassical beauties were bulldozed to build multi-level modern flats that have no relation to Greek influenced architecture. Eleni loved the old photo too, but admitted she wouldn't have inherited her own place to live if it was any different. In the elevator, Eleni pressed the button for the sixth floor, which wasn't her floor. She glanced at me and then Nikos with a mischievous grin on her lips. "I want to show you something."

We arrived at the top floor of the building where there was just one apartment with a doorbell nameplate that bore her cousin's name, Danae Telli. I looked at

Nikos, who shrugged his shoulders. Eleni fumbled with a key in the lock, and then we followed her into a square five-hundred-square foot studio. A few oak shelves sat empty in one corner. A matching bed frame with a white mattress sat in another corner, partially hidden by two beige curtains. A few framed photos of London hung on the dark vanilla walls.

Eleni slid open the another set of dark blue curtains against the back wall to unveil two balcony doors. A stream of bright light overtook the room. She whirled around and said, "It is yours."

"What?" Nikos and I exclaimed in unison.

"Not yours, Nikos, you have a flat," Eleni joked. Nikos's own spacious photography studio, which doubled as his flat, was also inherited from his family.

"My mother and I spoke to Danae after you left today. She has the other apartments to manage while she is at university in London, so she say it would be great if you could stay and maintain this. It will be a favor because she will not have to worry. No rent and no contract. You must only pay the *koinochrista*, you know, the water, the lights—"

"Utilities," I cut in.

"She say you can stay as long as you need!" Eleni clapped her hands with enthusiasm. "And I am downstairs!"

"And I'm around the corner," Nikos quickly pointed out.

Nikos and Eleni broke off in Greek as I scanned the flat. I loved it. It was simple and next to my best friends, and it could be mine—for practically nothing. It was so generous. A warm feeling ran through me. Was this another sign?

"But I don't know how long I'll stay," I said softly. "I could be gone next week!"

They stopped chatting and turned to me.

"You are not leaving in the middle of spring, and you're definitely staying for the summer with an opportunity like this," Nikos said very matter-of-factly. He raised an eyebrow and adjusted his eyeglasses. "Didn't we discuss this in the car?"

"Mom and I said it is one good way for you to think about your life here. Life on your own," Eleni piped in. She tapped her heel for a moment. "Nikos is right. Stay in Athens at least through the summer. It is only five months, and you can go back after if you want. But you need time. We think you do, and a Greek summer vacation will help. It will."

I squinted my eyes at her, I wanted to believe her. "The Greek summer cures many things." She nodded with confidence. "I know."

Although I thought I was going against all logic, I wanted to give it a try, even if it was for a few weeks. A new yet strange feeling of independence washed over me and it felt good. Something felt good after a long time.

"I'll take it!" I exclaimed.

An hour later, we were sitting on my *new* balcony's cushioned chairs with a *new* view in front of me, a confused maze of random rooftops covered with solar panels, satellite dishes, and laundry lines. No Acropolis, but it was mine and I already loved it.

Finally, Eleni got up, smoothed out her wrap dress

skirt and glanced at her mobile. "*Prepei na figo*, I must open the shop. We can call Danae later to thank her." She quickly kissed me on both cheeks before she rushed out the door.

"Feeling good?" Nikos asked, raising his eyebrows.

I smiled. "I feel like I'm doing something crazy."

"What's crazy about loving a city, having a life, and not wanting to leave your friends?"

"I feel guilty about it all, like I'm avoiding that fact that Greg just dumped me. Sometimes I avoid reality you know." I looked down.

"Has he called you?"

"No."

"Facebook?"

I shook my head.

"Skype, Twitter, postcard, telegraph?"

"None of the above," I said sadly. I looked up with a small smile and batted my eyelashes, "Not even telegraph."

"Eleni was right, he is a *malaka*." He laughed.

I looked at my cell phone sitting on the table. I told Nikos that Greg must have found out by now that I never took the cab ride, that I didn't get on the flight, and that I asked the moving company to hold my boxes in their warehouse for the time being.

"Do you think he'll call me?"

"I don't know, Ava *mou*." He rested his elbows on his knees. "I am glad, though, that you went with your gut."

"Really?"

"Listen, when I was living in London, I knew I wanted to be back in Athens, even though London is the place to be for fashion," Nikos told me after a minute. "Something in me told me I belonged in Athens. Okay, it also helped that my girlfriend dumped me, but that was just the bigger catalyst to make the move back."

"You mean Jenny, the English girl?"

"The love of my life. But that was years ago. In fact, I should thank her. It wasn't easy to come back, but I found my way home despite how difficult Athens can be. I needed this place to become myself again."

"But I'm not Greek. I didn't grow up here like you did."

He shook his head in disagreement. "That doesn't matter. It's about where you feel your heart is. That's what you do, you follow your heart."

"But look where that got me with Greg."

"A lot has happened to you since you came to Greece. You aren't that girl we first met from a small college town. You're more Athenian than you think."

"An Athenian," I repeated. I liked that.

"To me, you're Greek." He said rolling his r's, emphasizing a heavy Greek accent he didn't have. He checked his big, yellow sports watch. "I have to run to open up the studio. I have that teen actor coming in for headshots. Penelope's got a lot of work to do on his pimples."

"*Oh*," I said. "Not so glamorous."

"We do magic," he said. "We're that good."

I giggled. I walked Nikos to the door. *My door.*

"Follow your heart," he said. "You'll see later that you can't go wrong—ever."

I made my way back onto the balcony in time to see his little red car speed off. I lowered my elbows down on the handrail and observed my new neighborhood again. An old, overweight Greek man with a handlebar mustache whelped something in Greek. He clutched a wooden pole stapled with lottery tickets. Three teen girls giggled as they walked together arm in arm, taking up the whole sidewalk. A crowd of people practically fought each other to make it onto a trolley.

I wondered what Greg was doing and if he was even thinking of me. I wondered if I should really trust my gut. It had been wrong so many times before. Perhaps being independent and having my own life was just what I needed to get over Greg.

And that meant I needed to find a job.

CHAPTER NINE

THE steam rose up from the teacup placed in front of me by a housekeeper. As I lifted it, the porcelain slightly burned my skin so I quickly placed it back down in its saucer. I managed to do it a little too fast and a bit of it spilled over the side and onto the shiny lacquered wood coffee table. I grabbed a napkin and started to dab the spot. At least I didn't spill it on myself. That wouldn't look good to the possible future employers sitting in front me.

Ambassador and Mrs. Li glanced at each other. The sound of blocks clanked in the background as their six-year-old twin boys amused themselves. I was a candidate to be their English-speaking nanny.

"*Xie xie*," I answered in my best Chinese accent, Mandarin for *thank you*.

I learned some Chinese from my father and then studied it in college. I never thought I'd use it, but it turned out that it came in handy for a job interview—in Greece, of all places.

"*Buyong xie*," Mrs. Li responded, saying *you're welcome*. She smiled brightly. As she picked up her teacup, her diamond rings sparkled as they hit a ray of sunlight streaming in the room.

Each day I stayed in Athens on my own gave me more confidence and freedom than I ever imagined. The only thing I needed was a job—just to see if I could continue living in Greece. I couldn't rely on my savings forever, and I did have several bills to pay to keep up Danae's apartment. My marriage status hadn't officially changed, and so I was eligible to work in the European Union. I needed to take advantage of something good that came out of the whole divorce mess.

One afternoon during a visit to Nikos's flat, Penelope overheard me complaining about the difficulty of finding a job, even with my work status. She mentioned her parents' neighbors, the Chinese Ambassador and his wife, were in need of a nanny. I'd explained to Penelope that I didn't have nanny experience, but they simply wanted a native English speaker to focus on creative play a few hours a day.

Penelope's parents gave me a good recommendation, which led me to the interview. Otherwise, I would've gone back to the drawing board.

"It is too important to learn English well," Ambassador Li said with a thick Chinese accent. "We focus on this no matter where we live since we move to new country every few years. English with good accent, unlike mine, will be good to get them far." I thought the Ambassador would show up in a stiff suit, perhaps even covered with shiny government medals but he appeared quite relaxed in khakis and a Lacoste polo shirt. "Funny coincidence you from same university as my wife."

"Same university and same department," Mrs. Li said proudly. She folded her hands in her lap over her black A-line skirt. Her English was good too but with a much slighter accent. She'd explained earlier that she grew up in Shanghai and left to study business at my alma mater before working on Wall Street throughout her twenties. Now at forty-five, she had traveled the world for the past fifteen years, following her husband's career as a diplomat.

"Mei is their primary caretaker. She lives here full-time and would be by your side," she explained. "We just want you to talk to Wen and Ru and teach them words and play educational games."

"I think they like me," I said, looking in their direction. "I hope so, anyhow. I certainly like them." They looked exactly alike with round, ruddy cheeks and dark almond eyes. Their pin straight black hair was cut identically and framed their cherubic faces perfectly. They seemed well behaved, unlike the kids I used to babysit as a teen. Ambassador and Mrs. Li told me earlier they liked that I was a camp counselor at Cayuga Lake Camp in Ithaca for three summers during high school where I taught the kids how to paint, swim, and even sew.

They spoke between each other in Mandarin and I couldn't translate every word but I knew it was positive.

"We'd like you to start on Monday. We'll know about Wu's next post in a few weeks, so we can only offer you something temporary for now," Mrs. Li said. She blinked at me hopefully. "The hours and salary are okay with you?"

I bounced in my seat. "Yes," I said, but what I really wanted to scream out was that I was thrilled to have a paying job in Greece.

My legs felt light with happiness as I made my way through the front gate security at the Ambassador's home. I stopped to breathe in the fresh, late afternoon air in the heart of one of the upmarket districts in Athens.

More suburb-like than city-like, clean, wide streets with well-kept apartment buildings and homes lined the blocks of Paleio Psichiko. The Li family's freestanding home was just one of many. Others were hidden from view, secured behind locked gates and gorgeous tall oak trees.

I whistled on my way to the trolley station on the always-busy Kifissias Avenue. I could not believe it. Not only did the interview go well, but I genuinely liked the family.

Suddenly, I lost my balance after something swiped my left arm. I fell in a thud on the asphalt road. The screeching squeal of tires sliced through the air. A car's motor churned loudly near my head. I glanced to my left where green Jeep hummed just inches away from my body. I laid my head back down on the road. *That hunk of metal almost ran me over!* I lost my breath for a moment as fear gripped every corner of my body, wondering if I was injured and what if I couldn't get myself off the road. I shut my eyes thinking about the possibility of dealing with internal injuries. A car door slammed shut and quick footsteps followed. Next thing I knew, a man yelled above me in Greek, words I couldn't understand.

"*Eisaste kala?*" he continued to yell over me. He was asking if I was okay but I could only stare in the direction of his dark silhouette that blocked the sun straight above us. A few pedestrians rushed by his side to peer over me as well. The stranger continued to speak in English.

"Are you okay? Can you get up? Say something, please," he commanded louder.

"I think I'm okay," I squeaked. The crowd dispersed and we were left alone.

I wiggled my fingers and toes as he helped to transfer me to the side of the road. I didn't feel anything out of place, thank God. I looked out at where he left the Jeep's engine running. Some cars passed around its left side, and their drivers curiously turned their heads to see what had caused it to stop in the middle of such a busy intersection.

"You came out of nowhere," said the stranger, but his voice seemed so kind.

I was sure he was right. With the new job on my mind, I had actually forgotten to do something as simple as look both ways before crossing the street. I had done it a million times in Ithaca where the only witness would be a friendly forest creature, like a raccoon. In Athens, not looking both ways was a recipe for disaster, at least for a foreigner like me. My first few weeks in Greece, I was afraid to cross the roads after I discovered that cars don't slow down much for pedestrians, no matter who had the right of way. I usually stayed back and waited for lights to change as true Athenians made a run for it and literally missed the headlights of oncoming cars by a few feet.

"I'm just not used to pedestrian laws around here, but I also didn't look both ways," I admitted.

"I'm Alexandros." He offered his hand.

I accepted. "Ava."

"I'm sorry. Should you go to the hospital? How you feel now?"

"No, I wasn't hit really. It was just traumatizing." My pulse raced as I did a double take on the stranger. He had wavy brown hair with streaks of blond. His skin was tan and his Ray Bans hid his eyes. Even though I couldn't see them, I registered the fact I found him very good looking and at that moment I couldn't separate whether I was having an adrenaline rush from the near-death experience or the fact that this Alexandros was touching my hand.

"Can I offer you a ride somewhere?" he asked letting go of my hand.

"I can take a taxi."

"Please, let me," he pleaded. "Where will you go?"

I looked at him for a moment. He seemed sincere enough. And from what I had noticed about Greeks in general, they were always willing to help strangers and meant well.

I accepted his offer. "To the center by Evangelismos Park."

"Perfect. I was to pass there anyway." He stood up and brushed off his jeans from the back. His medium build suited the faded yellow T-shirt imprinted with *ITALIA*. His sunglasses were now perched above his forehead and revealed his dark green eyes.

Nice eyes. I smiled as he offered his hand out and I reached for it.

A few minutes later, I found myself in the very Jeep that almost ran me over. We were stuck in traffic on Kifissias Avenue, one of the city's main arteries, but Alexandros clearly had an obsession with the brake pedal, and it had been a big stop and go.

"Are you comfortable?" he asked as he turned to me, stepping on his brake at the same time, continuing to inch the car along. Motorcycles whizzed past us, weaving in between cars. Motorcycles were the fastest and easiest way to maneuver around the city. Then one motorcycle slowly puttered by. Its driver balanced a cardboard take-out tray holding four iced coffees with one hand while his other hand maneuvered the bike. I laughed to myself. That was *so* Athens.

"I'm fine, just a little shaky." I couldn't believe I was letting the guy who almost killed me drive me home. Only in Greece.

He glanced at me. "Ava, right? You're from America?"

"New York."

"I want to go to New York and see the Broadway," he said.

"I'm actually from Upstate New York. It's more country or *horio*, as you say."

He flashed a perfect, white smile. "It still sounds nice." He scratched his chin slightly. "I'm from a village too, outside of Thessaloniki. I love the country, but I love Athens too since I live and work here now."

"What do you do?" My guesses included drag racer, model, or movie star.

"I'm an actor."

Close. My pulse raced again as I thought how sexy that occupation was. I raised an eyebrow. "Really?"

"Stage mostly. I sing too. It is not easy to get jobs these days but I am okay. It's new for me. I changed my job two years ago. Starving artist, isn't that what you say?"

Sings too? Is this guy the Greek Hugh Jackman? Hot. "That's right. As long as you like what you do, right?"

"Have you been to the theatres around town?"

I laughed. "I take classes, but my Greek isn't good enough yet to understand a play."

"You're taking lessons? So you must like Greece." He turned completely toward me, diverting his attention from the traffic ahead. I calculated that we were about to bump a tiny two-seater Smart car from behind and send it flying into the Acropolis. I put up my finger to say something when he slammed on the brake.

"*Gamo to kerato mou*," he cursed at the car ahead.

I flew forward in my seat. In a jerk reaction, he pulled out his arm in front of my chest to hold me back. *Oh, that's nice.*

"Excuse the language. I think you know what I said," he said lightheartedly. He winked at me. "People can't drive in this city."

That was for sure.

"So you like Athens? What do you do here?"

I hesitated since it was a question I had been asking myself lately. I decided on, "I'm a nanny for the Chinese Ambassador. Or I will be." I sounded like I had a purpose. I may not have my husband here, but I had employment which was just as important to any educated working girl.

"You speak Chinese? Wait...are you of Chinese heritage? I lived in London for university and had many Asian friends, but you aren't quite..."

"I'm part Chinese. I speak a little, but I speak English to the boys I take care of."

"Well, that is good for you." He flashed that handsome smile of his again.

The cars around us began speeding up, breaking the bottleneck traffic. Alexandros began to speed up. There was no danger of getting a ticket because traffic cops didn't really exist from what I had noticed. That was a big change from Upstate New York, where I had gotten four speeding tickets in the past few years. He barely cleared two red lights and honked at a motorcyclist carrying a family of three before we cruised into my neighborhood. He started to talk about nightlife in

Athens, but I barely listened or responded; my attention was absorbed by his sloppy driving. When I told him where to turn, he hit the gas pedal, cutting in front of the five cars in front of us already waiting to make a left turn. I couldn't help but gasp.

"But you, you just cut him off!" I exclaimed pointing to the line we were supposed to be on.

He grinned playfully. "We don't need to wait behind those cars, do we?" The light turned green and he pulled into the driveway and parked his Jeep with an abrupt, wheel-screeching stop. I let out a sigh of relief. I had survived two near death experiences in under an hour.

"You should come to a Greek play. You don't need to know much Greek. I have a part in one on Patission. In fact, we have a dress rehearsal in a week. I call you and let you know the details." He pulled out a card from his wallet and handed it to me.

My heart fluttered. It was actually fluttering! My cheeks warmed up as I reached for his card. He was directly asking me out. I bit my lower lip for a moment. Should I have even felt that way so soon after my husband dumped me? I decided not to think about it and enjoyed the moment of feeling flattered. How often did that happen to me anyway?

I looked down at his card and back at him. He smiled again. At that moment I decided I would see his play. He appeared to be harmless and I could make more Greek friends. *Why close doors?* The important thing was, after all, he didn't run me over. I gave him my cell number.

"It'll be great if you can come and then I can buy you a drink. I want to after what happened today."

I jumped out of the Jeep. My legs trembled slightly from the crazy car ride. I shut the door and looked in the open passenger side window.

Another warm sensation flushed into my cheeks. "*Efharisto*. Thank you, Alexandros."

He tapped his chest with the palm of an open hand. "*Parakalo*," he said with a seemingly innocent boyish smile. "You're welcome."

CHAPTER TEN

NIKOS adjusted his glasses more than once as his gaze locked on something behind me. I turned to check out what could be so interesting at Palace, a cocktail bar one of our friends, Pericles, had just opened.

"Do you think they're from someplace exotic like Sweden?" Nikos continued to narrow his eyes toward the back of the bar with interest.

Indeed, two platinum blondes sat, not saying a word but giggling furiously. Each one twisted a lock of their identically styled long hair in one hand. As if on cue, they sipped two large pink cocktails in front of them at the same time. If I'd had glasses to adjust, I'd have done it twice too.

"I know a few words that will have them impressed with Nikos."

I loved to hear Nikos talk about himself in the third person since I had figured out it meant he was impressed with himself.

I sipped my chocolate martini and then asked, "You know Swedish too?"

"I know enough." Nikos barely looked at me.

"Pericles knows them, I am sure." Eleni held up her dry martini. "I don't think they are from Sweden. *Signomi.* Sorry, but they are bleached blonde Greek girls who can't appreciate real *kastana mallia*." Eleni lifted a fistful of her long, brown hair, then gestured back to the "bleached" girls. "I'm surprised, Niko. You can't tell that's fake?"

"Which part is fake? You mean their hair or...?" I turned around again to watch them both kind of bounce in place for no reason. My stool certainly didn't support any bouncing capabilities.

"Even Ava sees it," Eleni huffed. "Save your Swedish."

Nikos continued to stare, his eyes dreamy and soft. "I'll be ready." Knowing Nikos, he was probably thinking in Swedish.

"I should stop drinking." I folded my hands in front of me on the table.

"You drank a lot at the *bouzoukia* last night," Nikos said. "But you didn't do anything embarrassing." He placed a hand on his chin to give his next words some thought. "I would classify you as a calm drunk."

"Thanks," I said wryly. "That's an improvement."

Eleni stirred her martini. "Well, she had to celebrate for my name day."

It seemed like most of Athens was out partying the night before. Anyone named Konstantinos and Eleni celebrated their name day on May twenty-first. They happened to be two of the most popular names in Greece, kind of like the American names John and Sarah.

Yesterday morning, we stood in line at Eleni's favorite local *zacharoplasteio* or sweet shop. As tradition has it, the people who celebrate their name day buy sweets for their co-workers or friends. Because it was Saturday, she bought little cakes adorned with chocolate frosted flowers for friends and relatives that passed by her apartment to wish her a happy name day or *xronia polla*, which translates to *many years*. To continue tradition, she invited her friends out to her favorite *bouzoukia*, which was packed with name day parties at each table.

"I cannot believe Gus was there at the next table for his name day. Athens is too small," continued Eleni.

I had met Gus, which I learned was an English language nickname for Konstantinos, while in a whiskey drunken state during my first *bouzoukia* night which was the same night Greg dumped me. He actually recognized me and told me that he hoped I was doing better.

"I told him I'm doing fine," I said.

"You're doing great," Nikos said.

"I'm much better now compared to that first night. I was a royal mess." I rolled my eyes. "Seriously, is it too soon for me to go out on a date? My divorce paperwork hasn't even been filed yet."

Eleni leaned forward and shook her head at me; her dangly silver earrings sparkled as they caught the candle glow off the table. "What you say now? Ava, you are ready. You need to have some experiences. How you say—" she paused for a second "—rebounds." She smiled after she remembered the apparently difficult English word. "It must happen."

"It can't hurt to have experiences, but just be careful," Nikos said. "What is this guy's name again? These actors can be so full of themselves."

I pulled out Alexandros's card, which was tucked in my wallet and offered it to them. Eleni grabbed it. She adjusted her posture, cleared her throat, and then read his name off the card, "Alexandros Rouvas," in a very melodic deep voice. She then switched back to her own higher pitched voice. "If he hadn't put your life in danger, he'd be perfect." She shook a finger in my direction. "Just don't let him drive you anywhere again. We need you."

Nikos raised his chin up, unimpressed. "I haven't heard of him."

"We friended each other on Facebook already. Eleni and I checked his photos and he seems legit," I said.

"He's definitely handsome, a hottie as you say." Eleni slapped the card down on the table. "From our Facebook stalking session he seems to know lots of pretty girls, but his status is single."

Nikos leaned back to face her, twisted his lip, and folded his arms over his T-shirt emblazoned with a peace sign. "*That* makes him legit?" Nikos knew a ton of actors since he had taken their photos at one time or another.

I remembered another detail. "He said he's had a career change. He landed a small part in a play at that theatre I told you about."

"Let me see his text again," Eleni said excitedly.

I handed over my cell phone with the screen open to Alexandros's text. Nikos started reading my part in an American accent, which he did quite well.

"'Nice to meet you yesterday but still traumatized.'" Nikos tried to sound like me. "'LOL. Let me know about your play. Hope to learn more Greek. Ava.'"

Eleni then took over in her sexy male voice impersonation, which strangely, was quite good.

"'Hoped to hear from you,'" she said. "'Thursday night. Box Theatre. Call you Wednesday to confirm. Drinks after.'"

"No comment from Ava except giving him her smiley, winky face." Nikos nodded his head with approval.

He winked at Eleni and Eleni winked back at Nikos. I couldn't help but laugh.

"Oh, but there's more from Mr. Alexandros." Eleni cleared her throat. "My favorite part." She looked up from my cell phone with a solid look of determination. "'You'll definitely learn some Greek,'" she read in her deep, husky man voice.

I giggled with embarrassment just as our waiter placed down a third round of cocktails.

Nikos's attention turned to Pericles who entered the room. As Nikos waved his hand up, Pericles spotted us and tilted his chin up in our direction. In one hand Pericles held the stem of a martini glass half filled with a bright red concoction and a sliced strawberry secured on the rim. He lumbered over with his familiar easy stride wearing an oversized black Def Leppard T-shirt, black jeans, and black combat boots with the laces practically undone. Classic Pericles.

"*Geia sas paidia*. How are the three musketeers?" He set the drink on the table, pulled out a cigarette, and lit it up.

Eleni lifted up her martini to him. "We like your fantastic drinks. I never imagined you were a fancy cocktail man. You seem more...um, round of whiskey shots. No offense, my dear." She winked at him.

"Thank you, my darling. No offense. I am a man of many tastes." He nodded and turned his head to blow a puff of cigarette smoke away from us, swishing his low ponytail of long brown curls.

"Did you try this one?" Pericles raised his martini glass. "It is my favorite creation, the Strawberry Sunrise Surprise. *Teleio*, huh?" He sipped it daintily then faced me, "So, you converted to Greek yet?"

I laughed. "I'm trying. It's kind of hard."

"I don't know what they would do if you leave." He pointed his drink slightly toward Eleni and Nikos. "So you must stay."

"She just found a job," Nikos said proudly.

"And a man." Eleni scrunched her forehead. "Well...a date."

Pericles nodded his head with approval. "Good and good." He turned to me. "I know things are real depressing in this country lately, but don't let it get to you. People think I'm crazy to open this business with the crisis. I do not know what will happen, but I am happy I am doing it." He folded his arms tight in front of him, flexing his arm muscles slightly. "I feel it inside. I believe in it, so I'd regret not trying."

"That's what I'm doing now, giving Athens a try." I raised my fresh chocolate martini. "To my awesome Greek friends and this awesome new bar."

As they started talking amongst themselves, I thought about my first day of work the next day and then a few days after that, my first date.

I didn't need Greg. Things were looking up.

"Wen? Ru?" I looked down at one of the twins, his blue-black hair was shining in the sun. He had just creaked open one of the double doors to the ambassador's residence.

Wen or Ru blinked for a moment, giggled, and then sped off swinging the door open as Mrs. Li approached. Her snakeskin sandals clicked on the white marble tile.

She greeted me with a smile. "Ru loves to answer the door. Come in, Ava."

"Thanks." I smiled back. "I'm really excited to be here, Mrs. Li."

"Please, call me Amy."

After she gave me a tour of their home, she pointed out some essentials to my job including their massive collection of English language books, educational games, and DVDs in a second floor playroom. The twins found us in the playroom and slowed down as they entered. Their gazes locked on me with curiosity as they stepped lightly, approaching their mother. Amy smoothed her white linen skirt and bent down to their height, smiling as she spoke to them in Chinese. The boys, with their cheeks flushed a bright shade of rosy pink, both pointed to me at the same time.

"I told them you will be speaking to them in English so they will learn," she translated.

"Hello, there." I sat on the floor and picked up a little toy dump truck. "Who is Ru and who is Wen?" They pointed to each other then promptly ran off out of the room. I grinned at Amy. "They ran off somewhere." I swung around to see if they would come back in the room.

"But they certainly understand," she said proudly. "They're just shy. They need a little more time to get used to you."

For the last hour I kicked a ball around with the boys and counted in English. By six o'clock, I got ready to leave.

"I knew the boys would like you." Amy pulled her long black hair down from her bun. "I don't know my schedule for the rest of the week, but I will try to be around."

"They're great." I felt a tug on my jeans. One of the twins looked up at me with the little toy dump truck in his hand.

"Ru?" I guessed.

"Here." He over pronounced the word in a thick but adorable accent. "*Fo* you. I Wen."

"Oh, wow! Thank you, Wen."

"You are welcome," he mumbled softly and scurried behind his mother's leg.

The twins proved to be great students by the fourth day on the job, well-behaved and eager to follow my lessons.

"Fifty," I yelled out as I pushed Wen on a playground swing.

"Fifty," Wen yelled his voice drifting off in the air as he swung back up away from me.

I loved hearing them use a new English word knowing they learned it from me.

Wen flew up. His little body whizzed through the air, the chain on the swing creaking slightly.

"Okay, done." I stopped the swing. "Good job counting, Wen. Give me five."

He hopped off the black plastic seat, kicking up dust, and slapped my hand. He kicked up even more dust as he ran over to Ru who was playing catch with their full-time nanny, Mei.

I plopped down on a nearby bench. I lay back, feeling the urge to close my eyes for a moment and just feel the relaxing, warm Mediterranean sun on my face. It was stronger and more energetic than the Upstate New York sun I was used to my whole life. I heard a few loud giggles and opened my eyes and saw Wen, Ru, and some other kids tumbling about. It blurred before me like it was all so familiar. The monkey bars, swings, and slides cemented onto this particular Athens city park resembled the playground down the block from my house in Ithaca, New York.

Memories of my childhood rushed back to me. My father used to push me on a creaky, black plastic chain swing as he counted in his first languages: Spanish from his Mexican father and Chinese from his Chinese mother. Those moments were the highlight of my day and they proved to be rare. After my father left one day, my mom said he probably would never come back. Since then, I couldn't help but feel like something was missing from my life. Later, my mother had explained that his drinking problem was to blame and not me.

The twins continued to run about, their pin-straight hair flying in the air as they chased after two little girls. Wen and Ru were so lucky, I thought, to have parents that gave them the best, including an extra nanny like me *just* to speak English. I was unlucky enough to have had a father who gave up on me.

My cell phone rang. I dug down in my tote, thinking it had to be Alexandros who was supposed to confirm our time to meet that night. Wen screamed with such joyous laughter, making me laugh out loud as I slid the phone's screen to accept the call.

"Ava?" questioned a familiar voice without a Greek accent. It certainly wasn't Alexandros.

"Greg?" My cheeks warmed up quickly.

"You sound surprised." His tone of voice seemed too even, too cool, and too calm.

My palms started to sweat. "It's been a while." I hesitated. I wanted desperately to say something smart. I calculated how long it had been since he dumped me: one month.

"How are you?" he asked.

"I'm fine." My throat closed up. He was *finally* calling me and I had no idea how to act.

"I heard you're still in Athens," he said, but it more sounded like a question, like he wanted some sort of explanation.

"I decided to stay longer." I pushed the words out of me.

"Why?" His voice raised a notch.

"I guess I wasn't ready to go yet." I wanted to tell him that he didn't seem to understand that I couldn't just pick up and change my life again. I couldn't do it. I felt so unsure of myself.

Neither of us spoke for what seemed like an eternity. There was no noise on his end of the call, but I was sure he heard that I was at a park full of screaming children in the middle of Greece.

"Is there something you need?" I finally broke the silence.

"I just wanted to see how you are. I didn't call you sooner because this is a big change for us. I realize the enormity of what I did."

"Yes, it was." I cut him off, surprising myself. "Enormous. What you did."

"We weren't happy," he said, almost apprehensively. "I'm moving on and so should you."

What did he mean by moving on? Did he already find

someone new? I couldn't handle that kind of news. *What did he want to tell me?*

"Do you need something? Because I'm actually at work right now." As soon as I said it, I bit my lower lip and closed my eyes, preparing myself for his response.

"You're working?" He sounded like he was trying to stifle a laugh. He thought I was joking. "What could you be possibly doing? How long do you plan to stay there?"

I remained silent thinking I could've said something I didn't mean. Part of me wanted to say, *Come back and let's start again.*

"Ava?"

I swallowed my thoughts. "I'm here."

"I'm just concerned. Do you know what you're doing?"

"I'm fine," I blurted out, saying more would draw me to tears.

"I'll try to call you again. I don't want to disturb you at work, I guess." His words were suddenly hollow.

We said goodbye. I took a deep breath. As I tried to remember the conversation, my phone rang again. Greg was trying to call me back, I figured. I must've made a fool of myself sounding so damn needy—but I was. The truth was I missed him.

I looked down at the number. Alexandros. I took another deep breath and faked a smile as I asked, "How are you?"

"Great. You?" He questioned back with enthusiasm. The sound of honking horns and screeching brakes filled the background.

I forced myself to continue smiling as I spoke. I didn't want to sound like something was wrong. Alexandros didn't need to know he was about to take a depressed, about to be divorced girl out. "Excited about seeing my first Greek play."

"I'm on my way to the theatre to do some things before the show. Can you get to the theatre at eight?"

"That's fine."

"The ticket will be at the counter. I'll see you tonight." A horn honked. *"Ela!"* he shouted away from the phone.

Oh, God. Alexandros was definitely on the road again.

"Sorry, *koukla,* I wanted to say that I'm excited to see you tonight. Gotta run, there's all this traffic and as usual, people can't drive right in this city."

"Looking forward to it," I said through what had easily transformed into a genuine smile. He called me beautiful in Greek and he even said he was excited to see me. Someone wanted to see me after all. That felt so special at that very moment. I hung up and decided that I would have a very good time that night. Good times and positive vibes would keep my mind off Greg. Like Greg, I was going to move on too.

Bells rang in the distance as her gaze focused on me. The sharpness in her eyes and the stiffness of her face tensed up my legs as she continued to speak. Then her voice echoed throughout the small square room, also known as The Box Theatre. Although, I couldn't understand the Greek, I deciphered that she was asking a series of questions and I secretly hoped they weren't directed at me, but I couldn't be sure by the way she continued to transfix her gaze on me. I lifted an eyebrow at the thought.

Alexandros didn't tell me it was a one of those interactive performances that involved audience participation. She cocked her head in a furious nod and pointed straight at me. I dared to avert my focus away. I sank into my seat which was one of ten occupied in the theatre. The other empty twenty chairs, I had quickly counted, left a void in the room. The ten of us sat eye-to-eye with the four actors in front of us. I turned my attention back to the stage where they stood.

Alexandros stood barefoot off in the corner, his hands in the pocket of an oversized beige trench coat. A matching beige top hat covered his face, which was turned from the audience toward a white marble statue of a Pegasus. He hadn't said a word in a while, but each time he had spoken a few lines, I not only wondered what he was saying, but found it sexy that he commanded the stage.

The room brightened up. The actors remained silent as they shuffled a few steps to the center of the room, their expressions relaxed as their characters let go of them. Then they lined up in a row and bent forward to bow. I clapped which prompted the other audience members to do the same. I smiled at Alexandros as I applauded. He held the top hat in his hand and gave me a wink.

Minutes later, as I caught my reflection in a lobby mirror, someone touched my shoulder. My pulse raced knowing it was Alexandros. My first date, post-Greg, was about to begin. We greeted each other with cheek kisses.

He smiled that smile I remembered from the day he almost ran me over. My heart fluttered even though our meeting did have that teeny-tiny near death part to it.

He had changed into dark blue jeans, a blue T-shirt, and a black motorcycle jacket that fit his build perfectly.

"How you like it?" He was still smiling.

"Wow." I exhaled, still feeling my pulse race. "You." I pointed to him with two fingers and nodded my head. "You were great. I enjoyed watching you."

"Thanks." He put his arm around my shoulder.

I hoped he didn't feel my pulse racing through my body.

"It was a challenge," he said. "How can I explain? Well, it is not a regular play. Let's go and get a drink near here, and if you want to, we can go together to my friend's party. She's an actress too." He let go of me to wave goodbye to a few people in the lobby and smiled at me again.

"Sure." It sounded like a great plan: a drink together, then a party filled with Greek actors. He opened the door for me and I walked out feeling the cool night air tickle my arms. He took my hand and swung me around, taking me by surprise. I let out a nervous laugh.

"You look great." He eyed my dress.

I secretly thanked Eleni, who rescued me by letting me borrow her navy blue Prada sweater mini dress, which I'd paired with light gray tights and high-heeled booties.

"Thanks," I said in a small voice as I tucked a lock of my hair back behind my ear. I gripped my black leather clutch and caught up beside him to cross the street. In a minute, we were inside a small lounge with warm dark orange walls, soft lighting, and a mahogany bar. Alexandros pulled out two stools and offered me one. The place was almost empty at ten thirty p.m. It was still early for Greek standards.

"*Ti tha parete?*" The bartender raised his eyebrows at me and then at Alexandros, asking us what we wanted to order.

"*Mia bira* Fix, *Iacove.*" Alexandros ordered a beer, calling the bartender by name. He gestured to me. "And for the lady..."

"*To idio*, the same," I said.

Alexandros let out a whistle as he lifted one leg to straddle his stool. "Your Greek is good." He inched his stool closer to mine. "But I'm not sure you learned Greek tonight. It was Ancient Greek. I didn't want to tell you because you might not have come." He raised his eyebrow at me. A sly smile spread across his lips. "I guess you can say I tricked you."

"Ancient Greek? Thank God, I thought I was hallucinating or I really haven't been paying attention in class," I said with relief, and then add playfully, "but you tricked me." I touched his shoulder slightly before placing my hand back in my lap. My pulse was still racing, but I couldn't help myself from flirting more. His smile was too perfect. "I'm glad I came. I mean, it was interesting." I tried to somehow express myself by rolling my hands in the air. "The bells, lots of intense eyes, yes, good acting and the screaming part at the beginning was interesting."

"It has the theme of past and present." He searched my eyes for agreement.

"Right." I nodded and crossed my legs, not knowing what to say next.

"You had no idea, did you?" He gave me a double take.

I couldn't help but break out into a laugh. "Not at all." He laughed too.

The bartender placed our Greek beers in front of us. Alexandros picked up his drink and raised it to me looking straight into my eyes. "*Stin ygeia mas.* Cheers."

"*Stin ygeia mas.*" I looked into his eyes and we clinked glasses. I took a generous gulp, feeling my nerves start to subside with the first sip of the alcohol.

"I love to be on stage and express a character," Alexandros explained. "It is much better than what I did for the past six years."

"Which was?"

"Shipping. My whole family is in shipping, and that is why I moved to London to study and work. It was a job. Only a job."

"You should do what you love."

He smiled. "How about you, what do you love?"

"I managed marketing for a university in my hometown back in New York."

"And now you are a nanny." He raised his voice with the word *nanny*. "And here in Greece, not New York. That is so different." He cocked his head to the side throwing me a sideways glance. "It is sexy."

"Sexy?" I asked, confused about how nanny and sexy could possibly relate.

"You are a hot nanny. I wish my nanny looked like you when I was growing up."

My cheeks began to warm up with embarrassment. "Thanks." I was taken aback by his compliment of *sexy nanny*. That was something I never imagined I'd ever be called in my life.

"You changed jobs which is what I did. I made million dollar deals, and now I'm talking to a winged horse statue on stage. A big difference."

"You were good though, talking to Pegasus," I

countered. "This nanny thing, it suits me now though. It's hard to explain."

The beers washed away my nervousness as we talked about our lives and life in Athens. The most important thing I learned was that he hadn't had a serious relationship in years. He didn't even budge with surprise when I admitted that I was getting a divorce.

"You move on." He flipped a hand in the air. "That is life, for me at least. Some things are not worth to dwell on."

But I had a marriage. What Greg and I had was a life commitment. I kept those thoughts to myself.

"Now it's over." I sighed. "That's for sure." My gaze met his again. "Leave it." He nodded his head to the side as if to stomp on my point.

I wanted to argue about the importance of commitment, but it wasn't easy as his green eyes continued to search mine. He gently pushed a thick lock of my hair behind my shoulder. He leaned in, he gently cupped his hand around the back of my head, and kissed me fully. His lips were soft, warm, and gentle. I melted inside and apparently that made my stool wobble. I gasped, thinking I would crash backward out the window. If he wasn't somehow holding my head, I probably would've fallen.

"You're sweet and sexy," he breathed out as he released me from his grip.

Apparently, I didn't wobble too awkwardly. I managed to regain my breath and my balance on the stool. I was buzzed enough not to mind I almost made a complete ass of myself. Instead, a sleepy smile crept across my lips, my eyes barely opened. "You are too." I couldn't believe I had just kissed someone other than

Greg and it was amazing. Although, I couldn't even think of the last time Greg and I kissed anyway. A few minutes later Alexandros paid for our drinks and we headed out of the bar together.

"Ready to go to party?" He took my hand in his as we walked out into the cool Athenian night.

"I'm ready." The beer buzz knocked me a bit stronger at that moment making my knees a bit weaker. The night was young and I was feeling confident it would only get better.

CHAPTER ELEVEN

A SHINY, gold beach ball-like object bounded in our direction, missed us, and bounced lightly against the wall, only to be thrown back into the packed crowd of bodies in front of me. The ball continued to bounce above dozens of heads that took up the expansive hallway we were about to enter. I took a second to concentrate on where I stood exactly, where golden rubber balls could be thrown about so easily, but everything seemed to be in place as I continued to absorb the warm buzz of conversation, lounge music, and laughter. The beer buzz kicked in as I stepped into the party; the brilliant gold-and-white party lights and vanilla paper lanterns strung across the walls around me blurred. The only steady thing was the grip of Alexandros's hand as it clutched mine. He led me through the maze of guests all gathered in tight groups. Like clockwork, they shot their heads up only for a moment to eye us up and down as we squeezed by together.

A tall, leggy blonde with a tiny glittery gold top, matching scarf and leather leggings parted the crowd and approached us. "*Kalos ton*, look who's here!" Her flat-ironed hair shone in the amber glow of the room. She looked off to the side and brought up a martini glass gently to her thin but impressively striking red lips. Her completely straight posture, made me stand up straighter. When she finished her sip, she turned her smoky brown eyes on Alexandros.

"Anastasia." Alexandros eyed her up and down as well, a mischievous smile on his lips. Not the toothy, friendly grin he had given me all night. A pang of jealousy shot through me as I wondered how familiar they were. They gave each other a two-cheek kiss. "Nice party," he complimented her. "Love the gold theme."

He let go of my hand and introduced me. "Ava, this is Anastasia Filioti; she is behind the best parties in Athens."

Anastasia merely glanced in my direction but then looked completely away as she lifted her other martini-free hand to suck a long, skinny cigarette. She exhaled a puff of smoke before turning toward me and said in a flat, bored voice, "Welcome to my Gold Party."

My mouth opened slightly. *Is she for real?*

The word *bitch* came to mind. Before I could respond with something, I didn't know what at that moment, she raised her martini glass and took another sip of her drink. Her drink took a little longer this time, enough to make her oversized, gold bracelets jangle down her arm. She shifted her gaze back to Alexandros. Their gazes locked again as they spoke in Greek above me. If she was an indication of Alexandros's friends, I would need more to drink. My attention wandered around the apartment. Indeed, it was appropriately themed as a gold party. Strings of elegant white-and-gold lights lined the walls around modern, white leather furniture. Groups of small gold masks hung from the ceiling, and gold inflatable balls of different sizes continued to bounce randomly around the room. Glittered paper sculptures framed the living room window, which boasted a perfect nighttime view of the Acropolis. Its magnificent gold glow shone like it was lit just for the party.

To top it off, everyone followed the theme and donned something in gold. Men wore gold ties or shirts. Gold printed dresses and skirts clung to perfectly shaped bodies. I glanced down at my own outfit, which didn't have a touch of gold in it. *At least Alexandros is gold-free too*, I thought. Then I looked up to find Anastasia wrapping her gorgeous gold scarf around his neck. She pulled the ends down to bring him closer to her and stared straight at him. I became the only un-gold partygoer and my date was being seduced by the host.

Alexandros and Anastasia laughed. I cleared my throat and tried to listen in on their conversation from which of course, I couldn't understand a word. I looked down at my booties then back at them. Alexandros caught my look and stopped their conversation. "We should get drinks."

"I'll get them," I offered with a tight smile. I rolled my eyes as I walked away. I wasn't even sure if he heard me as another tall blonde joined in on their conversation. I quickly spotted the bar in the corner and promptly picked up two gold-rimmed martini glasses with a light yellow-and-pink concoction inside. I sipped one of them quickly. It was sweet, tasty, and strong. Perfect.

I glanced over at Alexandros. *Three girls* surrounded him. He was like a hot girl party magnet. I took a long sip of my martini, steeling myself, and walked over to give him his drink.

"*Geia sas,*" I greeted them all and forced a smile through gritted teeth.

"This is Ava. She's from New York." Alexandros

introduced me happily as I handed him his drink. He accepted it and placed his free hand on the small of my back. I glanced at him for a moment as a small feeling of confidence washed over me, like maybe I belonged.

The hot girls stared at me with blank expressions. All three of them blinked their long lashes at the same time.

"You like our drinks?" Anastasia asked coolly, looking down at me with half-open eyes. She raised her martini glass in one hand and placed the other on her hip.

"Nice," I said, feigning a smile.

The third new addition to his hot girl groupie crowd babbled in Greek and in response, Alexandros turned to whisper something in her ear letting go of my waist. I took another sip from my glass to realize I finished it. I drank it in a matter of minutes, yet I craved another. I made my way back to the bar, where I grabbed another cocktail. As I passed the window framing the Acropolis, I spotted a few people out on the patio. I slid the glass door and stepped out.

The city lights glittered just like the gold lights strung inside the flat. I stepped up to the balcony railing and held onto it with one hand, feeling the ground a bit shaky underneath me. I gripped my fresh drink in my other hand as I admired the Acropolis, closer than ever, shining in the dark of midnight. I closed my eyes feeling unsteady and hearing the Greeks around me speak too quickly for me to comprehend a thing. As I finished my second drink, I immediately wanted a third, but I couldn't bring myself to let go of the railing. I wished I could just be somewhere familiar. For the first time, Athens felt cold and distant.

"Nice view," a voice said from behind me, startling me. My empty glass slipped out of my hand and fell over the railing down to the cobblestone street below. I followed the sound of the crashing glass by lowering my heavy head over the balcony first and then realized someone was standing right next to me. It was Alexandros, giving me a flirtatious look with one eyebrow slightly lifted.

"Good thing I brought ammunition," he said in a very sexy voice. He held up two gold martinis, one in each hand. He offered one out to me, and I smiled wide. He was too charming.

"Just what I was looking for." I took a long sip. "Looks like you know a lot of people here."

"A few." He shrugged my comment off.

Then he pulled me closer to him, very close. I wanted to ignore him for ignoring me, but his attention made the world stop spinning.

"I'll meet you at the hall. I just have to give my card to a director Anastasia told me about." He gripped my waist tightly now, his hand rubbing the small of my back and sliding farther down. "I was thinking we could have a drink at my place."

"Meet you at the door." I needed to be out of the Gold Party. *Stay cool*, I warned myself as I walked back inside, feeling unsteady. I balanced my legs and heels to synch with each other reminding myself, *One foot in front of the other, Ava*. I couldn't bear to fall in front of these pretentious people. I finished my drink, placed it on a nearby table, and then claimed an open space in the hallway. I spotted Alexandros in the distance leaving the embrace of yet another two girls, one of which he patted on the butt. I rolled my eyes. Had he forgotten that I was still waiting for him? *What a jerk*. As I checked out which girl was coming onto him next, a small gold rubber ball bounded toward me, catching my vision. I caught it easily, a bit surprised by my drunken reflexes, and like everyone else was doing throughout the night, I threw it back out into the party crowd. Immediately, I a high-pitched squeal followed.

"*Prosehe*," a woman said in a very slow, exaggerated, and irritated tone. It was one of the bleached blonde hot girls Alexandros flirted with at the beginning of the party. But this time she clearly wasn't amused, her jaw cocked and her big green eyes pierced me with an uncomfortable icy glaze. She seemed half like she was high on something and half like she was just a natural bitch. She didn't recognize that she had already ignored me earlier.

"Sorry," I said calmly. She narrowed her eyes even more. A chill flew up my spine. "Everyone's doing it if you can't tell," I continued, trying to explain.

"Well, *the help* shouldn't be," she said slowly and viciously as she stared me down from head to toe.

She walked away balancing her body on her gold stilettos and almost tripped over herself. I was tempted to push her over when a woman yelled, "Cassandra *mou*." She stopped to talk to her.

The help? My body tensed up. Anger rose up inside my throat. Yes, my outfit didn't cut the gold standard for the dumbass party. Yes, I was of Asian descent, and yes, the maids and probably *her maid* came from Asia to work in Europe. But really, I was wearing Prada! "I'm not the help," I attempted to say, but they weren't paying the slightest bit of attention to me.

Then, Alexandros came up from behind them. As I was about to call out for him, he grabbed both of them by the waist. Cassandra slipped on her stiletto and the liquid gold of her martini glass flew out in my direction and splatted onto my chest, right onto Eleni's Prada dress. I gasped at the wet stain, my face hot with anger and humiliation. A dozen or so partygoers stopped in their little circles to observe the showdown between us.

"Oh, my God," I murmured in horror.

Alexandros dabbed a napkin on my chest. "It will come out," he said trying to console me.

"*Thee mou!*" exclaimed Cassandra giddily. Instead of apologizing, she just said oh, my God in Greek. Like she understood the meaning of apology.

"That was so mean," I said under my breath.

"Cassandra didn't mean it. It was just an accident," Alexandros said calmly. "She's high right now."

"Great excuse." I rolled my eyes. Alexandros looked at me, confused, and turned to say something in Greek to the girls. He waved his hand up, a cue we were going to get the hell out of there. He smiled as if nothing happened. "Ready to go?"

As we made our way out, I glanced back to see Cassandra and her friend laughing in my direction. She already had another cocktail in her hand.

"You must get out of those wet clothes." He took my hand and as soon as we were out the door, heading to his Jeep, he stopped to whisper in my ear, "Don't worry, my flat is close by."

I was tempted to kick him in the balls and hail a cab for assuming I'd hop into bed with him after his behavior all night. He was a jerk for taking me to a party full of cold and ignorant people, for ignoring me at said party, and for his arrogance. But with his warm breath in my ear, all logic abandoned me. Above all else, at that moment, I felt wanted and sexy. I needed it. It was too irresistible. I was turned on.

Everything was a blur on the way to his flat. I thought of Cassandra the Horrible Greek Girl and decided to say something as he moved his hand up my thigh.

I placed my hand clumsily over his. "So you know Cassandra?"

"She's a good friend." He smiled. There he was again with that dumb smile. He must've known how nice it was.

"Really?"

He pushed past my hand and glided his hand higher up my thigh, making me lose my train of thought. "She did the best thing all night," he said slowly.

I could only look at him in disbelief then back down at my, no, *Eleni's* stained dress.

"I have a great excuse to rip that dress off you," he continued.

Alexandros was obviously totally full of himself, but the next thing I knew I was in his arms at his front door. We kissed like crazy. The uncomfortable wetness of the dress clamped against my hot skin as he pressed harder against me. Dizzy with gold liquor, all I wanted to understand at that moment was that the best-looking man all the beautiful women at the Gold Party wanted, wanted me.

I woke up with fur, or something like that, tickling my face. I sneezed, jolted up and out of a bed which I immediately sensed wasn't mine. A cat screeched somewhere in the room and a white blur of fuzz dove under the bed. Sunlight peered in through half-closed curtains that draped two grand marble columned balcony windows. I was alone in Alexandros's room. I barely remembered the sex. I rubbed my eyes and caught dark streaks of navy blue and black makeup smeared on my hands. I needed to fix myself, Alexandros must be somewhere around, and I couldn't look like a total mess. I grabbed my purse on the dresser and rushed into an adjoining bathroom to wash my face. Upon catching my reflection, I calculated that I'd need more than a washing to look fresh. I touched the fine lines on my forehead which came as a result of dehydrating my skin after a night of drinking. Under the vanity mirror, my skin cast a strange yellow hue. My eyes wouldn't stop sagging at the corners.

"Get a hold of yourself," I said to the mirror. I washed off streaks of smoky eye makeup with soap then dug through my clutch to pull out my reinforcements. I smoothed out my skin with some powder, applied a bit of blush and pink lipstick. I lined my eyes with a hint of chocolate brown eyeliner to brighten them a bit. I finger combed my tangled hair then blotted the lipstick on a piece of tissue paper. I didn't want to look too made up after all.

I slipped out of the bathroom to reach for Eleni's dress which was half drooping off a chair. The drink stain and memories of Cassandra the Horrible flooded back. I hoped the bitchy, racist socialite hadn't ruined the dress. As I spot-washed it, I wondered how Alexandros could associate himself with such people. But I didn't really know him anyway. I let out a sigh of relief when the stain finally washed out. As I happily slipped it back on, I heard a vacuum whir in the other room. Alexandros was home. I walked out ready to greet him but instead find a short, plump, and dark-haired Asian housekeeper. She switched off the vacuum at the sight of me.

"Good morning. I heard you so I must vacuum, ma'am," she said plainly in a thick Asian accent.

I scanned the living room for Alexandros.

"Mr. Alexandros left already," she informed me.

"Oh." My voice rang with disappointment.

"Are you Filipina?" She smiled as she smoothed her apron over her chubby belly.

"No, but people tell me sometimes that I look like a Filipina." I nodded, not quite sure what else to say. "*Kamusta?*" It was the one phrase I remembered in her language; it actually meant *hello*.

She smiled warmly at my effort. "Oh, okay. Have a nice day, ma'am." She turned on the vacuum again. I gave her a double take and confirmed that she could pass for a relative of mine after all. I appreciated her politeness after a night with the rude Gold Party girls.

I left the flat, closing the door behind me and immediately pulled out my cell phone to check if Alexandros left me a text or Facebook message. Nothing. I put my hand up to my forehead and pulled my hair back thinking how I must've drunk so much but at least I wasn't that hungover. I reminded myself that I was thirty, not twenty anymore. I made a note to myself to act more mature if I was going to put myself out there.

I started my way down Dionysiou Aeropagitou, one of the ancient city's most beautiful pedestrian walkways, right where Alexandros apparently happened to live. I balanced my heels between the cobblestones noticing how the midday sun brightened my mood. Then, I came upon a view of the Acropolis. It hovered grandly above me, far more beautiful than it appeared last night from the balcony of Anastasia's apartment. In her world, for some dumb reason, I didn't fit in Athens. At that moment, by myself, a renewed sense that maybe I did belong there filled my thoughts. Fitting in would take time and I would need to somehow find my way on my own, no matter who walked in and out of my life.

CHAPTER TWELVE

I COULDN'T believe my own mother was agreeing with the man who left her only child. I slid my head down and out of view from my laptop's camera as we Skyped.

"It's been a month. A month, Ava," Mom said in her Mom-knows-best tone of voice. "It was perfectly natural for Greg to ask you if you know what you're doing. *I* don't know what you're doing there."

"Mom, I still can't decide." I lifted my throbbing, aching head back into my mother's sight. "Greg has no right to tell me what to do, where to go. He left me. Remember?"

"I'm not saying he has a right. I just see his point. You know I never agreed with him, really. You look terrible too. Are you sleeping okay there?"

I made a mental note to avoid Skype calls after too much drinking dates. I couldn't believe I even had to make that mental note. I wearily glanced at the clock and looked back at the screen. "I need to catch the trolley to get to work. Don't worry about me. I'll figure things out."

She shot me am unconvinced look, her green eyes full of concern. "Be safe. I saw that riot on CNN last night."

"It's safe here."

There was another strike a few days ago and a clash

broke out between the police and some civilians. The situations broke out frequently at Syntagma Square, located a half mile away from my apartment, ten minutes by foot. While that was happening, life went on as usual everywhere else in the city. Mom e-mailed me an article that said Greek hoodlums were storing their political messages in Molotov cocktails and threw them in random windows. She said that I was not an exception. I figured as long as I wasn't smack in the middle of the action and couldn't smell tear gas, I was safe. I didn't know whether I believed myself or not.

"Bye, Mom." I ended the conversation.

She logged off and I shut down my laptop and immediately put my head back down. The truth was that I didn't know what I wanted or what I was doing anymore.

It was Saturday and I loved thinking that I was doing overtime at a Greek beach. With Mei sick and Ambassador Li on a business trip, Amy asked me to work and help her take the twins out for an outing at Artemida Beach, one of many Athenian beaches less than an hour away from the city.

Wen and Ru plopped their plastic shovels in the sand surrounded by a few sturdy sand castles they managed to create over the past two hours. They were positioned among dozens of couples playing *raketes* or rackets, a paddleball-like game in which people knocked a tennis ball back and forth between two wooden rackets. The fluorescent balls whizzed through the air all the way down the beach, right to where the turquoise sea met the sandy shore.

Amy and I sat back on two rented lounge chairs facing the sea. I learned a bit about Greek beach etiquette from Nikos and Eleni. They wouldn't dare lie out on their towels. Lounge chairs enabled beachgoers to order an iced coffee or club sandwich from the beach bar, of which there usually was one with good-looking waiters and waitresses. Amy was familiar with the beach culture too, and we ordered iced coffees immediately. I relaxed under the umbrella shade and half listened to dance music pumping from the beach bar and watched people as they passed by. Some stopped to say hello to the twins, who looked especially charming in matching yellow swim trunks.

"Wen and Ru are such good boys," I said with admiration to Amy.

Amy rubbed a huge gob of white fifty sunscreen on her leg before she turned me. "You'll be a good mom one day. I think you have a special way with kids."

"I thought maybe I'd have a kid by thirty but, well, life changes."

"I had the twins at forty but I have to admit I was anxious when I was your age. It all worked out. I loved being single in New York, it was one of the best times in my life. I don't think another place could've suited me at the time. There was something about that city and my age, it just matched."

"I think that about Athens actually," I said. "Things are so familiar and unfamiliar at the same time."

"Exactly how I felt about New York." She pulled up her oversized black Chanel sunglasses above her head. "We're a lot alike. I knew that when we met."

"Really?" I took a deep breath feeling the urge to ask

her advice about my problems. "My family, my mom, really, wants me home. She's worried. I've been with her my whole life apart from now. I want to make her happy, but I don't know what will make me happy. I just don't think going back to Ithaca now would do it for me."

"Place is really important in your life." She paused. "There's this saying that you can fall in love at first sight with a place as with a person."

"If Greg was my person and it turned out to be a disaster, what will Athens be?" I laughed nervously.

"But places are different than people," she said in a more serious tone. "People choose to do things to us and vice versa. A city comes as it is for *us* to make our way in it. We choose our home and our way of life. We moved to five different countries and each experience was totally different but you know what? Each city was always home."

"It's nice how you followed him and he supported you." I was feeling sorry for myself, but I couldn't help it.

"Wu appreciates it. I don't know if Greg did from what you tell me. You need to find someone who can appreciate you, especially if you're going to be making sacrifices." She reached over and lightly patted my leg, offering me an assuring look.

Her cell phone rang. Their driver was a few minutes away. They planned to do some shopping before the stores closed at six for the rest of the weekend.

"The car is here. Do you want a ride back to the center?" She began to pack her tote.

The sea majestically glinted in the sun. "You know, I think I'll stay and relax a bit. The afternoon is too perfect to give up just yet."

After I escorted Amy and the boys to the beach

entrance, I made my way back to my lounge chair. I looked down at my yellow bikini. It fit a little too snug around my hips, and my belly rounded out over the top of the bikini bottom, more than usual, creating an unpleasant roll, a beer belly from too much drinking lately. I needed to watch my intake.

Too much beer intake had my thoughts running backwards to Alexandros and the annoying fact that he hadn't tried to contact me once since he took me to the Gold Party more than a week ago. I was trying to take Eleni's advice and avoid calling him. I banned myself from his Facebook page too. Nikos was sure he was just that kind of guy, into one-night stands. Both of them told me the Gold Party sounded ridiculous anyway.

"That Anastasia Filioti is a spoiled rich girl and no talent actress who cannot be trusted. *Malakismeni*." Eleni had tacked on female version of the word, *malaka*, with amazing spite. She calmly added, "It is no surprise her friends are jealous of you."

"Jealous of me?" I had asked as I recalled their perfect bodies, their designer clothing, and their glam makeup.

"You should feel flattery. Think of it, no one will make such trouble to make you feel bad in Greece or anywhere, unless they feel a threat," Eleni explained.

"You Greek girls are vicious, though," Nikos piped in, shooting Eleni a look.

In my numerous outings with my friends, I noticed how aloof and unfriendly Eleni could be to people she didn't know, including guys who attempt to hit on her or her friends. Nikos explained that was why he was more successful with foreign girls, since they were just friendlier than Greek girls.

"Why's that?" I asked.

"Our women are tough, and on first impression they seem bitchy, but that's only because they don't put up with any *skata*, bullshit, as you say."

"I can't speak about other women but I should be careful. There are many jerks walking here and there, everywhere! *Pantou!*" Eleni huffed. "Anyway, this Cassandra *malakismeni* wanted to spill the drink on you. You are too nice, but I would have spilled something on her right back, but like Nikos say it's because Greek girls are mean."

"You'll never see them again anyway and you are *not* calling Alexandros so that keeps you out of that *parea* too," Nikos said.

"It's just that he seemed to like me," I said sadly.

"Do not be naïve," Eleni said. "Move on."

That was sort of Greg's advice too, to move on.

"If only it was that easy," I said out loud, coming back to reality. I reached into my beach bag for my sunglasses.

"Ava?"

A woman stood above me blocking the sunlight. I lifted my hand over my eyes to get a better look.

"Clara Pappas?" I asked.

"I knew it was you." Clara threw her arms around me. She plopped down on the empty lounge chair next to me and reached over to give me the two-cheek kiss.

Clara and I grew up a few hours from each other. She was born and raised in Toronto by second-generation Greek parents. We always hit it off when we'd catch up sporadically at ex-pat community events. She was about to complete her Ph.D. in archeology. Recently, we'd sent Facebook messages back and forth in an attempt to get together after she found out I'd be staying indefinitely.

We started to discuss my new job and her thesis, and then we moved onto the topic of the impending heat wave which clearly had us both sweating profusely even under the shade of the beach umbrella.

"I don't blame you for staying in Greece, Ava. This place sticks to you despite the crazy stuff you can't get used to, but look, all this is just at our fingertips." Clara looked out at the sea. She always had a positive attitude, and I appreciated that about her.

She was right; the day certainly was lovely. The beach, although crowded, was full of people who enjoyed what they had. That was the way of life in Greece. A beautiful country with great weather created beautiful days.

I scanned the beach. "Who are you here with?" I wondered if some other ex-pats were around.

"My cousin and his friends. They're into windsurfing and extreme water sports." She rolled her eyes. "I came along to take a break from work, or babysit. Depends how you look at it." She pointed to some guys out in the choppy waves who hung onto some large neon kites. They were all so built—and good looking. I raised an eyebrow at her and lounged back in the seat.

"You call that babysitting?" I asked in disbelief. "I babysit two-foot tall humans with developing brains. You don't *babysit*. They're six-foot tall Greek gods who appear to be very developed."

"I suppose." She pulled her hair in a bun, brushing off my comment. "Too bad I have a boyfriend in Canada who is coming next week. You should meet him and all."

I was aware she continued to talk to me about something but I couldn't focus very well since I noticed that not too far from where we sat a very attractive, chestnut haired surfer put down his board and began to walk in our direction. That very possibility demanded all of my senses. His well-built chest and arms glistened in the sun. Slowly, but surely Clara's voice floated back into my consciousness. She was actually introducing him to me. I wished I had covered my body with my sarong earlier instead of drooling.

"Ava, this is Loucas, a friend of mine."

"Your friend?" I asked.

Loucas pulled up his white Ray Bans and revealed his light brown eyes which offered me a sympathetic look. He looked away and back at me quickly.

"*Harika.*" I smiled immediately registering a shy and innocent charm about him.

"*Harika*, nice to meet you too," he said with a heavy Greek accent, but for some reason I found it extremely charming.

"My cousin is waving me over. I'll be right back, guys. Gotta babysit." She rolled her eyes again before she hopped off the lounge chair. My gaze trailed after her. I was alone with a good-looking Greek boy named Loucas and I had no idea what to say to him. I slowly turned back toward him. "Please, have a seat." I offered.

He sat and asked, "Are you also from Canada?"

"A few hours from Canada. I'm American. I'm from New York."

He scrunched his forehead. "Where are you really from? I mean, you don't look American."

I playfully scrunched my forehead back at him. "Americans can look like all sorts of things. I was born and raised in New York. I have a mixed heritage."

"That is why you are so pretty, *poly omorfi*, we say."

I blushed warmly in the heat of the sun. I guess he wasn't so shy. Eleni would advise, *Don't believe a word*. I'd like to think he meant it though.

"America is nice. I want to go there for university study," Loucas continued.

"Wait, are you in college?"

"Yes, I study chemistry at the Athens University."

I nodded then propped my arms behind me to lift my chest up in an attempt to look skinny. I sucked in my stomach as much as possible but I had a feeling that wasn't working. I cursed myself for not doing sit ups in the morning but then thought I should actually start.

"Hot out today, maybe you want a drink from the cantina? I'm getting a beer."

I nodded and as soon as he turned his back, I fished for my sarong out of my beach bag and wrapped it hastily around my waist to hide my bloated belly and hips. I fluffed my hair a bit and readjusted my sunglasses on top of my head. I calculated I had a few more seconds as he paid for the beers. I rushed to grab my lip gloss and swiped it on before throwing it back into my bag. I swung my hair back as he approached me again.

"Here it is." He took a spot closer to me in a shady part of the sand under the umbrella.

I learned that he just turned twenty. As he admitted that, I thought about how he couldn't even order the beers in the States! I wanted to mentally check myself, but he was too cute. Flirting was harmless after all.

"What's your second star sign?" he asked.

Classic Athenian. If a Greek wanted to get to know a person he or she often asked about the second star sign. Nikos and Eleni taught me there was a second zodiac sign based on some odd formula that calculated one's birthday and time of birth and other numbers. I told him I'm a Pisces second sign and a Capricorn zodiac sign.

"What sign is your boyfriend?" he asked.

My boyfriend? Good way to get that in there.

I smiled watching him as he sipped his beer. "I don't have one."

He grinned. "I cannot believe this."

"I'm actually getting a divorce."

He spit his beer out slightly. "Sorry." He coughed. "Divorce?"

Did I say something wrong? I didn't know how to respond.

"Are you not in the twenties? Did you marry very small? I always had this idea of the marriage." He babbled on in his slightly broken English but I wasn't able to listen to the rest. There I was, a thirty-year-old about to be divorcee. There he was, a twenty-year-old Greek surfer dude studying chemistry. We had nothing in common.

"You are twenty, like me?" he questioned again.

I wanted to laugh out loud, but I pursed my lips in disbelief. He was a solid decade younger. Where did the time go?

"Twenty-one or twenty-two?" he guessed.

"Twenty-three actually." I smiled and took another sip of the icy cold beer. I stifled my laughter. I couldn't believe I just lied about my age.

He seemed satisfied with my answer. "*Eheis oraio hamogelo.* That means you have nice smile," he said.

"Thank you." I kept my smile up.

Clara joined us again. "Sorry, guys, I didn't mean to be gone for so long, but they needed help with this raft." She shook her head. "All those muscles together you'd think they could form a thought." She tapped Loucas on the shoulder playfully. "Oh, sorry, Loucas, I don't mean you. We like your muscles. I only make fun of family—and some friends." She lifted her shoulders and threw me a satisfied look of humor. I missed North American sarcasm.

"I go to help. Nice to meet you." His gaze lingered on me for a moment before he headed off in the direction he came.

We both watched Loucas's tanned, broad back distancing away from us. When he was out of earshot, Clara playfully smacked my thigh. "Do I sense something between the two of you?"

I placed my finger on my lip. "He is...what's the word? Hot." I nodded to stress my approval, pointing in his direction. "I'd see his picture in the Greek dictionary next to hot, wouldn't I?"

"And sweet. They are all so young and sweet." Clara chirped as if she we were discussing baby chickens. Clara, who also turned thirty this year, looked longingly at the group of boys, who were all gathered scratching their heads simultaneously. They were apparently still figuring out how to inflate the boat.

"You'll appreciate how old he now thinks I am." My tone of voice projected the juicy admission of gossip.

"So you exchanged ages? Of course you did. Isn't that funny how they ask that stuff here? What did you say?"

"I said I'm twenty-three."

"Go, girl. Why not, if you look it? You need to tell me your secret." She laughed heartily. "Now that you're single again, you gotta get your feet wet. That Greg was such a jerk. I think you need to just get out there. I wouldn't waste a minute. Gosh, if I were single I'd go for Loucas. Well, no, actually he's like a cousin to me." She curled a strand of her strawberry-blonde hair around a finger. "But you know what I mean."

"We didn't exchange numbers or anything."

"I have his number for you. I'm texting it to you right now." She pulled out her cell phone.

"I can't call him." I moaned. "That's so desperate. Eleni says that's a dating no-no in Greece. Besides he's practically a teenager, and I just had a bad date last week. Maybe I should keep it calm for now."

My phone mewed like a cat, which meant I got a text.

"Whatever you want to do." She winked at me.

I rubbed my bloated stomach in small circles. "I've been eating too much junk and this isn't helping." I pointed to the three half-eaten pizzas spread out before Nikos, Eleni, and me at Eleni's apartment.

"Who knew Clara was keeping *parea* with boys who are twenty?" Eleni poured more red wine into my empty glass. "That is nice he sent a text to Clara after you left, to ask for your number."

"He's young, but he has this amazing build." I lifted my eyebrows up and down. "Am I boy crazy lately or what?"

Eleni put down the wine bottle. "You get the attention. Why not? You are a *koukla.*"

"When I broke up with my girlfriend, I had four girls after me." Nikos pushed his plate aside. "No joke. Something about the post break-up period. I think you omit a scent that says, *I'm easy, take me, love me, need me.*"

"That is the truth," Eleni said matter-of-factly. "Things will change, Ava *mou.* One date can be a boyfriend later and you know what happens? No more *bouzoukia* nights with Eleni." She finished with the snap of her fingers.

"Well, I'm not going to sweat this one like Alexandros. I hated waiting for him to call." I picked up my third slice of pizza. "I don't care what Loucas does this time around. I know it can't mean something. It would be just to have fun. I have to admit, it's nice to have a guy like this starry-eyed—after me!"

"Something else I must bring up, you know what's coming?" Nikos asked.

I glanced over at Eleni who seemed to know exactly what he was going to say. "What am I missing?"

Nikos put up both hands in the air and exclaimed, "*Tou Agiou Pnevmatos!*"

I nodded my head up and down slowly, not understanding. "And that means what?"

"It's the first long holiday weekend of the summer," he said with the same excitement. "Usually people go to their villages, except you know my village is kind of in the middle of the Cycladic Islands."

"We go each year to the house of Nikos's grandma in Mykonos," Eleni explained further. "*Yiayia* cooks and we relax and go out." She gave me a double look. "You must go."

"Mykonos," I said flatly. I dropped my slice of pizza, not feeling hungry at all. Mykonos was where I had my honeymoon, not even a year ago, and there I was talking about going back as a single woman to one of the biggest party destinations in the world. "I don't know."

"You told us the ambassador's family will be on vacation too, so you'll be off until Tuesday. You have to come!" Nikos pleaded.

"I know but it's just that..." I mumbled.

Nikos and Eleni exchanged glances then turned to me at the same time.

"Mykonos is the best island. Do not let the *malaka* stop you from going to have good time with us," Eleni reasoned. She thought for a moment. "It is a new relationship with Mykonos. Come to be with Mykonos!" She spread her arms out wide.

I laughed nervously.

"If any island has worth, it's my island," Nikos said. "You're going. *Telos*." He clapped his hands together.

I took a big sip of my wine and turned to each of them. I didn't have anywhere else to go and the thought of being alone in Athens on a big holiday weekend sounded pathetic enough. Maybe it would be good for me.

"Don't let memories of the *malaka* ruin it, *parakalo*," Eleni pleaded.

I sighed. "I do want to meet your famous *yiayia* after all." I half grinned. "I'm in. Just for *Yiayia*."

"*Fantastico!*" Eleni danced in her seat.

"It'll be great," I said but I was still unsure.

I glanced into my empty coffee cup then around the café again. No sign of Loucas who was half an hour late. I was surprised but glad to get his call during work. I found out he lived in Neo Psichiko, not too far from the ambassador's residence. He and I agreed to meet after my shift finished at seven p.m. at a café called Anemos.

I called Eleni out of boredom. "He's still not here."

"Why you on time? Always. How do you get things

done in America?"

"Usually, Americans are on time."

"You know about the Greek time," said Eleni. "What time is it now?"

"Its seven thirty-five now, I calculated that I should give him fifteen minutes after because he's Greek."

"That's fair," she agreed.

"So I've officially been waiting twenty minutes."

"Officially, he can send you text, at least."

"I'm officially leaving now. I'm not calling him."

"*Asto*," she said, a common Greek phrase meaning *just leave it*. "*Filakia polla*, see you at home."

As soon as I walked into my flat, my phone rang. Loucas's name flashed across the screen.

"Ava, *hilia signome*." Loucas apologized when I picked up, saying he was a thousand times sorry. "Are you at café still?"

"No, I'm home now," I said coldly.

"My parents." He moaned.

"Oh, what happened? Is everything okay?" I asked thinking something terrible happened to them.

"We had big fight. They yell to me." He sighed sounding annoyed.

He had stood me up because he was yelling at his parents. "An argument?" I scratched my head.

"I know. I want to go for the windsurfing, a race, this weekend in Mykonos. Good wind. My parents yell to me I will get hurt in my leg. They want to go to our village in Kalamata. It is how you say...unfair."

"Oh." What else could I have said? He lived with his parents, which is common in Greece, and he was just twenty years old. I couldn't help but think his reason for being late was just so childish, plus he could've called.

"This is why I did not see you. Can I be forgiven?" he asked sweetly. At least he was apologetic.

"That's fine." I rolled my eyes, amused.

"Maybe I can go to you now?"

"Actually, I have plans." I didn't feel like waiting for him again.

"Oh." He sounded disappointed. "Where will you be this weekend?"

"Mykonos."

"Really?" He perked up. "You take the ferry or fly?"

"The ferry, with my friends."

"I want to see you. If I can go, we can meet in Mykonos," he said with excitement in his voice.

I hesitated for a moment. Did I really want to see him? I wasn't sure. "I'm staying with friends and don't know our schedule." Maybe he would get the hint.

"Great!"

Hmmm, I thought, something got lost in translation there. "*Geia.*" I ended the conversation quickly and hung up the phone.

CHAPTER THIRTEEN

ELENI peered into my field of vision. "Green maybe?"

Then Nikos joined her, his brow furrowed. "I disagree. Ava's definitely more blue."

"Great, I look like a sick Smurf." I moaned.

I barely kept my eyes open. Anything I did see bobbed slowly and strangely, up and down, left and right around me. The ferry seats, people, windows, and orange carpet repeated the same sinking rising and circling motion which my stomach unfortunately and obediently followed. As my luck had it, most passengers didn't mind the rocky journey including Nikos and Eleni who continued to chat in the seats facing me, munching on chips and sipping sodas. The first half hour was manageable but the trip began to look down after that, and I still had five hours left on the ferry ride. My first ferryboat proved I was way too sensitive to rocky seas.

Nikos continued to frown at me then said to Eleni. "It's balfour seven winds."

the strange wax and wane of the boat vibrated through my body as I leaned my head on the windowsill. I thought maybe it was all a sign that I should've stayed back in Athens. My cell phone mewed, cutting my self-sorrow. I pulled it out to find a text from Loucas.

Ava mou, I will come to Mykonos. Filakia.

I found myself smiling but that quickly faded as the

ferryboat jumped over a wave, or was it a whale?

"Loucas." Eleni teased holding a potato chip, totally unaffected by the movement. "He will come *telika?*"

I handed over my phone. I couldn't bear to read it again.

"I can't believe I feel so bad. I don't want to ruin the fun. I hope this goes away soon," I moaned.

Nikos reached over and patted my hand. "Don't worry. It'll be better when we reach dry land."

The journey to *Yiayia's* house didn't help either. I crawled into the backseat of Nikos's car and laid on my back as the cloudless, light blue sky whizzed by. I had arrived in beautiful Mykonos again, but couldn't even look out the window.

"Do you want me to stop?" Nikos asked from the driver's seat.

I closed my eyes for a second. I raised my arm up and gestured for him to move on and then turned my head back down in a dizzy haze. Wonderful, I was afraid memories of Greg would ruin my vacation, but instead I would be the cause of it.

Eleni turned back and rubbed my arm to assure me we'd make it to the house soon. *"Deka leptakia."*

Ten little minutes seemed like an hour. We pulled up to the house and my senses demanded that I should sit, stand, and lie down. Nikos and Eleni pulled me by each arm and guided me up a set of gray stone steps to *Yiayia's* house which looked like a perfect sugar cube adorned with bright blue shutters. As we approached, a little woman with short white hair and dressed head to toe in black, including black orthopedic sandals, came scurrying out. She flashed us a welcoming smile before she began talking rapidly in Greek and flailing her hands about. Nikos and Eleni both let go of me for a moment to kiss her hello. Before I could compose myself to do the same, she spit on me. It wasn't a sloppy and saliva filled one, it was actually quite harmless and of course, very strange. I stood there frozen as she came up to my neck, half an arm's length away shooting bursts of air off her lips aiming with a ferocity I'd never witnessed.

My lips formed a big O as I focused on Nikos and Eleni who stood there laughing. *Yiayia* then promptly kissed me on both cheeks and motioned us to follow her as she continued talking a mile a minute.

"*Yiayia* is Ptooing you because she's sure someone gave you the evil eye on the ferry. It's the only explanation why you feel so sick," Nikos said.

I raised my eyebrows. "Oh," I responded trying to register it all.

"She protects you from the bad, how you say, bad karma. *Yiayia* does it a lot and it works," Eleni said. She nudged me playfully with her elbow. "She likes you."

Eleni pulled out my blue crystal evil eye pendant from under my T-shirt and called out for *Yiayia* to turn back and look at it. Upon seeing it, *Yiayia* smiled and dozens of wrinkles curled up around her eyes. She clapped her hands while announcing something else in Greek. *Yiayia* resembled Nikos with the same small forehead and large nose. With surprising strength, *Yiayia* pulled me with her to enter her home, speaking to me in Greek.

"*Yiayia* says you'll be better once you have something to eat," Nikos said from behind me.

As soon as we enter the home, the warm aroma of chicken, pasta, and tomato sauce hit me. *Yiayia's* home cooked food. However, my usual appetite for devouring anything Greek didn't rear itself. Something else did in the pit of my stomach and it wasn't pleasant. I released myself quickly from *Yiayia's* grip to search for the bathroom.

Nikos directed me, "To the left."

I made it in time and washed up. I took a moment to compose myself, my cheeks flushed from making such an embarrassing entrance. I tiptoed back out into the hallway.

"*Po po!* You look very bad!" Eleni exclaimed as she stepped into the hallway from the kitchen. She held a large brown ceramic bowl in her hand. Nikos and *Yiayia* followed her, both with their arms full with kitchen equipment. *Yiayia* chimed in, her forehead wrinkled with concern as she offered some advice in Greek.

Nikos stopped licking some white sauce off a big wooden spoon. "You want to rest or maybe you need fresh air? We'll take you to a quiet private beach nearby."

I waved my hands in front of me and backed up towards the door. "I feel much better so don't worry. I can find my way." The thought of fresh air actually sounded much better than being enclosed in the sugar cube surrounded by food smells.

Eleni placed the bowl down on the table and walked toward me. "Are you sure?"

"No really, tell *Yiayia* I can't wait to try her cooking. Stay and help her. I just need a quick walk. I'll be back."

Nikos waved the spoon in the air. "Make a left out by the car, the beach is right there!"

I walked out dizzy with relief. Fresh air already felt

better than ferry smell, car smell, and *Yiayia* cooking smell. The sun shone bright and with each step of my sandals crunching on the small rocky path, I came alive again. I somehow found a clearing that opened up to a deserted sandy beach. I whistled as I took in the sight before me. Like a photo on a postcard, two small, rocky brown cliffs jutted sharply into the turquoise sea creating a hidden island cove. It was the essence of peaceful isolation. No one appeared to be around. It was just me and the beauty of the island's nature. The crystal water seemed to laugh, glinting like a diamond in the sun. The thought occurred to me that a quick dip in the Greek sea could get me back on track. I didn't want to waste a minute more.

I pulled off my T-shirt and scarf, jiggled out of my jean skirt, and kicked off my sandals. Strangely, as I stripped, I felt even more renewed. I quickened my step toward the water. Then, I threw off my bra. *Why not?* No one was around. I paused for a split second and decide to slide off my panties. *Why not?* I asked myself again. I was living in Europe, and there wasn't a soul around to notice me anyway.

Last year, on my honeymoon, I was shocked to see how many topless women were prancing about quite comfortably. I wondered then what that would feel like, but I didn't have the confidence to try. In my moment of rejuvenation it somehow felt perfectly natural and the perfect opportunity. Most importantly, I began to imagine how the refreshing, cool sea would feel over my naked body. There had to be a reason people skinny-dipped.

I started to skip faster, feeling the hot, fine sand underneath my bare feet. Within seconds, the water was up to my waist, inviting me to feel it more. I let out a long breath and gently fell backwards, releasing myself into the sea. *Heaven.* I closed my eyes as I floated backwards spreading my arms and legs out, the sun warming my body. The waves rocked and cradled me, holding me to help me relax. The sea filled my ears coaxing me to listen to its sounds, enveloping me even more. *How very nice.*

Some water splashed onto my face, but it was an odd splash like it came from somewhere or something. *Something?* I opened my eyes to find one huge, black eye the size of my palm, surrounded by chestnut brown fur. It blinked at me. A set of brown, furry nostrils then released a quick snort of air on my damp face.

I screamed at the top of my lungs and lost my floating balance. My heart raced. I scrambled to find my footing. What *the hell* was that? Was I hallucinating? Was I still feeling the effects of seasickness?

My heart continued to pound in a furious panic. I stood up and scanned the sea, confident I was about to confirm the first ever sighting of the furry Mykonos monster eye when I spotted the real perpetrator. A shiny, brown-and-white speckled horse slowly plodded away, his body halfway in the sea.

As I registered what the monster was doing, a frantic man's voice sliced through the air catching me off guard again. "*Tha se soso!*"

I quickly translated. He was going to save me? From what? I didn't need any saving!

I turned to find a man running toward the water. I searched my surroundings in a panic and confirmed he was, in fact, running toward me. I then registered that his Greek yelling was of course aimed at me, who else?

The horse monster?

A hot pang of pain shot up my foot. I stubbed my toe on something on the sea floor. "*Agggh!*" I yelled out, lost my balance, and fell back into the water. I popped my head out to see the stranger was dangerously close to me. I waved my arms frantically and jumped in and out of the water. "No!" I yelled. "I can stand and swim!"

I looked in the horse's direction to see it drying itself in the sun, swishing his long brown tail. I shook my head; why would I run to the horse? I turned back and the stranger had an alert gaze and a set jaw, a strong look of determination. I waved my hands in the air with the desperate hope he would somehow disappear. Then I attempted to swim-run from him but it was too late. He gripped my waist as he pulled me towards the shore. I resisted as much as my strength would let me screaming, "Let me go, let me go!"

"*Iremise,*" the stranger yelled back. "Calm down!"

We plunked down on the beach. The sand stuck all over my back and my behind. As I rubbed it off, I gasped in horror. In all of the commotion I had forgotten I was in my birthday suit. My blood drained down to my feet as I realized I had been *totally naked* in front of the stranger the whole time. The man, soaked in his T-shirt and board shorts, shook out his salt and pepper hair. Beads of water dripped down his face. Before he could say anything I broke into a run.

"*Perimene!*" yelled the stranger. "Wait!"

There was absolutely no time to change. I snatched my bra and underwear and then dashed to my pile of clothes and rushed up the beach path. I only stopped to slide on my sandals.

"Shit," I muttered, not sure which way to turn. My

chest heaved; my hair fell in a tangled heap over the front of my face. I was soaking wet, naked, and my damn sandals were on the wrong feet.

He was still yelling. I turned back to see he was getting on top of the horse; he was going to chase me with *the horse!*

I ran for it again not knowing if I was going the right way. Then, in my vision, like a saving grace, I spotted Nikos's red car and *Yiayia's* sugar cube. I ran up the stairs and opened the thankfully unlocked door. I slammed it behind me.

I turned around to peer out the door's window. No horse and no Horse Guy. I turned back around and exhaled long and deep.

"I'm safe," I said, panting heavily.

I regained focus to see Nikos, Eleni, *Yiayia,* and about eight other strangers, probably Nikos's relatives, gathered in the kitchen with various dishes and utensils in their hands. My sudden grand entrance froze them into place. There was complete silence.

"Ava?" Nikos and Eleni asked at the exact same time.

I flashed a stiff gritted smile as I stood there hugging my clothes in my arms.

"*Geia sas!*" I yelled out.

"*Geia,*" the crowd answered in perfect unison. Like clockwork, they looked away and got back to lunch preparations like nothing happened.

I then made a last dash for the bathroom.

Eleni bounced in place at the end of my bed impatiently. "So you don't know if he was handsome?"

Nikos held his glasses as he wiped a tear from his eye from laughing so hard. "*Yiayia* says there are a few horse riders who like to use her beach but this is new. I can't believe you were naked and chased by a horse." He continued to laugh. "I'm sorry, it's just unreal."

I laughed too, happy it was over and that I'd never see the Horse Guy again. Although, the horse was lovely. I wouldn't mind seeing *him* again.

"The tragic part is Ava cannot even remember if he was handsome. He say he wanted to save you," Eleni snapped excitedly as she playfully nudged Nikos on the arm. "*Einai para poly romantiko.* So romantic!" She sighed.

After I flashed Nikos's family, I regained my composure with a long shower. The rush of adrenaline helped me find my appetite again. From the moment we sat down to eat, *Yiayia* circled the table with more of her *magierefta* or home cooked, olive oil based Greek dishes. I devoured her *moussaka*, a Greek version of lasagna, baked with eggplant, minced meat, cheese, and white cream sauce. I tried a local favorite, smoked sausages called *loutzes* which were spicy and perfect. Just when I thought I couldn't eat another bite, *Yiayia* walked out of her kitchen with a plate of homemade *galaktoboureko*, a sweet milk and cream filo dough dessert. I repeated the word fifty times before I pronounced it properly, much to the amusement of one of Nikos's little cousins. I needed to order it back in Athens and I found repetition helped to learn crazy long Greek words. With our bellies full and going out time starting around midnight, we all agreed a nap was in order to give us enough energy to last the night.

"Go rest, Niko, we need our beauty nap," Eleni said

as she slipped under the sheets in her own bed across the room we shared.

"All right, ladies," Nikos said lightheartedly.

I shut my eyes, laid back to rest, and smiled as I heard him laughing to himself as he made his way down the hall.

CHAPTER FOURTEEN

IN one part of Mykonos's main town, called Little Venice, whitewashed cafés and bars sat right at the edge of the island and met the sea. I found an empty chair and stretched my legs out over the tiny sidewalk that separated me from a ledge that held back the water. The sea was black by night. The bright white of the moon highlighted the turning of the waves. I continued to follow the motion of the waves as they glided in, the sounds only interrupted by groups of friends laughing, making their way down the concrete walkway in front of me. If I really focused on reality, I would also hear the dance music that pumped in through the windows of the famous bar, Villa, I sat behind. Reality seemed so far at that moment.

Inside Villa, cramped in the center of a body-pushing crowd, Nikos, Eleni, and I, as well as some of Nikos's friends from the island, had raised our shots to a *kalo kalokairi* or good summer. I couldn't help but think of last summer, my honeymoon summer, my new marriage with Greg. I was in the same bar and my life was very different.

"*Ola kala?*" Eleni startled me as she placed her hand on my shoulder, asking me if everything was okay.

I straightened up and looked up at her. "Just thinking, Eleni *mou.*"

She blinked her long lashes and narrowed her eyes

playfully. "The *malaka?*" She pulled up an empty chair and wrapped one arm around me. We both looked out towards the sea. "Why don't you come back inside?"

"Don't get me wrong. I'm having a great time." I straightened my skirt. I hated that my depressed feelings were ruining her fun. I glanced at her and tried to change the subject. "That blond guy, Stelios, is totally into you," I said.

She pointed her finger at me. "I do not like the blonds. He is not my type and do not change the subject."

"Despite the sea, car, and land sickness, thanks for pushing me to go," I said. "Things have been off my mind most of the time thanks to you both."

"I hope you like Mykonos better," Eleni said hopefully. She took a big sip of her peach drink, which had a ridiculously long wooden skewer holding what seemed to be a mini fruit basket. On it was a big slice of kiwi, a slice of an orange, and a few strawberries.

"Your drink looks..." I paused giving it a look. "Fruity?"

She pushed the skewer out of our vision. "I will tell you what I know. Mykonos is our island. It can be for you too. Where else do you find this?" She put the drink back between us. The skewer wobbled. I laughed heartily.

"What is this anyway?" She stuck her tongue out at it. "It's the *laiki agora* of Mykonos in a glass." The Mykonos *farmer's market* in a glass.

I laughed and looked back at the bar behind us as an old Madonna song blared out with a new dance beat behind it.

"Let's go dance. Madonna calls!" I got up and offered my hand to help Eleni up, pulling her fruit drink free arm up with a tug.

"Really? *Bravo!*"

Enough about Greg, I decided. He didn't last another summer with me, but I was lucky enough to make good friends that were there with me. I couldn't waste another second moping on one of the most beautiful places in the world.

"You have a package."

I opened one eye registering Eleni's familiar voice singing in my ear. She sat on the edge of my bed, dangling a turquoise gift bag with a satin blue–and–green ribbon tied to it.

Nikos charged into the room. "Is she up?"

"*Tora,*" Eleni answered excitedly, saying the Greek word for *now.*

I rubbed my eyes to focus better and glanced at the clock which said 2:00 p.m. I rose up stiffly. I didn't want to sleep away the day in Mykonos, of all places.

"What time did we get back last night?" I croaked, my voice still full of sleep.

"Seven in the morning," Nikos said. He was already dressed and loudly munching on one of his *Yiayia's* homemade *tiropitas.* "Congratulations, *koritsia mou.* That's an early return home in Mykonos."

We had ended up in paradise. Well, Paradise Beach, to be exact. What seemed like a thousand fun party people converged at the beach club where we danced on the sand and where the drinks somehow kept coming. We made friends with a group of Greeks and then a group of Italians. The night flew by as we laughed and joked. As the sun came up we piled into Nikos's little car with five other people then tried to find some fast food in town. It all seemed quite funny at the time.

"Paradise Beach was a good choice." I stretched my arms, realizing I didn't have a hangover which startled me for a moment. "I had a great time."

Eleni adjusted a strap on her blue sundress. Her long brown ponytail bobbed up and down as she shook the bag again toward me. "*Anoikse tora*. Open. Now."

"All right. Who is this from anyway?" I asked.

Did Mom courier a gift to me, but for what? That would be weird. Or Greg? For our upcoming wedding anniversary? Too soon for that, scratch that—never. I read the card: *For the lady at Koutali Beach.*

I raised my eyebrows at Nikos and Eleni. "I'm that lady, I guess?" Then the salt and pepper haired Greek man who *thought* he saved my life rushed to mind. "The Horse Guy," I whispered.

Eleni nodded to agree. "That's what we thought."

I unfurled the ribbon and snapped open the stapled bag. I pulled out the rainbow pattern scarf I was wearing that day on the beach. I must have dropped it during my mad dash or didn't manage to pick it up at all, but the Horse Guy did.

"*To foulari sou!*" Eleni exclaimed. She wrapped the scarf around her neck, smiling intensely. She couldn't bear the suspense. "You did not know it was gone."

I pulled out a blue-and-green cardboard box with the word *DANOS* imprinted on the lid. An envelope tucked inside said:

Dear Lady from Koutali Beach,

Please find your scarf enclosed. I guessed which house is yours since there aren't many in this part of the island. I hope you don't mind if I offer you this token of relaxation. It's the least I can do since you seemed very troubled, bothered, and frustrated. I hope everything works out for you.

Sincerely, Stefanos

"Stefanos is the Horse Guy." Eleni clasped her hands together. "Written in English, with the hand, on beautiful stationary. *Exei class.* He remember you were a foreigner because you yell to him in English."

"Yes, such details. I can't believe it." I scanned the paper. "I think it's a spa weekend."

Nikos took the card from me. "It's a weekend stay at the new and exclusive Danos Relaxation & Health Spa near the main town, where we were last night." He paused, his eyes wide. "Do you realize Danos Hotels has some of the nicest hotels in Greece? They just opened this spa; it is supposed to be amazing."

Eleni read over his shoulder, "Good for one ultimate spa package which includes the massage and facial, specially prepared Mediterranean meals, and a one night stay at the deluxe suite. Please use the code word: *alogo.*"

Nikos and Eleni giggled at the same time.

"*Alogo* means horse," Eleni explained.

"It's a little too much." I replied. "He doesn't even know my name!"

"That's what the code word is for. Obviously, you left a good impression," Nikos said.

"I must've really left a bad impression, you mean. I want to thank him, but the Horse Guy didn't even leave a business card."

"You thank Voula Christou, who is the Danos Spa Director," Eleni said as she read the card again. "She signed the voucher. Maybe she can tell you how to contact the Horse Guy, that is, if you really want to."

I hugged my knees in front of me. "It's all so strange and unreal."

"This costs a thousand euro I think. Go to relax," Eleni said. "You *need* to relax."

"Besides, when will I be back in Mykonos to use it?" I asked. I continued to look at the letter as if I could actually check for more authenticity.

Nikos tapped my shoulder then pointed over to Eleni. "I think it's being taken care of."

Eleni held a cordless phone to her ear.

"She's asking about when you can use it," Nikos translated.

After a few minutes, Eleni pressed the phone off with a look of satisfaction. "I spoke to Ms. Voula Christou." Her eyes twinkled with excitement. "She tell me the spa is full because of the holidays but when I told her the code word she put me on hold. Then she tell me the spa can take you anytime, even today." Eleni beamed.

"We're here to relax and party and to forget about our troubles in Athens. You had such a great time last night and now this. You have to go," Nikos urged.

I remained unconvinced.

Eleni clasped her hands up to her face, grinning widely. "Ms. Christou, say it will take six hours with the lunch. Go by three, and we will go to meet you for dinner and then we go out and you will be *fantastiki*."

I imagined how nice a massage would feel and so would a sauna. I loved saunas. "You both think I should take it?"

"*Signome*, you were very messy yesterday," Eleni responded immediately.

"A mess," Nikos corrected her.

I smiled at the correction. "I was a messy mess," I added.

"Right. A mess." Eleni giggled. "Anyway, this Horse Guy know the right people to give you a something that is for free. It is Greece. *Siga!*" She flicked a hand up in the air.

"People know people," Nikos said. "Maybe he felt bad for you and he's being helpful. He thinks he saved your life after all."

"*Piyene*, go!" Eleni ordered.

After being wrapped, rubbed, scrubbed, rinsed, showered, steamed, massaged, and even lightly squeezed, the ultimate spa package lived up to its name. After six blissful hours, my face felt tight and fresh; my body was renewed. I even felt flexible. I didn't know that was possible.

It began with Ms. Frosini, my personal chef, who prepared a Greek chicken dish for lunch right on my hotel room balcony. As I reclined back on a lounge chair, I couldn't tell where the sea ended or the sky began. The blues before me simply blended so naturally. In the distance, the rocky terrain of the island created the perfect border to my view. Small, white buildings dotted the landscape and a few churches with sea blue domes broke the pattern.

Next, a personal masseuse, Georgia arrived with a stiff smile. She came up to my shoulders and her hair, pulled back in a tight bun, was pinned down securely with dozens of black bobby pins. I raised my eyebrows ather impressively muscular arms. She didn't waste a moment, inquiring about any pains I had in my body. She cracked her fingers, making me second guess what she would do to me, but Georgia worked out every knot in my body. Next, a facialist named Dimitra gave me an hour-long deep-pore facial using masks created from natural ingredients found in Greece.

As I made my way out of the steam room and pulled on a robe, I heard a knock at the door and Georgia peeped in. "The salon ready, Ms. Ava."

I reached into my purse to check my cell phone messages, since I was expecting a text from Eleni. I had one message and one missed call, not from Eleni but from Loucas.

Hallo. We arrived. See you at Villa tonight?

I picked up the phone and called Eleni.

"*Ola kala?*" she eagerly asked if I was okay.

"You can't imagine. There's this little masseuse with magical arms. Now, I'm going to get my hair blow dried and styled." I found myself giddy with excitement as I untangled my hair with my fingers.

"I knew it! We will go to meet you at nine thirty; then we eat before we go to Villa."

"So we're going to Villa again?"

"*Nai,*" she confirmed. "Why?"

"Loucas texted and he'll be there with his friends at midnight."

"More people is better," she said.

"I don't want to give him the wrong idea."

"Oh, Ava, you have stress. Relax. Didn't you learn how to relax today? *Tha perasoume poly kala,*" she said, saying in Greek that we'd have a good time.

I quickly texted Loucas back.

See you tonight.

CHAPTER FIFTEEN

I SWUNG my head around one more time still in disbelief that my thin, brown hair was capable of such buoyancy. I even caught the essence of the floral shampoo the hairdresser used.

I took a step closer in the mirror. My makeup was fine, no mascara or eyeliner streaks; then I readjusted my turquoise hoop earrings. I pulled up my full, white skirt around my matching white tank top making sure it fit in just the right place on my waist. To complete my outfit I slid on a new pair of turquoise jeweled flats, perfect for parading around Mykonos town in comfort, and headed out to the lobby.

Georgia waited there with her clipboard. "You have Aegean suite until tomorrow for late check-out. Include is early breakfast and late brunch. You call chef for choice you like."

"I'm not staying tonight, but I can use the room for the meal tomorrow." I didn't explain that breakfast would be unlikely knowing how my friends partied in Mykonos.

"Keep keycard," Georgia suggested.

"Is Ms. Voula Christou here?"

"She left. She come to job tomorrow at nine a.m. I leave your message."

"I'd like to see her in person, to say thanks," I explained.

Georgia reached for my bag filled with my toiletries and clothes from the afternoon. "We put this in your room?"

"Sure, I'll pick it up tomorrow."

"I give you good advice." She leaned up to tell me something more. "Too much tension you have. Relax. It is Mykonos." She smiled this time and squeezed my shoulder.

Georgia liked me after all, I thought.

"I'll try. That was the best massage, and thank you again."

"Enjoy Mykonos."

"I am."

Eleni whistled at the sight of me and scurried over in a short black and red dress and black wedge heeled sandals.

"Someone is ready to party." She swooned, taking my hand and dancing around me *bouzoukia* style. "You even smell like *nichtoloulouda*, my favorite flowers."

Nikos approached, pushing his red eyeglass frames against his face as he peered at the lobby columns. "This architecture is amazing." He then focused on me and immediately smiled with approval. "You look so relaxed, *koukla mou*."

"*Niotho yperoha*." I tested the Greek phrase I learned during my facial which meant *I feel wonderful*.

Eleni clapped her hands. "Now for wonderful food, then wonderful drinks, then we get to meet the wonderful Loucas."

"I heard the high school student is joining our *parea* tonight," Nikos joked, putting his arm around me.

"He's twenty." I nudged him softly in the ribs. "Anyway, he's just a friend."

A few hours later, I found myself making out with that wonderful friend after I'd downed my second wonderful pink cocktail at Villa.

Loucas had joined our group with four of his friends. One of them, named Andreas, was hanging on Eleni's every word all night. Nikos hit it off with four giggling tourists who joined the group as well, and they kept talking in a foreign language, so he was no doubt thrilled.

Like a big herd of grazing sheep, our group headed out into the tiny walkways that zigzagged through the main town known as the *Chora* connecting numerous shops, clubs, and even small residences. By day the walls gleamed of bright white, but at night they were muted shades of gray.

Loucas held me by the waist as we made it through the wide open door of a club called Blue. "I'm glad we met up finally."

"You're so cute." I grabbed his chin playfully. "And so young," I added. I didn't know what I was saying. I was showing how drunk I was, but I didn't care.

He looked up and glanced back at me. "I guess you're a *few* years older," he said.

Of course. He thought I was twenty-three.

At some point, the group switched clubs again. Loucas and I were following in the rear when he swooped me in the air and carried me into a small side street. I yelped with laughter feeling myself being lifted by his muscular arms. The next thing I knew he was facing me. My half bare back pushed against the coolness of a stone wall which helped me keep my balance. He bent down to kiss me. He pulled back my hair and whispered softly in my ear, "*Se thelo*." Then he breathed on my neck, kissing me there too.

"I want you too," I said back, almost out of breath. The mysterious empty little island street, the darkness that surrounded us, and the distant beat of club music all contributed to the excitement that overcame me. With my body loose and the alcohol guiding me, I was carefree. "Let's go somewhere." He kissed my ear again and again.

I rubbed my hands up and down his back, feeling his strong muscles under the palms of my hands. "Where would that be?"

"Maybe we go to my hotel room," he suggested.

I pulled back to look in his eyes. "Aren't you sharing a room with the guys?"

"Well, it bother you..." he said.

"Yes, it *bother* me!" I blurted out. I started to giggle at the thought of his friends walking in on our make out session.

"I just want you." He pulled me back to him and started to kiss my bare shoulder.

"I'm staying with *Yiayia*." I closed my eyes as I concentrated on his lips touching my skin. Suddenly, I remembered my hotel room card key for the Danos.

"Danos," I blurted out.

Loucas looked up. "*Yiayia* Danos?"

"No, I mean at the Danos, the new spa around the

corner."

"Alone?"

"Alone," I answer assuredly.

"We should not wait. We go." He scooped me up around the waist and off the ground a few inches. I started to giggle and then remembered I should let my friends know where I would be. With my feet on the ground again, I pulled out my cell phone and texted Nikos and Eleni.

At Danos 2nite. Long story. Am ok. Have fun!

Just as I pressed send, Loucas tucked me under his arm and we walked to the other end of town towards the hotel. I leaned on him as we dodged the other couples and groups making their way around the chaotic and unique hub that was Mykonos nightlife.

"This is the room?" Loucas grabbed my waist from behind.

I fumbled for my keycard. I turned around to tease him. "You're fun." I squeezed his cheeks. "And so cute."

"Thanks, *moro mou*," he mumbled, sounding congested.

I let go of his cheeks, realizing I was still pinching them.

"I need fun in my life." I swung back around to open the door to my suite. With a little click and the blink of a green light, we practically fell through the door together, still laughing from something I hadn't figured out yet. Loucas scooped me up and carelessly dropped me on the mattress, hovering over me. We kissed hard and I breathed him in, a mix of a spicy cologne and stale cigarette smoke from the clubs. He pulled off my tank top and ran his fingers through my hair. While holding my hair he pulled my head back gently and started kissing my neck. At the same time, he unzipped my skirt and slid it down slowly, one hand caressing my thigh. A happy numbness overcame my body. Both of us breathed heavily as we were touching, grabbing, kissing and licking. Then he rolled over and propped himself on one of the big blue oversized pillows.

"*Ela edo*, come here," he commanded. He motioned for me to get up.

I made a concerted effort to lift my body up off the soft bed but crashed back down. My next attempt, I crawled toward him with a goal: I needed to pull off his black fitted T-shirt. I couldn't be the only one topless. Then, there he was lying in front of me: tan, chiseled, and perfect. Just like on the beach. I stared for a moment, feeling the buzz of the alcohol run through me as I dragged my hand in a big clumsy movement over his chest.

"That's real nice—and fun," I purred. I bent down to kiss him on his chest, then his abs. I got down to his leather belt and fumbled trying to figure out how the damn buckle worked when I heard a strange grunt.

"Loucas?" I popped my head up to find him—snoring.

I slumped down next to him, snuggling my head on another pillow. "Better that way," I murmured and managed to fall into a dizzy, deep, drunken sleep.

I shot up straight out of bed wondering where I was

and what the hell that noise was.

Buzz.

My head pounded furiously. Not another hangover. I scolded myself as I rubbed my eyes. I scanned the room: vanilla walls, the smooth lines of modern dark wood furniture, lilies in the corner, and in my immediate vicinity, white sheets and covers in a tangled heap. In it was Loucas, hugging a pillow, snoring, and was that drool? I turned away, crinkling my nose. *Eww.*

Buzz.

I wondered who would be at the door so early, then again I glanced at the alarm clock to see it was 2:00 p.m. Mykonos wake-up time. I figured it was the chef checking on my menu. On my way to the door, I hastily pulled on the hotel's white terry cloth robe over my half-naked body, fumbling to close it properly as I swung open the door.

"*Kalimera,*" greeted a deep voice laced with a slight Greek accent. "I hope your stay is fine, Miss."

It wasn't my chef, but rather the Horse Guy. He gave me a slight nod waiting for my reply. There he stood in front of me with his salt-and-pepper hair. His hazel eyes complimented his brown trousers, boots, and a casual, beige button down shirt that hung close over his medium build. As I checked him out, he suddenly looked away and cleared his throat. Then, I remembered what I was wearing, practically nothing—again. I looked down at my bathrobe. Apparently, I didn't secure the sash tight enough, my breast was practically falling out. I quickly pulled the lapels of the robe closer together up to my neck.

"*Kalimera,*" I croaked, sounding like a hungover frog. As if teasing me, my head gave me a good pounding. I put up my hand to my head, which opened up my robe once again. I quickly put both hands back to the lapels and let out a nervous laugh. The Horse Guy stood there looking all put together—the opposite of me. My head sent another hangover pound and my wince at the pain caused me to close one eye for a moment but I managed to ask, "You, uh, are?"

"Stefanos, the man with the horse." He cocked his head slightly reminding me of George Clooney. In fact, he kind of looked like a Greek George Clooney. As I contemplated the resemblance he said, "I'm so sorry to wake you up. I just wanted to try to see you before you check out. I didn't mean to intrude. I just hope everything turned out okay with your stay."

"Thank you, y-y-yes, sorry." I stuttered. Was it so hard to speak, Ava? I scolded myself. "I meant to thank you and find you actually."

He nodded his head a bit, which set off a feeling of attraction in me. "Your name is?" he asked.

Oh, duh. Right. I kicked myself mentally for being so dumb. "Ava. Ava Martin."

At that moment, the door jerked open and Loucas, topless and wearing his jeans with the belt buckle open and hanging down, swung one arm around me and rubbed his eye with the other. He gave Stefanos a once-over. "The room service? Hungry."

My head boiled. I wished Loucas would disappear. Stefanos's eyes darted between us. With that George Clooney cock of the head, he offered us a cool smile and said, "Just ask for me if you need anything else today." He turned and made his way back down the hall.

Loucas called after him, "Um, room service, *kurie?*"

Stefanos rounded the corner without answering.

I called for room service and the operator informed me a special brunch was already on its way. Must have been Stefanos. I placed the phone down and began to get ready, the whole time thinking about the Horse Guy slash Greek George Clooney.

My jaw dropped as I took in my reflection. Bloodshot eyes, smeared eye makeup, puffy and dry skin. My once salon-spun, bouncy do resembled a bird's nest tangled down my shoulders.

"You're such a mess," I said.

"*Moro mou*, did you say something," Loucas asked from the bathroom.

I didn't answer him but continued to stare in awe at how low I had gone. The Horse Guy must've thought I was some crazy woman who couldn't get her act together or her clothes on properly. First I was seasick and then proved to be a Mykonos party girl complete with a boy toy in my bed.

Twenty minutes later, a shower, fresh makeup, and clothes gave me a more positive outlook as I walked out of the bathroom following the smell of fresh coffee and bread. That outlook died as Loucas continued to devour whatever he grabbed from the tray. He was a growing boy, I reasoned to myself.

I eyed the plates. One was filled with black bread, mini croissants, and other types of breads. There were mini butter croissants, chocolate croissants, and slices of sweet bread. Scrambled egg whites and hard-boiled eggs adorned another plate. An impressive bowl of cut up melon, apple, pear, and pineapple sat next to glass bowl of Greek yoghurt and two types of honey completed the buffet. I picked up a steaming carafe to prepare my cup of coffee when Loucas took a smacking big gulp of his food. I winced.

"*Moro mou*," he said.

"Me?" There was something about him saying *my baby* in Greek as I was trying to recover from a hangover that didn't sound right. I couldn't tell him not to call me that since last night, in my drunken state, I allowed it. *Or could I?*

He licked some honey off his finger. "Last night, I was drunk. Did we?"

I raised my chin upwards, pressing my tongue off of the bottom of my upper jaw and quickly pulling it back to make a definitive clicking sound. He understood the Greek gesture for *no, negative, dislike*. I turned off to the side for a second realizing I had just done something really naturally Greek without intending to.

He winked. "Another time."

I wanted to raise my chin and click my tongue again, but decided against it. Instead I said, "Good breakfast, isn't it?"

"But no meat."

"I guess there could've been some bacon." I said shrugging my shoulders.

"Bacon is not meat," he winked at me and got up, stuffing another piece of pound cake in his mouth. He swallowed it in a gulp. "I'm excited about the water. The waves will be great."

"You said."

He reached over to kiss me on the lips but I dodged the attempt and planted the generic two-cheek kiss on him. He stepped back and it seemed the excitement of surfing day took over any rejection I had just dished out. "I can call you later." He opened the door and waved back at me. *"Eisai koukla."*

I waved a hand and as soon as the door closed, I released a sigh. I couldn't believe I almost slept with him. He proved to be too young for me. I made a mental note that I needed to control my liquor intake. That was for later, though; at that moment, there were more important things to figure, including what to do about Stefanos. I wanted to see him again.

Nikos answered his phone sounding bored. *"Nai."*

"Are you up?"

"Ava! We didn't get home till eight. Eleni is sleeping still but we'll meet you in town for lunch. We got your text."

"I'm at the Danos about to check out. Loucas left."

"Are you all right?" he asked with concern. "You sound funny. Did he do something?"

"I'm glad he's gone actually. He's so immature." I brushed the thought away. I couldn't waste precious time. "I'm freaking out about something else."

"What happened?"

"It's the Horse Guy."

He barraged me with questions. "You met the Horse Guy? What? How?"

"He knocked on our door just about an hour ago and he saw Loucas shirtless and hugging me."

"Den katalavaino, Ava *mou,"* he said, telling me he didn't understand. "Why are you freaking out?"

"He arranged this amazing spa gift and I show up

at the door with a boy I almost slept with, obviously because I partied all night and well...It's rude, I think."

"Listen, the hotel stay was his gift. He must work there. That's probably how he got you in on one of the busiest weekends of the year."

"You're right, he did say he works here and to ask for him if we, I mean, I," I corrected myself, "need anything."

"You need to say thank you. That's it," Nikos advised. "It's simple."

I hung up and wondered why something that sounded so simple seemed strangely complicated to me.

CHAPTER SIXTEEN

"*Kalimera,*" I greeted the front desk clerk. The wall clock read 4:30 p.m., much later than I thought. *Why did time seem to go so fast in Mykonos?*

I corrected myself. "I mean *kalispera.*"

"*Kalispera.* Ready for check out?"

I nodded and handed over my keycard when I eyed the name on her tag, Voula Christou.

"I was looking for you yesterday, Ms. Christou. I received a gift."

She nodded. "Ah, yes. Ms. Ava Martin." She said my name quite easily. "How was the gift from Mr. Stefanos Danos? Was your stay relaxing?"

I pulled myself back for a moment again. I just heard the name Stefanos with the name Danos. That meant Stefanos was probably the...

Voula Christou continued to make eye contact with me, waiting for me to say something.

"So," I hesitated. There was the risk I would sound really out of the loop with how I even got the incredibly luxurious spa package. "Stefanos Danos, you said?"

She nodded. "Yes, Mr. Danos."

"Danos like Danos Hotels." I turned my body slightly to my right to point to the immaculate, shining white marble lobby behind me. She continued to nod. She must've thought I was an idiot.

I swallowed. "Well, yes." My voice mysteriously turned up a notch. "Amazing. It was amazing. Mr. Danos," I pointed to her, "and *you*, run a really nice, relaxing kind of hotel." I paused. "Spa, I meant. Oh, and hotel of course, it's like a five-star boutique hotel, like it says here." I pointed toward a big marketing placard on the counter but in the process I knocked it over. I wasn't doing much to repair her impression of me as an idiot.

"Thank you, I appreciate that," she said quite pleasantly as she picked up the placard.

"So, umm, Stefanos Danos, he was nice enough to stop by my suite today and he said to ask for him if I needed anything."

"Of course, Ms. Martin. Mr. Danos is working by the outdoor pool."

"Before I go back there to the outdoor pool," I said as I gestured behind me. "Just to be clear, Stefanos Danos is *the* Danos? Like the *owner* of the hotel?"

"Yes, Ms. Martin." She folded her hands on the counter and gave me an extra odd look.

"Thank you," I mumbled.

A tingle of excitement ran through me thinking I would see Stefanos again. I walked out onto the large patio and among the sea of hotel guests donning swimwear and basking in the June heat. I spotted one man with salt-and-pepper hair, fully clothed and concentrating on something on his tablet.

My chest tightened. My confidence evaporated and I thought that leaving the hotel and walking back into town would be a better plan. *What he must've thought of me!* My manners overcame me and I decided I needed to do the right thing and give him a sincere uninterrupted thank you as a properly dressed and civilized woman. I walked over with a new, but fake, confidence in my step. I cleared my throat and said, "Hello."

Stefanos didn't budge from whatever he was reading. I cleared my throat again and said a little louder, "Hi, Stefanos."

He looked up and gave me a double take. "Ava Martin." He said, placing his tablet off to his side. He got up to greet me.

In my more composed state, I took him in. He was a good amount taller than me, medium build and was looking at me with expressive, large, hazel eyes, batting a noticeable set of dark, long eyelashes any girl, especially myself, would love to have. Although his full head of George Clooney salt-and-pepper hair took my attention again. *It was sexy.* My heart fluttered. *Oh no, not again.* Since when was I attracted to older men?

"I just wanted to say thank you for this weekend. It was a generous gift." I shot him a hopeful look. "I was kind of surprised to see you at my door this morning."

"So I did take you by surprise?" He rubbed the back of his neck for a moment. "Do you have time? I'd like to have a coffee with you to see how your stay was."

"Okay." Damn it, heart flutter number two reared itself. "But I don't want to keep you away from your job."

Stefanos didn't seem to hear me as he raised his arm to catch someone's attention. Two pool attendants brought over another yellow lounge chair and a small table.

"Please," Stefanos said. He patted the arm of the chair next to him. As I took a seat, he asked me, "What will you have?" A waiter stood by.

"An orange juice, please."

Stefanos ordered a cappuccino. "So," he started,

taking a deep breath.

"So," I interrupted nodding my head. "I guess you are a big deal here at the Danos."

He grinned. "You can say that our family name is pretty well known around Greece." He leaned forward making steady eye contact with me. "That's why you got the best staff. I know it may have been a shock to get such a gift from a stranger, but after seeing you on Koutali Beach that day and how you looked..." He did the George Clooney cock of the head. He smiled, easily resting his elbows on his knees. "I'm glad you took it up."

I blushed and my cheeks warmed up. He's glad? I must've looked horrid. "I got seasick on the ferry over from Athens. It was my first boat ride. I thought a cold swim would help me recover from my deliriousness."

"That explains some things."

"I thought I was alone," I said, my voice raised a notch. I let out a giggle that went on a little too long.

"Usually, you would've been alone. Only a few Mykonians live out there. My horse likes to smell people, as you found out." His mouth slowly parted into a mysterious smile.

There was a lot behind that smile, I decided.

"I have to be honest," he continued. "I just felt bad such a beautiful girl seemed to be in such an awful state."

Beautiful and awful state in the same sentence, I registered. I shuddered as I recalled my naked run for the hills.

"This morning, I wanted to say—" He paused as the waiter placed our drinks down.

What could he have wanted to say about the morning?

Sorry to disturb you, I just wanted to check how your absolutely free five-star spa weekend, courtesy of my famous family hotel, is going. Sorry that you and your rude, hungry, surfer dude date drank too much.

I was proving more and more to Stefanos that I could keep it classy.

"About this morning, I didn't mean to disturb your stay with your boyfriend."

"Actually, he's not my boyfriend," I said sharply. "A friend."

He shifted in his seat and said nothing.

"From Athens," I added abruptly. "We know each other from Athens."

"Athens," Stefanos repeated.

"We met recently." I picked up my juice and put the straw to my lips, but didn't sip it. I put the glass back down. He needed to know that I wasn't into Loucas at all. "Well, not that recently." He must think I sleep with people at Mykonian hotels that I met "recently." I picked up my juice and bit my straw. *What am I saying to this man?* I asked myself.

Stefanos opened a packet of brown sugar and stirred it into his cappuccino. He threw me that odd smile again, his eyes crinkling at the corners. Heart flutter number three reared itself proving that I was definitely into older men and I never knew it. Still, he said nothing. I couldn't take the silence; I had to say something, anything.

"Everything was perfect. I want to thank you personally for being so generous to someone, well, you never met until today."

"Met *officially* until today," he corrected me. "Even if we didn't meet in person, it would've been my pleasure to know you took up my gift."

"I wanted to call you, but you didn't leave any contact

information."

"It wasn't my intention for you to find out my family name or that I own the hotel. I didn't want that to make you feel uncomfortable."

Silence again. I took a moment to think about what was so attractive about him. He didn't have Alexandros's arrogance and he seemed to be a far cry from Loucas's immaturity. He didn't look like Greg at all. It was this mystery behind his eyes and smile; they were hiding something.

"Actually, I was hoping to see you again," he said. "I hope you don't mind."

"Not at all." I beamed, my heartbeat quickening. "I'm glad to meet you too. *Harika poly.*"

I learned that Stefanos Danos was Greek American, born in California, but his parents moved to Athens around his first birthday. He returned to California to study at Stanford University and worked in finance before coming back to Greece in his late twenties to take over the family business. He had a passion for horses and especially loved Indianos, his beautiful brown and white horse that I had the pleasure of being sniffed by. Indianos lived at his home in Mykonos, which happened to be his favorite island.

As I explained where I was from, I a curling scream from the pool, "*Baba!*"

Stefanos raised his eyebrows toward the pool craning his neck, his eyes searching for the child behind the yell.

"*Baaaabaaaa!*" screamed the same voice with urgency. I turned to see a young boy, about the age of four or five, wearing a snorkeling mask and blue floaties on his arms.

"Excuse me, Ava." Stefanos walked over to the pool's

edge where the little boy had already swum to meet him. He had a son. After a few minutes Stefanos walked back to his seat, rubbing the back of his neck. He glanced at his watch.

"Is everything okay?" I asked.

"That's my son, Christos."

Then it dawned on me. Of course he had a wife! Why didn't I think of that? "Is your wife here?" I scanned the patio. I imagined she'd be upset to see her husband speaking to some strange woman, especially one looking at him too much.

"I'm divorced."

Divorced? He was of my people, well, my future people. I perked up in my seat. I figured he would understand me just fine.

"Christos is spending the holiday weekend with me. His nanny felt ill, so I took him to work."

"I'm getting a divorce too actually," I admitted.

"I'm sorry to hear that. I hope it's for the better."

I nodded my head. "I think so."

"I hate to cut this conversation short but I have to take Christos back to the house." He grabbed his tablet. "I'm going back to Athens tomorrow, and then I have to fly out on business for a week." He looked at me for a moment, a moment too long, making me look away. "But maybe we can continue this conversation in Athens after my trip."

Then, from the corner of my vision, I spotted Nikos and Eleni creeping by the wall behind Stefanos. Nikos had his hands in his pockets as he peered in our direction. He pushed back his glasses for a better look. Meanwhile, Eleni tiptoed in her flip-flops, as if we could hear them flop. I waved my hand out to them. "Oh, my friends are here, I should go too."

"About Athens?"

"I'd like that," I answered trying to figure out his smile. I guessed I'd find out soon enough. We pulled out our phones and exchanged numbers.

I smiled wide, my pulse quickening as I offered my hand and made physical contact with him. "Thanks again, Stefanos, for everything,"

He held my hand with both of his, gripping just strong enough. "My pleasure. *Harika*." He let go, walked past me, and touched my shoulder slightly. He took his son's hand and they disappeared back into the hotel. Nikos and Eleni rushed over, their faces shining and hungry for details.

"*Kouklos*." Eleni whistled. "Like a Greek George Clooney."

"That's what I thought," I said dreamily.

"He is. I must admit," Nikos said. "I hate him. What languages does he know?"

"That was him," I said happily, ignoring Nikos. "The Horse Guy."

"*Loipon*," urged Eleni. "He likes you. I can see. How old is he?"

"He told me he's forty-nine."

"Old enough to be your dad," Nikos said. "And what does he do here?"

"He's Stefanos Danos."

I shocked Eleni and Nikos into silence, shocking myself at the same time.

"You know? From the Danos Hotels?" I explained further.

Nikos dropped his voice a notch. "We know, Ava. *We* told you about the Danos Hotels."

"I did not know that was him; he never has a photo in the papers," Eleni gasped. "I wonder why he does not like to have publicity. He is good looking."

"He's really down to earth. He just thought I needed a spa break after seeing me, in his words, in an awful state. I don't think he cared that he met Loucas, or I didn't think he did. I couldn't tell."

"He will call you?" Eleni asked. "I saw you both type on your phones."

"He says he will." I pursed my lips thinking he might not. "There's something mysterious and different about him. There's just one thing, though."

"What could that be?" Nikos asked flatly. "This guy is nice, rich, and a Greek George Clooney."

"He's divorced," I said.

"So are you," Eleni threw back.

"I don't have a kid though," I countered.

"Oh," they said in unison.

"That was his boy?" Eleni asked. "Who cares? Go on a little date, the kid will not come." She shrugged her shoulders in amusement. "I hope."

"I never imagined myself liking a man old enough to be my dad, with a kid," I said.

"You also didn't think you'd be divorced," Nikos said.

"Or hanging out with a twenty-year-old student," Eleni said. "By the way, where is Loukako?"

Nikos and I laughed hearing Eleni use the diminutive of Loucas's name. In Greek, anyone's name or any noun for that matter can be made "cute" by changing its ending. Using the diminutive on people's names was sweet use of words, and another part of the language I liked.

From a Loukako to a Stefanako on one crazy party

island, life was taking a lot of unexpected turns. I wondered if I was ready for where it would lead me next.

CHAPTER SEVENTEEN

THE white-and-gray tiled floor shook beneath me. I watched each foot as I ran down the station's steps, hoping not to trip, but still make the next metro. I made it to the platform only to see it thunder away. Just as the noise subsided, my phone stopped ringing and it immediately displayed a just missed a call from Loucas. I decided I should call him back. In Greece, it would be rude not to. Maybe, he wouldn't pick up. I dialed but he answered on the first ring.

"Hey, *baby,*" Loucas chirped in a baby voice, dragging out the word baby.

I smirked. He was using a baby voice with me. When did we get that serious? "Hi, Loucas." I couldn't help but imitate his tone of voice.

"*Moro mou,* let's go for some drink in Gazi tonight."

"Actually, I," I stammered and twisted my nose for not having an excuse ready. After Mykonos, I had no desire to see him again, at least not romantically. Even though he was terribly cute, I figured I just didn't have anything in common with him. Why waste my time? We were in different phases in our lives, and I didn't need to complicate things with sex.

"I have to, uh, wash my hair?" I finally lied. Maybe he never heard that lame line before.

"Okay," he responded seemingly unfazed. "I miss you though."

I pulled the mobile away from my ear and twisted my nose up again. He had to be kidding. *Is this what the twenty-something girls had to deal with these days?*

I placed the phone back to my ear and said, "Maybe another time."

"Not this weekend because it's the basket finals."

I laughed inside when he said the word *basket*, which to Greeks meant *basketball*. I guessed the final syllable was just too much to tack on.

"Panathinakos will play against Barcelona," he said with much more excitement in his voice. "All weekend I am at a friend's house in Vouliagmeni."

"Totally do your basket guy thing." I envisioned them weaving baskets.

"If you change your mind I want to know it, because I want very much to see you again," he whined, but added on quite abruptly, "but not this weekend."

"Not this weekend." I repeated.

The metro thundered into the station again.

"Sounds like you must leave," he said. His baby voice reared itself again. "Miss you."

"*Bye-yee.*" I hung up and let out a sigh as I tucked my cell phone in my purse.

The metro screeched to a halt. The door to one metro car stopped squarely in front of me. As I zipped my purse closed, a jumble of arms and legs converged around me even though the doors hadn't opened yet. I figured out early on that many Greeks didn't like to queue because it seemed everyone wanted to be first. That always made me nervous standing in line anywhere, even in a store to pay for something, because people would cut in front of me and I'd lose my place. After it happened a few times, I'd lift my finger in protest, only to place it down again, realizing that it was just another one of those strange daily experiences from living in Greece.

The lack of subway queues was another of those things I had gotten used to. I often stood off to the side as passengers clawed past each other. Between those blocking the doors to get in and those compressed inside trying to get out, it all was rather annoying or amusing, depending on how my day was going. With so many people trying to squeeze in, the crowd pushed me aside as another throng of people rushed to make the closing doors. The next thing I knew, the metro doors snapped shut in front of my face, and the steel and metal churned away. I found myself alone on the platform.

I plunked down on a gray metal bench and looked upto find an array of marbled ancient Greek sculptures, chiseled and mounted on the wall across the tracks. Just as I was thinking how the guidebooks were right—the Athens metro was like an underground museum—a sharp voice cut my train of thought.

"Pou prepei na allakso traino an thelo na pao stin Omonia?"

The accent was undoubtedly American. I turned to find a brunette, middle-aged woman standing with an array of shopping bags lined down her arms. Her cheeks were plump with pink blush to match her track suit.

"Do you speak English?" I asked, almost a hundred percent sure that she did.

"Oh, sorry, dear, I didn't realize you're not Greek," she said in a perfect American accent.

"I'm American too." I loved to meet Americans in Greece. I spoke freely, without thinking about grammar or cultural differences. Good, old, easy American English. I smiled. "I'm from New York."

The shopping bags rustled about her. "Cool, I'm from Chicago. Anyway, I think I'm going the right way." She pressed an index finger on a glass case enclosing the metro map. "Yep," she confirmed. "I'm visiting relatives and I forget where everything is from the last time I came."

"How long are you staying?"

"Not short enough. This city is driving me nuts!" She slapped her hand upward in midair, which jiggled bags about her. Her pout quickly disappeared and turned into an exaggerated smile. "But I love New York. Are you on vacation?"

"I live here."

"What?" she asked, dipping her voice in a strange deep tone. "You choose to live *here*?" She started to shake her head in disbelief.

I flinched. *Was it so hard to fathom?* Yet, my cheeks heated up with embarrassment at her question. "Um, yeah."

"Good for you." She shook her head. "I'm half-Greek and all, but I can't stand it. You should go back, *go back*, save yourself."

I pinpointed her Chicago accent as she elevated her voice. A few folks nearby glanced in our direction. If only I could remind her that most people actually understood English in Athens.

"Um, I like it here," I said in a small voice.

She continued as if she didn't hear me. "Things are unorganized, everyone's on strike all the time, nothing freaking works; the country is falling apart with the debt they put on themselves. And if you haven't noticed, people are just plain rude!" She circled one hand in the air, just like a Greek would do to make a point. Two of the shopping bags slid down her pink velour arm. *"Go home,"* she lowered her voice into a vibrating purr, her eyes as wide as saucers.

I narrowed my eyes, wondering how to respond. I had this new urge to defend Greece. "Greece is beautiful."

"You're just crazy then. There's nothing that beats America. We got it all. I lived in Miami; we got beaches too."

The metro whizzed up. I walked away from the Chicagoan, hoping she wouldn't follow me. She wiggled up next to me on the platform. "What did you do in New York?"

I glanced at her again. I couldn't be rude and ignore her. "I was in marketing."

"Oh, yeah." She flipped her hand out. "You can't beat that here. You *know* what people get paid here? Now what are you doing?"

"I'm a nanny." I found myself saying my new job like a question.

She gave me a double take. "So you're here for love then?" she asked fluttering her lashes.

"Actually, no," I muttered. A pang of hurt shot up inside me as thoughts of Greg, the reason I was actually living in Greece in the first place, raced through my mind.

Exhibiting proper Greek metro etiquette, the Chicagoan firmly planted her body right where the doors opened. I squeezed myself in with the crowd, the Chicagoan sandwiched next to me with her shopping bag glory. As the metro sped off, my cell phone rang. In the packed car, I'd be sure to elbow someone if I reached for it.

Over the ringtone, the Chicagoan said, "No job, no

love, don't give me the line you're in love with Greece."
She laughed, cocking her head back.

Like usual, even though the metro was packed, it
was dead quiet. Her cackle resonated over the lull of the
metro wheels sliding down the steel tracks. A few gazes
darted in our direction.

I scrunched my forehead and tried to distract myself,
turning my attention to an advertisement about some
new toothpaste. I could actually read the Greek. My face
heated up as I thought about how upset this stranger
and her judgments of my life made me. Why did I care
about what someone who didn't know what I had been
through these past months thought? An announcement
blared over the loudspeaker calling out the next station
in English and Greek.

"*Signomi.*" I excused myself as I inched my way past
a few passengers to get ready to disembark. The metro
halted and tears begin to well up behind my eyes. The
doors opened and I heard her voice one last time.

"Nice to meet you," she yelled loudly towards my
back and over the passengers that helped to push me
out of the overstuffed metro car.

I stood on the platform, which I quickly realized
was the wrong stop. It didn't matter. I sat on a metal
bench and looked down at my hands. A tear fell on
them. I closed my eyes and a disturbing vision of the
Chicagoan's face circled around in triplicate. Her eyes
squinted, finger pointed at me, her lips screwed as she
mouthed the words, "*Go home.*"

She was right. America *was* wonderful. Was she a
sign? Was I making a mistake? What did Greece have
to offer me now? My cell phone croaked like a frog to
remind me someone had called. Stefanos. Suddenly the

invisible weight on my shoulders lifted.

I wiped my last tears, straightened my posture, and glanced around to find a few people who knew how to mind their own business. The fresh air hit me as the escalator ascended up. I'd walk home and at that moment, that home was in Athens. That was my choice.

I glanced at the clock as I placed the last dish I washed away. I had called Stefanos back, and he'd said he'd call me in a few hours. All the waiting had me thinking about him.

"I hardly know Stefanos, but something about him intrigues me," I confessed to Eleni as I wiped the counter down.

"Intriguing?" She flipped through a Greek gossip magazine.

"You know, interesting, very much of my interest," I translated.

"Then Stefanos is intriguing." She was practicing how to say the word. "What time will he call?"

"Anytime around now. I hate waiting." I threw down the dish towel.

"I thought you say you were not to wait for men." Eleni glanced up at me then back down at her magazine. "Talk first, do not be so, how you say *sfikti*? Uptight!" She proudly found the exact English word she wanted.

"We had a conversation, if you recall, and I liked him," I said firmly. "Right away."

"How do you decide? I never like anyone right away." I knew that was true. She was suspicious of every guy. They need to earn the right for her to actually be nice to them. That was Eleni.

"I think my tastes are changing. I won't hold the divorce against him. That would've been a no-no before."

"Life look different when you're divorced too," Eleni said. "The point of view, it changes." She flipped a page. "*To paidi*, the kid?"

"That I am not sure yet. But I need to learn more before I close my mind. See? I'm open to new things."

"He also has money."

"Probably, but I don't really care. I do care that he *doesn't* seem to care about showing it off."

She nodded and flipped another page. "He seems mature. He is forty-nine."

"Mature, yes. Nineteen years older than me mature. I think I can appreciate experience, especially after the whole Loukako ordeal."

"Poor Loukako. I think he really liked you."

I smiled. "I guess, but I just don't feel it. Now, with Stefanos—"

"I know."

"Know what about Stefanos?"

"I know why this is all," she paused, "intriguing—" she smiled when she remembered her new English word "—and you hardly know him."

"Do tell."

"He is chasing you and he is chasing you still!" She slapped the magazine down onto the couch.

"Maybe, you have a point." I rubbed my fingers on my chin. "That's never happened to me. I mean, the chase even began on horseback!"

We laughed.

"Alexandros did *kamaki* on you, but it was just to get you in bed and not talk to you again. *Malaka.*" Eleni flipped her hand in the air to make her point. "Loukako likes you but you don't like him. Your choice. Now, Stefanos seems serious about getting to know you. Too much effort. Is it not fun to be chased? Especially if you want to be?" she asked brightly.

The phone rang. We both looked at it.

"Ah, *tha figo*." Eleni made her way to the door. "It's the Horse Guy, chasing you on horseback."

She air kissed me good night on the way out the door. "Good luck. *Ta leme avrio*."

I winked at her then picked up the phone. The caller ID informed me that it was Stefanos. I took a deep breath; I needed to sound nonchalant.

"Hello?"

"Ava? Hi, it's Stefanos. Sorry it took me so long to call you back, I was at an event at the hotel."

"No worries. I'm glad you called." I liked his voice and somehow, I relaxed into it a little.

"Not yet out on the town?"

"It's eleven p.m., on Wednesday," I said as if he was crazy to think I'd be heading out. In fact, it was a valid question because it was about the time when Greeks typically finish dinner and might head out afterwards. "Nope, no plans."

"So you're well aware of going out time in Greece."

"Any day of the week too." I laughed. "Believe it or not, I am used to it now, I just forget. America is so different that way."

"You're becoming like a Greek. Not a Chinese-Mexican-White girl as you say—from boring Upstate New York," he said lightly.

"Just a Chinese-Mexican-White girl living in exciting Athens, Greece now."

"Well, if I was there in Athens now I would ask you out."

I smiled.

"But, I am here on this island and I should try to get some sleep, I guess. The staff here in Corfu has me on a tight schedule. I've got a big breakfast meeting at seven in the morning. I was hoping to get a workout in at five."

"You're going for a workout that early?" I believed in minimal getting ready time in the morning.

"It gives me energy for the rest of the day. I never used to exercise so much, but now it's becoming more important to me. I'm learning some of the most important things in life later than I should."

Hmm, what does that mean? I kept the question to myself and instead said, "*Bravo sou.*"

"*Bravo mou.*" He chuckled. "Good for me. So is your hometown really boring like you say?"

"Ithaca is pretty, but also pretty boring," I said in my most bored voice. "Athens, on the other hand, is way too exciting."

"It's too bad you're thinking of leaving. But I understand it. Divorce is a process, it can be really painful."

"I guess you know with your divorce and," I paused for a second, "with a kid."

"I do, believe me, I do. But that story is for another day. Anyway, I believe that things happen for a reason."

"My friends say that all the time. I think I'm turning into a believer."

"I'd love to call you tomorrow," he said.

"I'd like that."

"*Kalinichta.*"

I dropped the phone on the floor then stretched over

my covers, feeling the cool sheets against my bare arms. I couldn't help but smile. He showed all signs of interest and wanted to talk to me again. As Eleni said, Stefanos found me worth chasing. The man I loved found me worth dumping. I was too tired to ask myself why as I slowly shut my eyes and let drowsiness take over me.

CHAPTER EIGHTEEN

"SEASICK, skinny-dipping, and a Horse Guy?" Amy shook her head as she opened a cupboard, reaching for two Chinese teacups, when suddenly she turned her attention to the corner of the room. I glanced over to see the Wu with a big smile on his face, his hands outstretched and reaching to pull down the cord of an iron dangling off the kitchen countertop. It was like she had eyes on the back of her head. I helped to recover the iron.

"Irons are not for little boys," Amy scolded Wu.

He responded with a blood-curdling scream and plastered himself onto the marble floor. His cherubic face morphed into a plump tomato, his eyes shut tight with tears. After a few seconds, he suddenly stopped. Amy embraced him, rocking him back and forth.

"You know, Wu counted to one hundred today in English," I informed Amy, glancing at Wu and giving him a supportive nod.

Wu's teary eyes blinked. He understood I had just said something good about him.

Amy kissed him on the head as he wriggled free to run off into the living room.

She patted down her trousers and stepped back to the counter to pour Chinese black tea into two matching teacups. "So what happened? You fell in love after he arrived on horseback like a knight in shining armor?"

"Hmm, I wish." I sighed. "But get this. Do you know who the Horse Guy turned out to be?"

"Well, who?"

"The owner of the Danos."

"Ah," Amy said. "Now I see why you're intrigued. You met Stefanos Danos. I don't blame you."

"You know Stefanos?" *How could Amy know Stefanos?* Eleni was right. Athens was like a small town, not a city of five million people.

She pursed her lips as if trying to remember some details. "Ah, yes, of course, I met him at our embassy event at his hotel. He's handsome. I was surprised at how quiet and reserved he was, but I think that's what makes him mysterious. He had brought his wife, a Greek woman from South Africa who was very stunning."

My heart dropped. He had been married to someone stunning? And not that long ago?

"So he's divorced again?"

"Again?" My heart fell even further.

"I think he has a son from the first wife, the South African Greek is the second wife, if I remember..." She looked off to the side, trying to recall something. She took a sip of her tea and wrinkled her brow. "Just be careful," she warned.

I frowned. Stefanos hadn't mentioned multiple wives. Then again, why would he? Anyway, I was getting a divorce, and maybe I would get married again one day, so who cared how many marriages he had? I wondered if I should care, actually.

"We had a short and sweet conversation on the phone last night, so I didn't learn all that much about him."

Amy reached across the counter to pat my hand.

"Just have fun, don't take anything seriously right now," she said with an assuring nod. "Besides, kids can make things complicated. I want to see you happy." She paused and searched my eyes thoughtfully. "I sound like a nagging mom."

"You are like the nagging older sister I never had." I patted her hand back.

Amy proved to be a good sounding board. There was no way I could talk to my mom about dating again whatsoever anymore. Greg—and the fact that I ignored her advice about him—had forever tainted my ability to talk about my relationships with her.

Amy giggled. "Older sister? I like that; it makes me feel young."

"I'm glad we have these talks," I said feeling appreciative.

"Whatever you need, just ask. You're like family now."

There they were, piled in a haphazard mahogany red pile in front of me—*kerasia* or cherries. The kind I couldn't resist. The little fruit store called *Frutopigi* which translated to *fruit spout* always caught my eye when I walked back home. I pulled out a paper brown bag from the counter and shoveled in two scoops. The cherries were sitting next to their in-season neighbors, flesh colored peaches and nectarines, and little baskets of shiny red strawberries. I loved the rich flavors that fruits always proved to have in Greece. The *Fruitopigi* was one of many corner fruit shops in the city, and along with the weekly neighborhood farmers markets it was clear that Greeks preferred to eat food in season. I would be like a Greek, I decided, and stick to early summer fruit salads. The diet needed to start.

Should Stefanos see me naked again, I told myself with a smile as I stuffed a few nectarines in another brown bag, *he won't even recognize me*. Minutes later, I swung my soon-to-be salad in its plastic bag as I whistled and strolled back home where I would happily wait for his call.

Just as I polished off my super healthy fruit salad later that night, the phone rang.

"*Kalispera*," I answered feeling a lightness in my chest knowing who it was.

"*Kalispera*," Stefanos replied.

I sat down on the couch. A smile spread across my lips. "How was your day?"

"We had a big meeting, which went well. What's on my mind is coming back to Athens to see you this weekend."

"So, you're asking me out this weekend?" I teased.

"I plan to. Is that okay?" he asked with the same playful tone.

"So I hope you don't mind if I ask you something." I pursed my lips for a moment. I wanted to get to the point before I committed to our date.

"About?"

"The twins' mom, Amy Li, mentioned that she met you."

"Amy *Li*." He stretched out her last name.

"The ambassador's wife. The family I work for," I tacked on.

"Ah, yes, I went to their embassy event at my hotel.

There are so many embassy events, and the ambassadors change all the time. I can't keep track."

"She said you were mysteriously handsome."

"Sounds like a good thing," he said, sounding intrigued. "Don't tell her, but I mostly don't like those events. Too many stuffy people."

"And she remembers meeting Christos's mother, a South African Greek woman."

"Anna, yes," he said as if recalling a long lost friend.

Anna, I mouthed to myself.

"That's not Christos's mom," he said after a pause. "Anna was my third wife."

"Three wives?" A knot suddenly formed in my stomach.

"Not at the same time." He sounded amused. "Actually, Christos is my son from my fourth wife, Despina."

"Four wives?" I repeated. *Was that the mysterious thing he had going for him?* It didn't sound promising.

"I've lived a few lives."

"Yeah, I guess." I couldn't imagine having committed to four different people, four different times. The decision to commit to Greg—one guy—was a huge in itself.

"I can tell you about it, if you want to know."

"Yes," I gulped. *How exactly did four wives happen?*

"I was twenty-one when I married my American wife, Jennifer. We divorcedwhen I decided to move back to Greece. Then I met Katerina after I moved to Greece, and we got married and had my other son, Thanos."

"You have another son?" The stomach knot ballooned up inside me.

"He's fourteen and lives with his mom in Toronto.

She's a lovely woman, but we were young and stupid, you know? We parted ways amicably."

"Oh." He has a teenager.

"And then I married Anna, but we didn't have any kids. We divorced seven years ago and I met Despina and had Christos right away, but we've been divorced for the past year now."

A Jenny, or was it Jennifer? Some Greek women's name. One American. *Too many women!* I opened my eyes wide and found myself scratching my head.

"You're quiet. I hope I didn't scare you," he said. "My personal life isn't something I'm too vocal about. People tend to be way too judgmental, in my opinion, about things like marriage and divorce."

"It's just..." I paused and considered what he just told me. I did know what he meant. When I've told people I'd be divorced, I felt like a failure or just plain embarrassed especially when reactions morphed into the most pitiful of looks. But *four* divorces? I couldn't help but ask myself if I was a hypocrite for being uneasy about that. "It's just interesting to me," I finally said carefully. "I'm getting divorced now and it's stressful enough to think about doing it once."

"It's just complicated with Thanos, which is a long story. I wish I saw him more, but I don't get along with his mother anymore. Christos lives in Thessaloniki."

"Okay." I wished I could've said something smarter. The stomach knot had settled in by then.

"I hope you'll be available this weekend still because I have some ideas."

"Ideas?"

"Check your in-box. I just sent you something."

I headed to my laptop and found a message from

Stefanos. I clicked it open to find an attachment.

"A pdf."

"Open it."

I opened up a colorfully designed map of a chunk of Athens and a few nearby islands. The second page was an itinerary.

"Wow. Is this what you've been doing in Corfu at all your meetings?" I teased. If he went through this trouble to make a map for me instead of doing whatever a CEO did, I was already feeling a bit better about him. "It's impressive."

"Sort of." He laughed. "If you'll go out with me this weekend, you'll find out all you wanted to know and not know about me."

"Something more than four marriages?" I regretted saying it at the moment, afraid he'd take it wrong. The fact was, I hadn't decided if a four-times divorced man should be off-limits to me. I didn't think four-times divorced people existed until that moment.

"Maybe," he responded in a friendly enough tone. "That's why the date goes on for two days. I figure you'll have a lot of questions."

I laughed and scanned the page further, giving it a double take. He wasn't joking. I cleared my throat. "Your schedule says we meet at twelve on Saturday and return at ten at night on Sunday. I'll be back in time for work on Monday afternoon so that's good." I paused. "If I agree, I'd like some details on this elaborate plan."

"Fair enough. You told me last night that you're unsure about whether you'll stay in Athens or not. Think of this extended date as a tour of the city you haven't gotten to know yet and an insight into what you'll be missing if you leave. I don't think, at least from what we've discussed so far, that you've been to any of these places. Including Hydra Island?"

"No, none of these places." My pulse raced thinking about the whole idea which seemed overwhelming, even touching. He had put so much thought into this date, or trip rather. "Well, I've heard Hydra is beautiful."

"I would love to take you there. But before that, we'll start at Mount Immitos, then down to Vouliagmeni, then Piraeus, and then a boat to Hydra. I have the day in Hydra planned. I'll book two rooms, so don't feel pressure. It'll be fun. Will you come with me?" He said it all so easily.

I rapped my fingernails on the kitchen counter and pondered his question for a moment. *How could I not?* Why should I close the door on what sounded like an amazing date, or trip, or hybrid trip-date. Whatever it was, I had already moved on to wondering what I should wear. Visions of which dress would suit a little Greek island like Hydra wafted through my mind when he asked, "Or you can just think about it?"

I snapped back to reality. "It'll be fun," I said brightly. "Yes, I'll go."

I figured I was taking Amy's advice. Stefanos seemed thoughtful and fun and that's what I needed. Fun with someone I liked. Okay, so he had four marriages. I brushed the thought aside. I was in Greece and had an amazing opportunity to discover Athens with a very nice and handsome, George Clooney look alike who also happened to be a Greek hotel magnate. *I mean, what could possibly go wrong?*

CHAPTER NINETEEN

"**I**T'S hard enough to choose one date outfit," Eleni moaned, "but now we must pack you for a weekend!"

I opened my closet doors. I decided immediately I had absolutely nothing to wear and I hated all of the clothes I ever bought or made. "Help!"

Eleni shuffled to my computer. "I must see this map." Her morning cappuccino steamed out of her favorite mug emblazoned with the word *pringipessa* or princess in yellow neon Greek letters. The bright morning sun streamed in the window, a sweet reminder that in a matter of hours, Stefanos would pick me up.

I stuck my head back in my closet. "My e-mail should be open." As I contemplated which sandals screamed "Hydra," Eleni gasped.

"*Perimene!*" she exclaimed strangely.

"What happened, is it my laptop?" I turned around to look over her shoulder. "It's prone to viruses."

Then I understood why she said the Greek equivalent to *hold your horses*. Above Stefanos's e-mail titled, *Athens This Weekend*, an e-mail from Greg titled, *Still in Athens?* sat there unopened.

Well, that said a lot, I thought.

"Damn it." I scowled. A cloud seemed to dull the streaming sunlight that filled the room. "What does he want?" I asked, clenching my fists.

"Still in Athens?" Eleni asked raising her hands in the air. "What kind of *malakies* is this?"

"*Malakies*. All bullshit. Exactly," I spat out. I made a crisp, flat clicking-like sound with my tongue, expressing my annoyance.

Eleni gave me a double take accompanied with a sly smile. "Ava, you're Greek, I knew it!"

I rolled my eyes. I was proving to be a Greek tongue clicker, go figure. "He doesn't need to know anything," I said.

"Do you want to open it?" Eleni asked in a small voice.

"Hell, no," I said hotly. I hastily grabbed the mouse and pounded on it to delete the message.

"You did the right thing." Eleni placed her coffee cup down then seethed, "*Malaka* is back."

I stalked over to the balcony windows, feeling heavyhearted. I could never confront Greg with all of my anger like I just did in front of Eleni. How could I have been so weak when it came to him, the person I chose to be my husband? Maybe I was missing Greg. I was definitely missing *something* in my life. I buried my head in my hands. My eyes felt warm and I rubbed them gently. Eleni pushed the wooden desk chair back on the hardwood floor and then I heard her paddle in her flip-flops toward me. "Tell me," she coaxed. "What are you thinking?"

The tears welled up. "I'm not okay," I mumbled.

"I know you are not okay." Eleni began to stroke my back lightly.

"I just feel so lost." I exhaled feeling my chest puff up, feeling short of breath, and feeling tired of just *feeling* pathetic. "As soon as he contacts me, I suddenly feel empty and alone, just like when he called me a few weeks ago."

"What do you mean?"

"I'm thirty and I have no order in my life. He left my world upside down. I don't know where to go, what I should be doing, what my priorities are." I hated how I sounded desperate and unsure. "I feel like I should know something by now."

"You are figuring things out. You go through big changes. What is wrong with taking it easy?" she asked softly.

"I've always had order, Eleni." I caught her look as the sunlight casted a brilliant glow on her makeup-free face. I'm sure I was one of the few to see it "unpainted," as the Greeks would say. Her brow furrowed and her lips turned into a slight frown.

"It was just me and my mom in a small town. I knew for sure for so long that I could never leave her. I had a career there and I was good at my work. Then I met Greg and I loved him and he turned my world around. I left all of that security with my mom for this silly pipe dream that maybe Greg and I could have children together. We would give them the kind of stable life I never really had growing up."

"*O babas sou*, your father," she said cautiously.

"Yeah." I wiped a tear away. "To this day, I still think every day why, why he never tried to see me. I mean, doesn't he miss me?" I had never admitted that to anyone, even my mother. A silence hung between us. "What did I do wrong to him?" I asked in a small voice.

"You did not do anything wrong. How could you? You were *ten*."

"But that's not how I feel." I sobbed and pressed my forehead hard against the warm glass pane. "I failed my father, and now I have a failed marriage. My mom saw it all along and I couldn't see it. I hate that all of these feelings are just flooding back now."

"*Agapi mou*," Eleni coaxed gently.

"And with Alexandros, look how I went crazy for him and he forgot about me." I pressed an open palm against the window. "I don't want to make the same mistakes. I feel so broken. It hurts so much to know that I'm so," I paused and admitted, "dispensable."

"You are not a thing to be thrown away!" Eleni exclaimed with her usual gusto. "You are a beautiful friend, like you are a daughter. You were beautiful as a wife and as you would be as a girlfriend. If someone cannot understand, that is *malakies*."

I looked at her hopefully and silently. Was she right? Was it all really their fault and not mine?

"Forget Alexandros, he's a *malaka*." Eleni waved her hand sounding annoyed that she even had to mention his name.

"But it feels like I'm so easy to walk away from."

"You are not, Ava *mou*. You have met wrong people." She paused. "At least you are going on dates again. You must learn *siga siga* after your biggest love lesson, your wedding with Greg. Although..." She threw me a serious look, narrowing her dark brown eyes at me.

"Yes?"

She looked up at the ceiling for a moment, recalling something. "As we say in Greece, *tria poulakia kathondan ke eplekan* pullover."

"Something about *tria*, three, *poulakia*, birds, *kathondan*, sitting," I attempted to translate. "Three birds are sitting? And there's a sweater?" I shrugged my shoulders.

"It means that three birds are sitting and knitting a sweater." She twirled a strand of her thick brown hair and let out a hearty laugh. "This doesn't mean something to you, does it?"

"You definitely lost me." I sniffled.

"It means you don't understand what is really going on around you," Eleni explained further.

"You mean that I'm in my own world, as we say." She wasn't the first one to tell me that.

"Right. No matter how much we told you about Greg, you could not understand how he was to you."

"I realize that now." Too late.

"*Den einai kako*. It's not bad," she continued. "You like to think the positive about people and that things will be okay. So, you avoid some things that are the truth. I tell you Greg was a *malaka*, and Alexandros is another kind of *malaka*. Loucas just wants sex, but that is your decision."

"I suppose," I sighed.

"Sex isn't bad." Eleni arched an eyebrow. She smiled and then she let the smile fall as she went on. "As for your dad, I don't know what happened, but I do know that it had nothing to do with you. You were a child, and he was an adult. He was wrong. Maybe he will find you but that might not become. Many years, too many, passed. Be strong with yourself. Do what you need to be happy."

"I'm trying." I forced a smile. "I guess I shouldn't regret anything."

"Never regret anything. Things—"

"Happen for a reason," I chimed in to finish.

"A good reason." She nodded. "Whether you stay or go, you make your own choices now. Your mom wants you to be happy, but whether you stay here in Athens or move to New York City, it will still be too far away from her if it is not Ithaca."

"I do miss her and all that, but after living completely on my own..." I paused for a moment. "I feel like I need to go back because I owe her."

"Your mom loves you without reason, no matter what will happen. You don't owe anyone anything."

"Maybe part of me thinks that way because she didn't leave me, like my dad did. I can't bear to talk to her so much lately because I feel like a disappointment to the one parent who stayed by my side my whole life. How ungrateful am I?"

"You are not ungrateful; you are hurt and with confusion," Eleni said. "You know a few things *for sure* now."

"Like what?" I asked with interest. What in the world could I possibly know?

"You are not to follow Greg anymore; that is over. *Telos*."

"True."

"You want to live in Greece. That could change. For now you know this is home."

"Right." I felt a tiny bit better realizing that I did know *something*. "I need a job to keep my work status in the European Union. After Greg files the divorce papers, that could be it and there's my decision made for me." I looked down at the floor.

"He does not file yet, so you have time. Use it to figure out what you want."

"Life is getting harder here, the unemployment, the strikes, and the demonstrations." I glanced back up at her. "I think that Chicago woman on the metro had a point. America is better in some ways. I could work again in marketing easily, no language barriers, back to good old meritocracy." But there was nothing magical about that, was there?

"I support you in for all of those things as long as we can combine it with a question," Eleni said. She crossed her arms and shot me a stern look.

"Which is?"

"Forget everyone, forget the papers you must file, and forget citizenship. If you want something, it can happen. What does Ava Martin really want?"

It was a good question. "I wish I really knew," I said sadly.

She hugged me tight. "You will."

"Stefanos seems to think his date will help me decide about Athens," I said. I sat down on the couch to wipe the last of my tears.

Eleni eyed me up and down, her eyebrows raised high, with her classic look of concern. "You okay?"

"I'm fine now." I pursed my lips into a thin smile. "Let's get to the map."

"Yes, the map!" She hopped to my desk and opened up the e-mail. Scanning the page she said, "Stefanos did much work on this, *po po*." She waved her hand in a small circle expressing something positive.

"Notice that one star is on Hydra." I pointed my finger to the little island just outside of Athens.

"Hydra *einai para poly omorfi*," Eleni said expressing how beautiful Hydra was in Greek. She placed both hands on the desk and turned to me, narrowing her eyes slightly. "How you feel about the sleep there part?"

"I don't know actually." I shrugged my shoulders. "He told me he's booking two rooms there because he doesn't want me to get the wrong idea."

"That's fine," she concluded. "I never imagined a first date like this. It will be fun. I wish I could come."

"The whole mysterious ex-wives thing though."

"Oh, Ava." Eleni waved her hand out. "He's almost fifty; it would be strange if he was not married before. I dated a man once who was forty-three, divorced. Well, one date it was. I didn't like his cologne." She scrunched her nose. "You know my sensitivity to smells."

I giggled. "But four wives?"

"Who says you'll be the fifth? It's just a date. *Endaksi*, okay, a two-day date. Trip and date?"

"I just like him. I don't even know him. Maybe that's why I can't stop thinking about these things."

"Calm down and have fun. Like Amy said, you should not be too serious about things now."

"I'm definitely not ready for a commitment again anyway. Not now."

"Besides," Eleni said, "you do not meet a man like Stefanos Danos every day. I'd have to kill you if you didn't take this opportunity. Don't close the door on anything."

I poked her shoulder. "Maybe he has cute friends."

"Maybe, to be seen," she said. "You have fun first."

"I still don't know what type of guy you *are* into, you know that?"

"I love Greek guys," said Eleni flatly. "Specifically what type? *Einai mystico*."

"A secret," I translated.

"Okay, we have to get you going. Jeans for the day one." She shuffled through the hangers in my closet. "Do these fit okay?" she asked holding out my dark blue Armani's.

"God, I hope so," I said. "Why is dating so much stress?"

"You are the one with stress," she muttered as she opened up my underwear drawer. Maybe she was right.

I was sure the circulation in my upper thighs would get cut off. I envisioned an afternoon in the emergency room where the Greek doctors would have to cut off my Armani's. They were too tight but Eleni said I looked hot. Why did hot have to mean uncomfortable? Who made that stupid rule?

I fingered my *mati* necklace as I waited at the stoop of my building with my weekend tote at my feet. I had never done something like this before. Stefanos could be a weirdo, but my gut told me he wasn't. I sighed concluding if I couldn't stand him, I could always take a taxi home—well, before I ended up in the middle of a Greek island. I gulped.

At that moment, a vintage dark blue Land Rover choked its exhaust in front of me. Stefanos turned off the engine and jumped out stepping towards me with a boyish grin. He wore light khaki cargo pants and a plain vanilla T-shirt, bringing out his tan and making me notice how nice his George Clooney hair complemented him.

"Back from Corfu," I said grinning as I approached him too.

"You look lovely," he said.

We kissed each other on the cheeks, and tplaced his hand on the small of my back. I pulled away, making sure he wouldn't catch the little pooch welling out over the waistline of my jeans.

"Thanks," I said.

I reached for my tote but he immediately took it from me.

"I can do this." He carefully placed my bag into the trunk next to a big picnic basket and his own overnight bag.

"It's great to be back," he said as we climbed into the car. "I'm not so much into business traveling. If I can avoid it, I do. This is different though."

I strapped on my seatbelt. "There are so many places to see."

"Where is your favorite?"

"Well, here." My cheeks warmed up. "Actually, Athens is the only other city outside of the East Coast of the United States that I've been to. And Athens is the only other place I've lived besides Ithaca."

"Really?" He glanced at me slightly before turning his attention back to the road.

Ah, a normal driver, I thought with relief.

"You're out with a real small American college-town girl," I warned him.

"All right then real small American college-town girl," he responded with a playful smile, "do you remember our first stop in this big city?"

"Up there in the mountains, according to your fabulous map." I pointed out the window towards the rocky peaks that bordered the eastern edge of the city. He nodded and lowered his sunglasses over his eyes.

"It's just ten minutes away, and then it's all nature."

"Hey, city boy, just remember that I grew up in Upstate New York, where we're surrounded by nature."

"Touché." He laughed.

The Land Rover growled up a lone road that led into the wild thickness of Mount Immitos. The concrete jungle of Athens morphed into a proper forest. With my window half opened I took in the essence of the dry rocky brown earth and green foliage. Singing birds and humming bees overtook the drone of the SUV's roar at times. I scanned the way for butterflies, but didn't see any.

"You don't have to be very high above Athens to get an amazing view." He parked in a small clearing. I hopped out and stood at the edge of the cliff where I immediately spotted the ancient city center, the Acropolis, towering around the old city. From there the modern city expanded endlessly from that recognizable core, a sea of dusty white concrete that crept up the edges of the cliffs and to my west, down to the sparkling sea.

He opened the trunk to pull out a big basket. He laid out a blue blanket over a patch of grass. A slight breeze wafted the fresh scent of pine towards us.

"Need some help?" I asked.

"No, it's ready actually." He rubbed his hands together. "I made sandwiches. I hope you'll like them." He pulled out some clear plastic containers. Inside were four different fancy sandwiches with numerous luncheon meat and vegetables stacked between loaves of black seeded, plain white, and croissant-like breads.

"They are so gourmet." I eyed them quite impressed. "Definitely not peanut butter and jelly." I kneeled next to him on the blanket's edge.

"I don't know how Americans eat that." He threw me a look.

"I love it toasted with warm milk," I said. "It reminds me of the good days of my childhood."

He looked up at me for a brief moment, but went back to pulling out the silverware packed inside the basket.

"You know, all days were good really." I caught myself. "P.B.J. every day!" I scolded myself, there was no need to get into my childhood issues in the first hour.

"I didn't make these, but I thought you'd like to try them." He pulled out a small box of little cheese pies. "They're from a famous bakery near my house."

"They smell amazing."

I picked one up and took a bite. The *tiropita*, with its perfectly flaky filo dough and feta cheese filling, melted in my mouth. Just as good as Nikos's *yiayia's* version.

"I'm glad you like them." He reached into his pocket to pull out a leather fold. He unrolled it and pulled out a yellow plastic bag of what appeared to be smoking tobacco, rolling papers, a small plastic pipe, and a roll of tiny white cylindrical filters. He rolled up his cigarette in a matter of seconds. When I moved to Greece, I discovered most people still smoked and even preferred to make their own cigarettes with their arsenal of supplies.

"So you smoke?" My heart sank. I couldn't help but feel disappointed.

"I do, unfortunately. I know most Americans don't these days. I hope you don't mind?" He glanced at me, raising his lighter.

"No, go ahead," I answered.

"I only smoke a few each day, which is better than most Greeks. I bet that sounds like an excuse. Is it a turn-off?" He turned his head to breathe out a long cloud of curly smoke into the fresh air.

"Not exactly. But it isn't a turn-on," I tacked on as sweetly as possible.

He answered with a smile. I remembered that mysterious look I couldn't decipher *and* those long lashes. We remained quiet as we both took in our city laid out below us. I wondered what else I would discover.

CHAPTER TWENTY

"HERE are your clues about the next stop: hot, deep water, and steep rocky cliffs."

"We're off to a seaside volcano," I teased Stefanos.

"Something even better than scorching lava," he deadpanned.

The Land Rover jerked us around down the mountain. With one hand on the wheel, he looked over at me. "So far so good?"

Before I could answer, my cell phone mewed. I opened a text from Nikos and Eleni who wondered the same.

I texted back: *So far so good. But he smokes.*

A little while later Possidonos Avenue came up in our view, a main city artery that ran along area beaches. "This looks familiar, I'm sure," he said.

The Saronic Gulf and its blue-and-green waters swirled into a tantalizing calm in the distance. We passed the colorful beach bar entrances then turned off onto a small road away from the sea. We drove into a gate that led us to a small lake, but what called my attention was the looming earthen colored mountainside that sliced sharply into it.

"Here we are," he announced.

I whistled.

"This is actually a spa." He got out of the car.

I hopped out too, and walked up to a white sign. "Lake Vouliagmeni, the sunken lake," I read. "It was once a large cavern that collapsed it says."

"The water is constantly twenty-four degrees Celsius which comes from the mountain we just visited. It continues deep inside the mountain, but it's never been fully explored if you can believe it. A few amateur divers have drowned trying. It's that big."

"It reminds me of the gorges in Ithaca. And you know Ithaca is gorgeous," I said wrinkling my nose at the famous pun I grew up with. My neighbor Mindy's car and, well, most of Ithaca's cars had bumper stickers emblazoned with the local saying, *Ithaca is Gorges.*

His eyebrows squished together, not getting my joke. "Really? Well, this lake is one of my favorite places in Athens."

Over the sound of splashing water and laughing children I asked, "Why is that?"

He turned to me and smiled. "It's just something you wouldn't expect to find here. It's out of place, but at the same time it belongs. It's so different, something you'd see in the mountain, maybe, but here..." He stared out into the lake, his lips thinned out into a slight smile. "I don't know if you know what I mean."

"I do, more than you know." While my relationship with Athens was just rounding out at eight months, I understood what he meant. Lake Vouliagmeni was out of place. I followed him across the labyrinth of deck furniture. A waiter then led us to an empty table in the corner with a huge white umbrella above it.

"We can go in if you want." He grinned with the George-Clooney-like nod. "I now know you can swim."

"Ah, good one." I chuckled slightly as I looked out at

the water, curious to feel just how warm twenty-four Celsius really was. I couldn't bother to calculate what the temperature was in Fahrenheit.

"Let's drink some coffee first," he suggested.

"It's about that time of the day. When I first came here, I couldn't believe how much people drank coffee and for how long. I remember seeing a couple having a coffee at the café outside of my apartment and two hours later after getting back from errands they were *still* there!"

"We have a coffee culture."

"Now I'm part of it," I said. "It's part of life here."

First dates, business appointments, and friendly gatherings happened over a cup of coffee. A hot version in the winter and a cool version in the summer can be cradled by a Greek for hours. I had discovered that coffee was also about watching people and being watched. Eleni and Nikos were always very particular about which of the million Athenian cafes they'd spend the afternoon in.

My train of caffeinated thought was interrupted by a waiter placing two glasses of water and an ashtray on the table. He greeted us with a friendly, "*Geia sas.*"

"*Ena frappé, metrio me fresko gala,*" I said in Greek. I ordered a cold instant coffee, with two spoons of sugar and fresh milk. When ordering coffee, the amount of sugar was a very important detail.

Stefanos ordered a plain cappuccino. As the waiter walked away, Stefanos said, "You really try to speak Greek, which I think is great for someone living here less than a year. It's a hard language."

"I like languages. It's just different to actually learn and speak a language with natives. I get so flustered. I need to get better if I plan to stay."

"There's a lot that's great about Athens, and a lot that is just terrible right now," Stefanos mused. "The situation with the economic crisis is affecting everyone. I could see that it would influence your decision about whether or not to be here."

"In the past months I've seen a difference." I rested my chin on my hands.

"What do you see?"

"My best friend's family business is struggling, and they work so hard. Many of my Greek friends have lost their jobs, and their younger siblings say they have no hope of finding something even though they all graduated college. Just sitting on the bus, I notice on every major road that every other store is for rent. Not to mention all of the strikes and protests. I hear those constantly because I live so close to it all. Then the strikes mean I can't get around because the metro and buses aren't working. I won't even mention when the taxi drivers strike too." I had a lot to say even if I wasn't a Greek. I had a lot to feel and I felt for them. He looked at me silently. "People are angry and want change," I added.

"And you still want to stay?" He pulled out his cigarette kit.

"I haven't made up my mind, but besides the bad, there's the good. I like how people are trying to stand up for what they believe in. Maybe they blame their culture's way of doing things or corrupt politicians or each other, but they go out and they say and do something. I may not agree with the violence but going out there and taking action, well, I think it's something bold to do as a people. The crisis will pass. It has to and who knows, maybe I'll be here to see things improve."

"Tourism is hit too. You know our flagship hotel is right near your apartment on Syntagma Square."

"It's a gorgeous hotel." With its neoclassical architecture and large marble staircase, The Danos Syntagma was a national landmark. "The protests are always stressful, but we've been okay this year."

"But tourists are still coming, I'm sure. You have one of the most central hotels in town," I said.

"If they research, they might choose another hotel because they know the inconvenience of staying in the center of the city. If something happens, I imagine it can be scary for a tourist. We have the tear gas, threats of fire, and the metro is shut down without notice. It's a challenge, but I try to have a positive attitude with a hope that attitude will be passed to the staff. There are lots of things we avoided and lots of things that we are careful about from a business standpoint. I don't take anything for granted because you never know what can happen. That's what I've learned over the years."

"That's a good way to look at things," I said.

"Do you want to work in marketing again? Did you look for a job here?" he asked, his voice slightly muffled as he balanced the cigarette between his lips.

"I think I need to know how to speak Greek more proficiently, and that takes time. I'm just taking it easy now after my divorce."

"How is that going?"

"Greg hasn't filed yet, and I don't know what he's waiting for." I shrugged my shoulders. "I actually don't want to know because his work visa enables me to stay here legally. Otherwise, as an American, I'd have a three-month vacation visa like everyone else."

"No kids, so no issues," he clarified.

"On the contrary, there are issues, but no kids," I corrected him.

The waiter placed our coffees in front of us.

"You like the national drink?" He eyed my iced coffee. He lit his cigarette coolly, took a big puff, and exhaled the smoke into the air above us.

"I fell in love with the Greek frappé when I first came." I swirled the pink neon straw around in the tall glass, disrupting the top foamy layer of coffee to mix the standing middle layer of milk into the cold instant coffee mix. I tried to sip it slow but couldn't help but take big un-Greek like sips.

"Speaking of kids and divorces, how about you? Besides little Christos, you mentioned on the phone you have a teenage son?" My stomach twisted a little saying it.

"Thanos." He adjusted his position in his chair.

"Thanos Danos?" I had to smile at a rhyme. "Sorry."

He grinned. "In English, it does sound funny, I know. The Greek tradition is to name the first son after the father's father."

"No, it's nice. The tradition too," I added. "How often do you see him?"

"He's in Canada with his mother, Katerina. Katerina and I had a big falling out, so it's complicated, actually." He took a puff of his cigarette and looked out at the lake.

"Oh, okay." I hoped he'd elaborate.

"I support him financially." He placed the tiny sugar spoon gingerly into the foam of his cappuccino. "His mom finds excuses for him not to come to Greece, and with my work schedule, it's not easy to find the time to fly to Canada."

"But he's your son," I pointed out.

"Katerina has said so much bad stuff about me that Thanos probably doesn't think very well of his father."

"Yes, but he's your son, and he wants to see you," I said firmly. "Trust me."

"You think so?" He raised an eyebrow. His tone indicated that he was half-asking and half-surprised at my assertiveness.

My pulse raced. Poor Thanos. I knew how he felt. "I can't believe what I'm hearing!" I blurted out forgetting that I was on a date and that I was probably not supposed to be inserting myself into this situation. My own childhood feelings bubbled to the surface. "You're his father. He expects you to be there. Who cares what his mother says about you? How will he know if you don't make an effort to go to Canada? Maybe it's hard for him to come to you, but he's just fourteen." I wanted to put my hand in my mouth. I could not believe I said what I did. He calmly looked out at the lake again and back at me, apparently surprised at my passionate reaction.

"You have an opinion on that." He tapped the cigarette into the ashtray between us.

"I do. And I'm sticking to it. I have experience with my own dad and mom and, well, I really think if you want to see someone, you will."

"Makes sense." He gave me an intense look.

"When was the last time?"

"I hate to say," he admitted.

I decided not to push my last question. "Anyway, he's your son. Don't you love him?"

"*Of course,*" he said quickly and with emphasis, his hazel eyes dancing with emotion.

"Don't you want to make sure he knows that?" I

asked softly.

The pained expression on his face sliced through me. He sighed. "I need to think about things I guess. My priorities are also a part of my mistakes."

"Work versus family?"

"It is so obvious?" He shifted in his seat again.

"You're driven, but when it comes to relationships maybe you have issues." I sounded like a fortuneteller.

"You mean my four marriages?" He took a sip of his cappuccino, all the while his eyes were set on mine. My stomach flipped with that look. "Will you hold them against me?"

I sipped my sweating frappé to avoid answering. "What matters is whether you're happy now, I think," I finally said.

"The truth?" He looked at me, took a breath, and placed his hand on the back of his neck for a moment. "The truth is that I need to make changes in my life."

"Sometimes change happens or it happens to you," I said after a pause. "That's what makes life *life*."

"I should talk to you more about my problems," he said raising an eyebrow.

"I only wish I could apply it to myself." I swirled the hot pink straw again to hear the ice clank against the glass. "Maybe it's time for that mid-afternoon swim?" I suggested knowing that I'd have to squeeze into my bathing suit, but at that point the sun was high above us, and I decided I no longer cared what he thought of my hips. He could take me as I came.

"Perfect timing." He got up. "I'll get our bags."

"I hope you don't mind I said those things about Thanos and your relationship with him and all," I said later as we sat down to a late lunch. I pressed my fingers against the bottom of my wine glass. He chose a famous Greek restaurant called Hermes. Like the other restaurants right next to the water in the Passalimani or Zea Marina area near the port city of Piraeus, it featured a tranquil view of a small harbor lined with boats. Piraeus, one of the largest ports in the world, stretched out in the distance.

"I feel comfortable talking with you," he said.

My mind started to settle. Maybe I shouldn't have brought it up again, but awkward silence filled the fifteen minute drive to the restaurant. I didn't want that feeling to continue. So I spoke honestly, which was something I wouldn't have done with Greg. I would have second-guessed myself. I realized it was a little attempt to change.

He took a sip of his wine. "It's just more complicated than you think." His face reddened as he forked a piece of *melitzana*, or fried eggplants in olive oil, from the plates we were sharing Greek style.

I changed the subject. "What a view!"

"This is the nicest area of Piraeus and this place in particular is famous. It's real *politiki kouzina*, which means the Greek food from *Constantinopoli* or Istanbul. They add a special touch to the food that's different, if you notice."

"Paprika, some other spices," I guessed. I grab another forkful of the vegetable dish. "I've had a few of Eleni's mother's dishes. It's my favorite kind of *kouzina*. Any special food from the island we're going to?"

"You'll see." He kept his gaze on me as he waved over

the waiter for the bill. "Are you ready to go and find out?"

After he paid, we made our way past the closely spaced tables which were all occupied. As I slipped between a few people waiting by the reception area, I bumped into someone's chest, a strangely familiar chest , and looked up to see Loucas. We stood there for a moment looking at each other in silence. My tongue tied as my skin started to get hot. He was standing there with his parents who glanced at me and back at Loucas before they passed us quietly.

Loucas stood there. Stefanos stood there. I stood there. *Not again.*

"Ava," Loucas said finally, wincing. "What are you doing here?"

"Just ate," I blurted out robotically. *Was I supposed to call him? I couldn't remember.*

His gaze locked on Stefanos rather than me. "My parents love this place," he said.

"I'll wait for you outside." Stefanos inched past Loucas.

I looked after Stefanos, who turned out into the street. "I'm just out now with my friend."

He scratched his head. "Is not that the hotel worker from the Danos?" Loucas folded his arms, those muscular arms.

"Yes."

"You know each other?"

I stood in silence. "We do...now," I finally said.

"Ava, he is old like my parents, or yours." He shrugged. "*Kali diaskedasi,*" he tacked on in a lower tone of voice, telling me to have a good time. He walked past me, raising his brow slightly.

After he was gone, I muttered, "Have a nice dinner."

Just then, my cell phone mewed with another text from Eleni.

Update us when you can.

I held off on the text, hoping Stefanos was waiting for me outside. I scanned the crowd of late afternoon strollers. I let out a sigh.

The best date I had ever been on was ruined.

CHAPTER TWENTY-ONE

THE sky began to morph into a brilliant swirl of orange and gold. I checked my watch again. It had been almost fifteen minutes since I'd left the restaurant. Did Stefanos leave me behind because of Loucas?

"Sorry, I was trying to find a *periptero* that sold my filters."

There he was standing behind me, pointing to the small square kiosk across the street neatly lined with snacks, a cooler of beverages, and racks of magazines and newspapers.

"I didn't know how much time you'd need," he continued. He clutched his cigarette paraphernalia wallet in one hand as his car keys dangled in the other.

"I thought you left," I said in a small voice.

He cocked his head slightly. "Why would I do that?"

I decided to just smile. I'd overreacted, I guessed.

"Shall we?" he asked.

We walked up a quiet side street away from Passalimani. Our footsteps echoed softly as we marched up the uneven pavement. "About that back there," I started.

"Your friend. I remember him. How is he?"

"Good." I crinkled my nose. "He's a friend. There's nothing between us."

He looked over and grinned knowingly. I decided to

just stop talking—for once.

On our way to catch the ferry, we got back on the topic of Hydra and off the subject of Loucas. We drove through to the Port of Piraeus, where office buildings of different heights, from different decades and design, lined around the expansive docks. Tourists pulled their luggage behind them as they caught an escalator down off the pedestrian bridge that connected the port to the Athens metro line; others gathered under tented waiting areas. Hydrofoils and ferries parked at their gates sat ready to go on their daily scheduled runs to Greece's islands. A few impressive cruise ships docked near the harbor added to the sea view and the city skyline that twinkled in the distance.

"Are you sure about the ride?" Stefanos asked.

We had discussed whether or not I would get seasick. The ferry ride back from Mykonos actually went fine, so I decided that I'd take the risk on this small trip to Hydra as long as the forecast called for calm waters, and it did.

"I'll be okay."

"We park here." He turned off the engine and turned to me. "Did you know that no cars are allowed on Hydra?"

"So how do they get around then, horses?"

"Ever ride a donkey?"

"You're kidding." I wondered how difficult it would be to balance myself on one. "I'd love to try," I said.

"It's the best way to get around actually," he said it like he meant it.

The Flying Dolphin Ferry's engine puttered as it slowed down over the calm sea cloaked in early evening colors. Over the last hour and a half, as we crossed the Aegean Sea, we drank another round of coffees and talked about nothing in particular.

The silky navy blue color of the sky offered a striking contrast against the warm yellow glow of Hydra's main town sitting at the edge of the dock. There, the ferry parked next to lines of small boats and a few large yachts that all together sat like a captive audience in front of a dazzling bright stage of cafés and shops before them.

Stefanos flagged someone in the distance, and then touched my arm lightly. "Can you wait here for one moment? I must speak with that man. We do business together."

I nodded as he waved and called out again to someone. I turned my attention to the bustling dock when a rush of adrenaline tickled me. I was about to discover another Greek island. I walked on as more passengers disembarked the ferry. A few leathery tanned men pushing metal wheelbarrows scurried about and found customers who needed a way to get their luggage moving. With no cars on the island, wheelbarrows apparently got the job done. Then, I observed the other way things get done on Hydra. A handful of lovely donkeys swatted their tails about. The handlers petted their heads adorned with colorful trinkets. They paused to ask tourists if they wanted to buy a donkey tour around the town.

"*Omorfi kopela!*" yelled a rough, deep voice that grabbed my attention away from the adorable donkeys.

I turned to find a fisherman in a little yellow fishing boat. I understood exactly what he had said and turned around, to see if there were any "beautiful girls" in sight. Nope, it was just me.

The evening lights of the harbor glinted off his round gold eyeglasses. A hand rolled cigarette hung loosely from one side of his mouth as he held a silver fish in each hand.

"*Efharisto,*" I said thanking him.

He dropped a fish, and the cigarette dropped as well. "*Milas ellinika?*" His eyes seemed to fill his eyeglass frames.

"*Poly ligo,* very little," I responded. "I'm from America."

"English I can speak. I speak the nine languages! Now I speak the Chinese!"

I looked around. *Wait? Did I say I had Chinese heritage?* "But I'm American, not Chinese," I added with a small smile.

His voice boomed. "Are you ready?" he asked with his eyes round and wild.

I wondered if he was kidding. That would be kind of impressive. No wonder Nikos loves his languages.

"I joking to you." He laughed heartily still clutching one fish. "I know the eight languages. You know we Greeks say, 'It is Chinese to me!'"

"Yep, you sure do," I said. "We say, 'It's Greek to me.'"

He bellowed out a laugh like I imagined Santa Claus would. "Where are you from?"

"New York."

"*Kalos irthes stin Hydra.* You know what I said? Welcome to Hydra!" He spread his arms out freely. The fish wiggled. "Hydra is the best beauty in Greece and pretty ladies come for visit to the beauty."

As I stood there not knowing what to say he asked in a loud whisper, "Would you like to buy my fish?"

"Actually, no...I'm just visiting," I responded.

His face melted into a big, sad frown.

"It looks nice though," I consoled him.

"What is your name, *koritsara mou?*"

I hated when I didn't understand what people were calling me in Greek. I needed to learn that word.

"Ava."

"Pretty name," he exclaimed with an even goofier smile and pulled out a knife. "A-V-A?" He spelled my name for me.

I stood back and my heart skipped a beat. *What was I getting into now?* Then before I could make a run for it, he began to scrape the fish with the knife in large English letters A-V-A. "I name this beautiful fish after you, a beautiful girl from China." I looked around again for a girl from China.

"Umm, New York, actually." Then I began to laugh heartily. After all, this lanky, bespectacled Greek guy just gave me a compliment. Plus, I never had a fish named after *me!* Or scraped with my name. I wondered if that was common in Greece.

A group of three foreign girls next to me started to giggle. The funny fisherman directed his attention to them to speak in Dutch or German, and they responded with even more laughter. They looked over the fish with interest. He had to add three more names to that fish. Maybe his tactics worked after all.

"Thanks for waiting," Stefanos said. His eyes were already on the girls and the goof. "He has a crowd." He raised his brows in amusement. "He's definitely animated."

"He was doing a little *kamaki*," I said. I'd never forget the Greek word I learned for the incessant flirting techniques Greek men like to test on tourists.

"I'm impressed you know this word, although I'm sure you've had experience with it," he said with a smile.

"I'm no longer a tourist, though."

"So it would be just plain flirting."

We walked past the shops, which were full of early evening visitors, and restaurants waiting for their dockside tables to fill up. We turned a corner and climbed a few flights up stairs to a small whitewashed building.

"We've arrived. I may not have a hotel on this island, but I know this place is one of the best. It's owned by a friend of mine," he said. There was a small sign painted with the hotel's name, *Mati*, the Greek word for eye.

The warm smell of pine and cinnamon matched the smooth vanilla color walls and the dark wooden beams that lined the ceiling. A collection of blue and black glass evil eyes hung from shiny ribbons and decorative ropes. The front desk manager walked in to greet us.

"Two reservations, under Danos and Martin," Stefanos said. He added something in Greek which I couldn't catch.

"Yes," confirmed the manager. "The two best rooms upstairs."

He reached in a drawer and pulled out two sets of keys. We followed him upstairs, where he let us into a large suite. One wall was lined with balcony doors that introduced us to a panoramic view of the docks below.

"How you like, miss?" the manager asked.

"Very nice." I walked to the balcony doors and smiled at the beauty before me. The nighttime expanse of the Greek sea appeared never-ending. The manager then led Stefanos to his room next door. Just as he plodded back down the stairs, Stefanos popped in.

"I'm glad you like it," he said sounding pleased.

I looked up at him. "It definitely has charm." I lifted a *mati* sculpture off the bedside table. "I love these eyes."

"You know they protect its owner."

"I know," I interrupted pulling out my necklace from under my tank top. "I believe in it."

He inched closer to me to examine my pendant. I looked at his eyes looking down at my neck and my pulse started to race. I hoped he wouldn't touch me or he might feel just how attracted I was to him.

"That is a beautiful one," he said with admiration, keeping his hands to himself. He looked into my eyes and paused before he said, "It's looking after you, then."

I patted my necklace softly looking down at it and avoiding his stare. "Well, so far, so good."

He turned to leave. "I thought we can walk through the town then go for dinner there. Want to meet in an hour? Is that enough time for you? I need to make some calls anyway."

"Yes. See you soon." I smiled warmly as I closed the door behind him. I needed to make some calls too. I dove onto the bed and speed-dialed Eleni.

"*Ti kaneis re*? How is it?" Eleni asked eagerly.

"Is Nikos on?"

"*Na'mai*," he said joining in. I heard him crunching on chips.

"Well?" they asked in unison.

I cleared my throat and said, "I like him, but..."

"He smokes," Nikos cut in.

"He does, but that's another thing," I quickly said. "We ran into someone."

"Alexandros," Eleni gasped.

"Guess again."

"Loucas?" Nikos asked.

"Loucas," I said.

"Ha, I got it first," Nikos said happily.

"*Panagia mou,*" Eleni swore. "You can't walk down the street without bumping into your cousin or your drunken *gomeno* from last week."

The Greek word for fling or a non-serious boyfriend was *gomeno*, but I hardly thought that Loucas was anything close to that. We didn't even do anything together. *Thank God.*

"We walked out of a Pasalimani restaurant together as he walked in."

"Maybe Loucas and Stefanos have matching second star signs," Nikos suggested.

"Anyway, Stefanos didn't seem to mind. He even asked about him. Loucas seemed annoyed though," I whispered loudly.

"Maybe he really liked you?" Nikos asked. "By the way, why are you whispering?" he mockingly asked in a loud whisper.

"He's next door."

"*Oh,*" Eleni jumped in. "*Telika,* you have separate rooms. Good."

"He decided," I said. "I think I like that."

"You can always just choose one room later," Eleni teased.

"*Eleni,*" I scolded her. "I have to get ready for dinner. I have to shower too, and I only have an hour."

"*Kali diaskedasi,*" Eleni said.

"Have fun, but don't do what Eleni would do," Nikos warned.

"Niko!" Eleni yelped.

Laughing, they both hung up.

Exactly an hour later, I heard a small tap on the door. I took one last look in the mirror, readjusting my strapless bra then smoothing out my white sleeveless bandeau dress. The dress took me a while to sew properly based on a simple pattern I found in *Sewing Times* and I had finished it just in time to leave New York for Greece last year. I admired my creation for a moment and the fact that I could create my own bespoke style. I adjusted my *mati* necklace and hooked on a dangly set of earrings with white and blue stones to match. I checked my purse, which stored my lip gloss and my wallet. Ready.

I opened the door to see Stefanos standing there, looking handsome in a fresh pair of jeans and a white linen top.

He looked me up and down right away. *"Eisai mia koukla."*

"I am?" I asked, looking down at my dress.

"I love this dress on you."

"I made it actually," I said proudly, swinging the full skirt slightly.

"Eheis talendo," he said sounding impressed. "Simple and beautiful."

The weather remained steady and comfortably warm for our stroll through the small streets of the main town. On either side of us the doors to the jewelry and clothing shops were wide open and one in particular caught my eye. "This is pretty." I examined a few linen dresses hanging outside.

Stefanos walked in. "We can go look." He touched my shoulder slightly sending a tingle up my arm. "So, Ava, this is what you like. I didn't realize you design clothes."

"I never made my own design. I make clothes from patterns, more as a hobby to pass the time. In the end I have something simple and beautiful."

"I like that; it's creative," he said. "Who taught you?"

"My mom knows the basics, but I took it further and kept making outfits to suit my body."

He took my hand gripping it tightly and twirled me around.

"Your body type, if you ask me, is..." He paused to make something like a cross between a hissing sound and a *pssss* sound. It was the typical Greek gesture for emphasizing something really nice. I laughed. He made the *pssss* sound again. I laughed even more as we walked through the shop. Stefanos wandered off in one direction as I got lost in a rack filled with colorful skirts when someone started yelling nearby in Greek and then in English.

"Hello, are you listening? I'm talking to you. Do you have this in extra *extra* small?"

That eerily familiar voice came from a woman holding a large beige tunic in front of her face.

"Excuse me?" I asked.

The tunic came down. It was Cassandra. Gold Party. Cassandra the Horrible.

"Oh." She stared at me. Behind her green eyes, her brain began to slowly recall that she, in fact, had met me before.

"I thought you worked here," she huffed coldly.

Without being high, she still looked like a horrible person. She looked meaner than I remembered, with her chiseled cheeks and over plucked, thinly arched brows. Her skin was bronzed and her hair was even more platinum than I remembered. I hated that I liked her body.

"Some things don't change; you still look like the help." She narrowed her eyes.

I winced not knowing how to reply. *Damn,* there were no drinks handy to throw on her annoyingly super tight, pink sundress. If only Eleni were here. Before I could retort, she looked past me and her expression turned to one of happy surprise.

"Stefane?" she asked saying Stefanos's name in the Greek vocative tense and in a too friendly and too familiar tone of voice. They greeted each other with cheek kisses.

How could Stefanos associate himself with such a mean woman and even worse, two-cheek kiss her? I had learned early on that cheek kisses for Europeans were as sexual as pulling weeds, but obviously they knew each other well enough. Ex-girlfriend? I hoped not. That would be the end of the date. Then, I admired for a moment just how cute he was. Okay, maybe not. They continued speaking in Greek then Stefanos introduced me.

"Ava, this is Cassandra Spoudaia."

"Hi," Cassandra cut Stefanos off. She forced a smile, flashing her perfectly white teeth. "Your friend and I, we met at Anastasia's party. You should have come. It was wonderful," she purred then broke off into Greek again. A few minutes later, they said their goodbyes and she skipped out the door without so much as another glance at me.

"So you went to one of Anastasia Filioti's parties?" Stefanos asked, raising his brows and grinning.

"How do you know Cassandra?"

"She works for the hotel. She's in public relations. Her father's a good friend of mine."

She was an employee and not an ex-girlfriend or wife, for that matter. I breathed a sigh of relief, although it was a small sigh. She still seemed to have an eye for her boss. "She works?" I asked. I pressed my lips into a fine line.

Stefanos half-grinned; he understood what I meant. "You mean because she is what you say, a party girl? She is actually good at what she does because she is so social and knows a lot of people."

"Well," I told him, "this is the second time she's mistaken me for the help."

His brow creased with concern. "Really? Was she rude to you?"

"Don't worry about it," I said tightly.

Stefanos hesitated, and then nodded. But I could see him filing the information mentally away, and I was glad he didn't come to her defense.

So much for Nikos's words of encouragement that I would never see her again. Why did she, out of all the women in Athens, have to work for the man I was beginning to like?

CHAPTER TWENTY-TWO

STEFANOS offered his hand to help me down the shop's steps, which somehow led to hand holding. *So soon?* But there we were, his fingers enclosed between mine causing my heart to thump faster. He didn't let go even though our hands were clasped all wrong with my thumb squished between his forefinger and middle finger. However awkward, the gesture was so nice I relaxed and just leaned into him as we walked. As I looked up at him, I found him already looking at me. I smiled, and not knowing what to say and wondering what he was thinking, I eyed our surroundings instead. The cobblestone path was filled with people strolling, shopping, or just sitting and watching the world pass by.

"The town is really alive," I observed.

"Now that it's summer, all of Greece is really alive." He let go of our uneasy hold on each other. He made a sort of a pinching gesture with both sets of his fingers. "Despite the crisis, we find ways to enjoy life. How can you not, when you live in a place like this?"

"It helps to have resources. There are pay cuts and all of that unemployment," I pointed out with seriousness, wondering how the hotel magnate would respond.

Stefanos looked ahead with thought. "I admit, I'm lucky. During any time in Greece's history, if you know how we were during the wars and after, we may not have been rich as a country, but there was always spirit. We expressed ourselves through music and dancing. Good friends and family always mattered."

He didn't seem materialistic despite his inherited success.

"You didn't have to have much," he went on. "I admired my grandfather because he was in that position before he opened the first hotel. He taught me my biggest lessons, including not to take anything for granted."

I thought about my mom. "That's great to have family you admire."

We ended up at a seafood restaurant identified by the big fish painted on its sign. The dining patio seemed to float high above the sea. "This view is ridiculous," I breathed out.

"Oh, you don't like it?" he questioned grimly, looking as if he was ready to turn around and leave.

I laughed. "Ridiculous is actually a good thing," I assured him.

He smiled back, a little uneasily. "Besides the great view, their seafood is really top quality. I think you'll really love it." He took a seat.

We ordered a salty fish roe dip called *taramosalata*, fried calamari, and a whole fish to bake. The waiter invited us to choose the exact fish we'd like.

Stefanos nodded toward the back of the restaurant. "Would you like to come with me?"

I would pick my own fish? Why not? When in Greece...I followed him inside.

The warm mix of smells immediately took me in. The essence of oregano and roasted potatoes hung deliciously and thickly in the air. Several cooks and helpers yelled back and forth in rhythm. A grill sizzled, a casserole pot clanked against another, and in the middle of it all, a tiny Greek *yiayia* dressed all in black, her silver hair pulled back in a net, sat at a small wooden table peeling carrots. As we walked in, she smiled revealing her gums.

"*Ekei einai, kyrie,*" she creaked out in a high-pitched voice towards Stefanos. She nodded her chin toward a dazzling iced table full of pink, blue, purple, gray, and white raw seafood.

I gasped. There in front of us was the big, white fish the goofy fisherman tried to sell me. There the poor thing was, my name and a few others on it. Stefanos and I both broke into a giggle and looked at each other at the same time.

"I guess I know which one we'll choose," he said.

Two hours later, Stefanos refilled my white wine glass emptying out the bottle. We shared the "Ava" fish, which was baked to perfection with lemon, olive oil, and Greek herbs.

My feet were light and I felt like I could say anything, and I did. "I'm so happy right now," I announced.

He smiled and leaned in. His eyes crinkled at their corners. My heart melted as I met his gaze.

"Tell me more," he said cocking his head slightly.

"Greece is so beautiful and I'm a part of this, sitting here, nice company and great food. There's so much more to life than what I ever imagined. I guess I have Greg to thank for that."

"Greg?" His smile faltered.

"He brought me here after all. He may have left me, but I don't think I would've ever left the security of Ithaca if I didn't..." My smile faded as I admitted the truth. "If I didn't fall so much in love." My lips turned down into a pout. I couldn't help it and at that moment a happy couple passing by giggled in their embrace, holding hands, I was sure, the right way.

He leaned in closer over the table. "We do things for love," Stefanos said with sympathy. "I know I did."

"Four times," I blurted out putting up four fingers. That didn't sound right and that didn't look right, I thought as I lowered my hand. Maybe he would take it wrong. I covered my mouth. Stupid wine or stupid me rather. "Oh...I meant—"

"No, you're right." He pursed his lips and rubbed the back of his neck. "What can I say?"

"I didn't mean," I stammered. "I mean, it's a good thing to get married four times because four is better than never, I guess, right?" My voice quavered. There I was in complete moron mode.

Stefanos grinned and then looked me in the eyes a bit strangely, in a way no one had ever looked at me before. He definitely thought I was a moron.

He raised his glass. "I propose a toast."

A feeling of relief washed over me. A toast meant we were changing the subject. "Okay," I agreed.

"To beautiful Greece."

"I'll toast to that any day." I took a long satisfying sip.

I can't say I was drunk as we walked up to our rooms.

The wine buzz had worn off fast, and after the awkward mention of Stefanos's four marriages, we continued to pass the time talking and laughing for two more hours. There was something about him I really liked. He was quiet, low-key, and had a look that made him mysterious. His eyes hid something I had a growing desire to discover.

When I met Greg, I was just as enthusiastic but in a more innocent way. It might be the new emotional baggage I carried as a soon to be thirty-year-old divorcee or maybe it was because I knew about the baggage Stefanos carried. I was experiencing a more mature attraction. Maybe I was getting carried away. Maybe I was just a one-night stand on a two-day date to him. At that moment I wanted to see what it would be like to kiss Stefanos Danos, my Greek George Clooney, my Horse Guy.

Just as I turned the big metal key into the lock of my door he spun me around and gently kissed me on the lips. There was my answer. It was exactly what I wanted.

I returned the kiss. We stopped for a moment and I quickly opened the door and we fumbled in as one body. He managed to push the door closed behind us as his lips deliciously tingled the skin on my neck. I pulled him closer and took in the smell of his cologne, sweet and musky.

He took my face lightly in his hands. "Shall I go?"

Startled by his question I blurted out, "Why would you do that?"

"I don't want you to get the wrong idea about why I took you here."

Even if that was the case, I didn't care. "Stay," I ordered then kissed him hard, tasting faint tobacco and our white wine. We fell back on the bed. For the first time in a long time, my head wasn't spinning from alcohol or nervousness or any of my endless insecurities. I felt only the pleasure of being with him. I had decided to go with the unrealistic assumption that nothing could go wrong after that night.

With the sun warming my face, I opened my eyes slowly and felt a new lightness in my body. I smiled to myself. Why couldn't I wake up every day like this? Stefanos slept silently next to me on his side. I slinked toward the edge of the bed hoping to fix myself a bit in the bathroom before he woke up. As I did, his arms pulled my waist back into the center of the bed.

"*Kalimera*," he said sleepily.

I relaxed and fell into the warmth of his embrace.

"Good morning." I turned toward him and tucked a strand of hair behind my ear.

He stroked my bare arm. "Did you have a nice time yesterday?"

"I did," I said playfully. I closed my eyes again and enjoyed his caress. "Did you?"

"Definitely." He changed position to prop himself up against my side. I sensed him staring at me. I wondered how awful I must look with my makeup smeared off. The thought of gargling some mouthwash crossed my mind exactly when he gave me a sweet lingering kiss on the lips.

"That's something else," he said, smiling at me then getting up to walk towards the balcony window.

"You mean?" I asked, daring to hope that he's

referring to the sex we had.

"The view, that's why I love this hotel, the sea looks like it goes on forever."

I smoothed my hair down as his back was to me, still wondering what he thought about last night.

"I'll take a shower next door and get ready to check out. I'll meet you in an hour?" He turned around to look for my response.

"Great, I'll be ready," I said a bit disappointed.

"By the way," he said as he stood by the bed, "the last day with you was great and last night..."

He searched for the right word. His eyes danced slightly before he spoke, as if the inspiration for his thought just came to him.

"It was beautiful." He smiled then kissed me on the forehead. "See you in a bit." He walked out shutting the door quietly behind him.

My jaw dropped slightly as my pulse raced. I wanted to run after him and kiss him more for being so sweet and for saying such nice things, but I couldn't be too excited—yet.

I put down my half-eaten croissant. "What's the plan for today?"

We finished our leisurely breakfast at a harbor side café. My body relaxed surrounded by so much beauty. We sat just a few feet from the sea where a surreal view of clear blue and green water met the beige rocky shore of Hydra. I could even make out the rock formations underneath the calm lap of the waves. In the distance, a tiny beach with a group of morning swimmers spread out a few towels on some open, flat space. They treaded water, looking so calm. The island had a small and very tranquil feeling compared to Mykonos. It was a different charm but equally enchanting.

Our ferry would leave for Athens that night but I was already wishing I didn't have to work tomorrow. I sipped my cappuccino and took in the perfect warmth from the rising sun and appreciated the fresh, light breeze that continued to sweep under the bamboo covering above us.

"Have you ever been horseback riding?" Stefanos asked.

"Never."

"I have a friend here with a horse and I could give you lesson one."

"I'd love that. But I'm not very coordinated."

"I'm sure you'll be fine. Then we move on to the donkey."

He didn't laugh. As I wondered if he was serious, his phone rang. I peeped to find Cassandra's name and her photo flash across the screen. I wanted to stick my tongue out, but I stopped myself.

"*Oriste*," he answered the phone quite professionally. They continued in Greek for a few minutes. His voice lowered right away. It wasn't good news.

"Ava *mou*," he said. I liked the ring to that, but I didn't like what he said next. "We can't go horseback riding actually."

"Oh." I frowned.

"Cassandra left the island this morning to go back to work at the Syntagma hotel. Looks like there is going to be a demonstration at the square based on some new austerity measure that will be debated into the night inside parliament. It's an emergency weekend vote, so things could get heated, and it could affect the hotel. I need to get back as soon as I can. There's a ferry in half an hour. I'm sorry."

"No, of course, you have to work, keep the hotel in order." I understood completely.

"I will make it up to you. I had a great time with you." He stroked my hand.

"I'm glad I came," I said. But inside, I wondered if it would all vanish like smoke. I wondered if once we got back to the mainland, he would feel the same.

"Definitely the most romantic sex I have ever had in my life." I moaned and fell down onto my bed face first.

"Better than the *malaka*?" Eleni asked, taken aback by my sudden revelation.

I propped my head up resting it on my hands. "No comparison."

She lied down next to me. "After divorce comes the great sex from another person," she said thoughtfully.

"One other thing," I added, excited to spill the gossip. "Guess who mistook me for a shop worker while we were in town?"

Eleni narrowed her eyes at me. "Who?"

"Cassandra Spoudaia. The girl who spilled a drink on me at that stupid party."

"That is her last name? Interesting." Eleni's lips curled into mischievous smirk. "You know the meaning?"

"Spoudaia?"

"She's not Cassandra the Horrible. She is Cassandra the Great!" Eleni rolled her eyes. "*Einai teleio*, it is perfect."

"Ugh," I muttered. "She works for Stefanos at the Syntagma hotel."

"I cannot believe it. What I say about Athens? It is a village?"

"She was so irritating. She was rude, and even when Stefanos introduced me, she was just horrible," I continued, slightly shaking my head. "I'm just glad she's not one of his ex-wives."

"What is her work for Danos, organize cocaine parties?"

I laughed. "Actually she's his PR manager." I air quoted *PR manager*. "He says she's good at what she does because she knows everyone."

"I am sure she knows everyone and I am sure that I know how." Eleni lifted a brow with a huff. "It's important to know people, but she sounds like a rude *malakismeni*."

"She's the daughter of one of his friends," I added flatly.

Eleni sighed heavily. "Do you see how things are in Greece?"

"I wished you were there to tell her something mean yet smart to put her in her place."

"You know I would. Well, it looks like she will be around if you continue to see Stefanos."

"I feel good about him." I beamed.

"I want to hear your stories but I am late for the birthday party for my cousin. It is too far from here." She grudgingly pulled herself up from the bed and made her way to the front door. "*Krima.* A shame that you did not spend more of the time together. So you had a romantic kiss goodbye then."

"It was nice." I blushed. "My romantic weekend got cut off by political turmoil. How about that?" I sighed. "Anyway, did you hear about the demonstrations?"

"Nikos told me he wants to take photos. I thought about it too, but my family wants me to go to the party."

I shuddered. I didn't like the idea of Eleni in the middle of the chaos. "Is it safe?"

"Nothing is safe. Anyway, I need to take a stand at some point. I don't know if I told you, but I have gas masks for next time."

"Wow, are they Gucci?" I joked.

She pulled a face. "They are very ugly but useful of course."

"I wish I could go for support, but the last thing I need is another run-in with the police. I was practically given the death penalty for not validating my bus ticket." I rolled my eyes. "You, on the other hand, can talk your way out of anything."

She laughed. "I might stay at my parent's house. *Geia!*" She closed the door behind her. Then she opened it again to yell out, "I need more details!"

I kept busy behind the whir of my sewing machine for the rest of Sunday. I had reached for the fabrics I bought to make some summer scarves but then inspiration hit me for the first time, in a long time, to start a bigger project. All of my attention focused on a great pattern for sailor shorts. I had bought gorgeous twill navy blue fabric that I envisioned would contrast well with my Monastiraki buttons. I had never made shorts or pants before so finishing this piece would be an accomplishment if I could manage it. I had to make them just right to accentuate my curves. Or to hide them, actually.

I hummed to one of my favorite CDs for sewing sessions, an oldie but goodie, Pearl Jam's *Ten*, all the while thinking about the days that had just passed with a smile. I cut the fabric, imagining myself wearing the finished product on a trip to another Greek island with Stefanos. He'd tell me how lovely they looked, how original the buttons were and, of course, I'd reveal that I made them myself.

After a few hours, my inspiration fizzled. I'd managed to botch the pattern three times and wasted fabric in the process. I stashed the materials away feeling my stomach grumble. I was so absorbed in sewing, I hadn't eaten a thing since I left Hydra earlier that morning. My stomach growled again, and knowing I had no food in the fridge, I would have make a big sacrifice on my diet and head out for pizza. Classic excuse, but I started to crave it. I needed to take a walk anyway, after being cooped-up next to my sewing machine most of the day.

The warm summer night had already set in on Athens as I made my way out. I expected the usual din of cars and motorcycles to buzz on Vasileos Konstantinou Avenue, but the road remained traffic-free. One word came to mind: *demonstration*. I'd completely forgotten about it.

I turned three hundred and sixty degrees and my pulse started to race as I took in the thick eerie calm around me. It was like nothing I could ever imagine in the States. Many paced slowly almost cautiously. Some huddled in groups with crossed arms, darting gazes and glaring, protruding eyes. They carried signs and placards. Several were loaded with backpacks and some had gas masks hanging off them. These Athenians were demonstrators. They were of all ages, men and women, dressed down, and ready for what was to come. Large groups of young men donned dark colors and wound large handkerchiefs around their necks. Their focus aimed toward a crowd that gathered in the distance, off to the side of the road. I craned my neck to see more, my hands shook slightly as my curiosity propelled me to step quicker to the crowd too.

Along with the groups of demonstrators stood groups of Greek police, some posted near navy police buses with iron window bars that were being used to transport dozens of armed officers at once and to block roads. I turned back to see one parked across the four-lane intersection as a troop of identically armored officers quickly headed down. Their white helmets bobbed in a perfect line. Each one carried a large, transparent body shield. I slowed down my pace suddenly; I had never been so close to a real demonstration. I should've turned back but for some reason, I couldn't. The fact that Stefanos's hotel was just around the bend kept me walking and I couldn't pinpoint why.

I reached Syntagma Square, where I wiggled my way into a dense crowd that packed the road in front of the city's center point. A young man in a wheelchair passed in front of me, a gas mask ready in his lap. Two women about my age followed him wearing stylishly ripped jeans, oversized D Squared hoodies, and summer scarves wrapped around their necks. The girl with a ponytail gripped a construction mask in one hand and a Juicy Couture purse in the other. My gaze darted over the crowd quickly, searching for Nikos. As I scanned the faces surrounding me, I couldn't help but feel the energy of their concerns. I decided that I'd just go down to the main part of the square, and then I'd turn back. I could always run if something happened.

To my surprise, I found myself alone in the square. My attention wandered to the marble steps that led out of the square to the street right in front of the Parliament building. I tiptoed to try to see something, but couldn't from where I stood.

How dangerous could it be?

The square was practically deserted and I had hopped up those marble steps for many months now. I started up, with no one in sight, on the empty steps.

Then, commotion. In an instant, an intense energy, a crazy fast rumble surrounded me. People rushed out of nowhere and everywhere. It was a frantic mob, without an inch between them headed down the steps in a mad rush, and straight toward me. My heart thumped wildly; my fingers lost feeling. I turned around to head back down the steps, but not fast enough. My feet were slower than I wanted. My heart continued to beat out of control as I tried to maintain my balance but I learned quickly that the mob was one entity and much more powerful than me.

A much larger body knocked me down. I screamed as I landed hard on the corner of a marble step feeling a jolt in my back. There was no time to feel any pain as I scrambled and tried to push my way back up to breathe air but the bodies and legs and arms struck me from every direction and from every corner. Something or someone swiped me on my cheek and a backpack scraped against my shoulder. I couldn't even scream any more. Rather, I focused my energy on trying to stand up a third time. Then a force pulled me up, my arms led and my body followed. Two young men in black, long-sleeved T-shirts continued to drag me straight up. They yelled passionately and frantically to each other in Greek. I didn't know what to think, but an enormous feeling of gratitude swept through me knowing they saved me from the madness of the stampede. Still gripping my arms, they led me down the steps and off to the side letting me go at the same time. As I looked at one of them in the eyes, my own eyes began to tear as I tried to apologize and thank him in Greek. I couldn't think fast enough and he cut me off before I could mutter a word.

"*Eisai kala?*" he asked if I was okay at the top of his voice. His eyes danced with concern but that was all I saw of his face, a green paisley scarf secured the rest of it.

Before I could answer, he turned his attention away and screamed angrily in Greek at whoever was behind me.

"*Malakes! Malakes!*" they screamed in unison. I turned around to find out who they hated so much.

Right behind me, on the top step, a line of stiff backed riot police formed. Each uniformed officer protected himself behind a tall, clear body shield. In unison, they stepped down like a march of robots, one step at a time. Their white helmets gleamed. My mouth opened wide in awe. My jaw felt like it was about to drop off my face.

"*Kitakste ti ekanan stin kinezoula!*" One of the young men's long curly hair, loosely secured by a bandana, flew about as he threw his fist furiously into the air.

I understood enough to understand that they were blaming the police for what just happened to me, "a little Chinese girl."

How did I get in the middle of this? This could only happen in Greece—to me!

"*Malakes!*" they screamed again.

My hands shook. I somehow became the physical divide between armed riot police that represent the government and a mob of angry demonstrators who hate the government. The eyes of the young men held a fearless, determined gaze. They were ready to release the anger inside of them, something that I could never do. They screamed, jumped in place, and continued to call the riot police terrible names.

Then, one rioter threw a rock, which sailed over my head. Silence overtook the commotion as it hit one of the officer's shields with a thud. That was the catalyst for something I decided I shouldn't be around for. I almost lost my breath as I turned around to find an escape route.

A young man grabbed my arm to get my attention asking me loudly. "*Eisai kala*, are you okay?"

"I'm fine," I said in a panic. But I wasn't okay. *At all.*

"Go, run, you should not be here! No safe!" His blue eyes were wide and bloodshot. Their gaze excited me in an even more furious panic. "Go," he commanded aggressively and let go of me.

Freed from his grip, I ran to the side of the square and turned around to observe from a distance. The crowd began to lift their handkerchiefs and scarves up on their faces. Gas masks were out too. I turned to run but it was too late; the piercing sting of the tear gas was immediately unbearable. The sounds and the atmosphere engulfed me in a surreal haze. It was all an open opportunity for vandalism, rock throwing, gas bombs, anger, and danger. There was a message each side wanted to get across, and that was what it had come down to.

I ran back home, blinking furiously as my eyes continued to sting and tear. When I finally made it, I blindly made my way to the kitchen sink to wash my eyes out.

Suddenly, I glass bottles smashed outside. I slid the kitchen door shut to avoid the taste or sting of any more gas that could seep in. I grabbed a kitchen towel to protect my face when the phone rang. I answered it to hear Eleni command, "Turn on the TV!"

As my eyes watered, I switched it on to see local news coverage of the protests. I didn't understand the commentary but the pictures told it all. In a matter of minutes, the situation had gotten from bad worse.

"It is chaos," Eleni cried out.

"I hope Nikos is okay." I wanted to tell her I was there but I didn't want to get her upset either. She did warn me.

"He is. He knows what to do but you see what happened?" Eleni's voice trembled.

"What?" I asked confused at the tremor in her voice.

"The Danos hotel is on fire!"

Then I caught what was right in front of me. A few cutaways of several historic city center buildings. The video told the story, flames swept out of the Danos Hotel. My heart fell.

"I need to call Stefanos." My stinging eyes were the least of my concerns suddenly. "I hope he's okay!" I was right there by the hotel, but what could I have possibly done.

"Do not go. You promise—*einai poly epikindeno*, it is very dangerous," Eleni pleaded.

It was too late for that but I let out a quick sigh, thanking God I got back in time. "Okay," I said and hung up. I dialed Stefanos, but it went to voicemail; then Nikos called.

"Don't think of coming down. You saw the hotel?" Nikos asked over the screams and commotion of people in the background. A fire truck siren blared.

"I feel so bad. Are you okay?"

"I am. Just stay at home. Promise me."

"I promise, Nikos. Be careful."

Just a mile away, it was really happening. My city was burning down around me and there was absolutely nothing I could do.

CHAPTER TWENTY-THREE

"HOW close are you to the protests?"

"Mom, I'm fine, don't worry."

Mom called me the next morning in a panic. She explained that she had a bad dream, woke up, and turned on CNN to find breaking news coverage of Athens on fire. She rightly believed Molotov cocktails could smash through my windows.

Amy texted me earlier to see if I was okay, knowing I lived in the center. I texted her back that I was fine and I would see the kids in the afternoon, as usual. The ambassador's residence, like other Athenian suburban homes, remained insulated from the targeted chaos of the city core.

"It's my job to worry," Mom said with concern. She added almost desperately, "I miss you."

"You too." My heart swelled. I did miss her. "Maybe I'll come back to visit," I added. I didn't know if I said it to make her happy or if I meant it.

"Really? When?" she asked with surprise.

"I'll let you know."

"I'm driving up to Rochester tomorrow to visit your Auntie Lu." Auntie Lu was a friend of my grandmother's whom my mom made a point to visit once in a while to keep her company in her old age.

"Give her a kiss for me, then." I glanced at the clock; it was ten in the morning, which meant it was three in the morning in New York. "Get to bed, Mom, or you'll be tired while you drive."

"Stay safe, okay?"

"Trust me, there's no chance of anything bad happening to me. Don't worry." I wasn't sure if I was convincing myself anymore.

After I hung up, I got up to check my back in the mirror. I earned a huge black and blue bruise from the stampede. It throbbed as I lifted my shirt higher to examine it.

"Shit," I breathed out with disappointment. It grew even bigger from what I remembered, spreading from the middle to the lower part of my back. I iced it last night and even fell asleep on the ice pack watching Greek news. There it was, the painful proof I was a total moron putting myself in the middle of a riot.

I learned on the Web the fires were targeted at the banks that were housed in some neoclassical buildings located near the parliament. Some small businesses were destroyed in the process. A total of thirty fires burned in the city at the same time. From what I had learned so far, no one was seriously injured. Stefanos's hotel suffered some damage as well, but it was still open for business. I had no word from him and I was worried.

With a few hours left before work, I was deciding whether to head to the grocery store or run errands near the ambassador's house when my cell phone rang. Greg's name and smiling face flashed across the screen making my stomach turn. I was curious enough to find out just what he wanted.

I swiped the phone from the counter momentarily forgetting about my monster bruise and winced feeling it throb from my quick movement. "Hello?"

"Are you okay? I saw the fires on TV and wanted to make sure you're fine. I don't know where you're staying." He expressed concern, at least.

"I'm fine," I answered flatly. I was surprised he would call me to check on me.

"Are you?"

I really wanted to say, *What the hell do you want?* Instead, I repeated, "I'm fine."

"So, you're still in Athens?" There was judgment in his voice. I reminded myself that he had no right to care anymore.

"You know I love it here." There. I was glad we were capable of a civil conversation.

"Listen, Ava, I've been doing a lot of thinking and I think our separation put a lot of things into perspective."

What was he saying now? I wondered. "Like what?"

"I miss you." He almost sounded...desperate.

My heart stopped. "What?"

There was a pause between us that lingered a bit too long.

"I said I miss you," he continued more evenly, even kindly.

I didn't know what to even say. My heart pounded with anticipation.

"But I know we can't be together," he concluded swiftly. "I miss you, but I know it's not for the right reasons."

As if the pause button was lifted, my back started to throb again. My head pulsed from realizing that I had the hope, for a split second, that he wanted me back and that I could possibly want that too. But he didn't. I wanted to cry out, *Why are you calling me? Why are you ruining my life?* But just like last time, I couldn't say anything to make him understand how much he hurt me. Instead I asked, "Is that what you called to tell me?" My mouth curled into a heavy frown.

"I think we should be honest about things between us," he said plainly.

He shouldn't talk about honesty.

I closed my eyes and managed to say, "I have some food on the stove actually."

"Right," he said. "I don't want to keep you from things there. Be safe."

I dropped the phone on the couch and looked at it for a second. Then I screamed out, but of course, no one could hear me. I grinded my fists into the couch feeling my body tense up. No one could know how pathetic I felt all over again.

My cell phone rang and there was his smiling face, his name. He was calling me back. I switched it off feeling a surge of hurt in my gut.

Screw it. I needed fresh air. I couldn't be bothered to change my leggings and oversized tank top. Forget about doing my hair. I pulled it in a ponytail and folded it into my old, torn up New York Yankees baseball cap, one of my favorite possessions. It made me feel hidden, almost invisible although it probably accomplished the opposite effect in Greece where women didn't wear baseball caps. Even men don't. I pulled on my Converse and slung my leather cross-body purse over me.

A fresh cool summer morning greeted me encouraging me to clear my mind with a walk and I knew where to go. The traffic on Vasileos Konstantinou Avenue was back. Cars and motorcycles whizzed by as I headed up to Vasilissis Sofias Avenue exactly where I found myself the night before.

Police remained on every corner. This time, they weren't doing anything in particular but talking, swinging *koumboulois*, and watching the world walk by. After a brisk half hour walk, I reached my destination, Strefi Hill. I trudged up a natural dirt path and ducked slightly as I made my way between low-hanging trees. I watched my step for different reasons. Drug addicts claimed parts of the hill at night and who knew what was leftover on the ground. It wasn't the prettiest—or cleanest—hill in Athens, but I enjoyed a sense of relief, even joy, every time I reached the top where I usually found myself alone. As I stepped up to an open clearing there it was, the reason why I kept coming back. I breathed deeply as I took in the familiar sight. Athens was spread before me; the tops of buildings like clay models placed in haphazard directions proving there was no perfect rhyme or reason to planning the modern version of one of the oldest cities in the world. I stared with admiration at the Acropolis, directly across my line of vision; steady and secure where it always had been for the last two centuries. Nothing destroyed it, not even earthquakes or war. It looked like perfection to me.

I scanned the city below my feet and spotted the Danos Hotel off Syntagma Square. There was Kolonaki, my old neighborhood where I shared a home with Greg and right across I scanned the pathways and trees of Evangelismos Park that spread across part of my new neighborhood. I spotted the Hilton Hotel and the old marble Olympic Stadium. Then I searched towards other areas I've come to know like Gazi, Thesseion, Psiri, and then focused towards the calm of the sea towards the Port of Piraeus where I'd escaped to the islands. It was all familiar and real.

I closed my eyes and appreciated the fresh smells of trees and flowers, a mix of nature that the hilltop offered. The late morning breeze warmly tickled my skin and my thoughts wandered making my heart swell with pain and love. Tears began to run down my cheeks in hot running streams. Things went on and moved on below me. Under the steadiness of the Acropolis, people's lives continued whether or not they agreed with the political changes, changes perhaps they believed were out of their control in the end. Here, in this foreign city I had unexpectedly found my own place. I adored it as I faced my own chaos, confusion, and insecurity. I sat awkwardly on a large flat rock, taking care how I positioned my sore back. I lifted my eyes again and found myself blindly admiring how it was impossible to tell where the sea ended and sky began. This was my Greece.

I couldn't blame Greg or my father for anything anymore. I needed to change something. A year ago I didn't know this place and now it was familiar and recognizable—it was home, a home I was not ready to change. I was an outsider slowly becoming an insider, knowing what to expect, what to say, and how to act. It was more of a home than Ithaca was at that moment, which was why I couldn't leave, but there was no denying I belonged to both worlds. I was being pulled in two directions and didn't know which path was right for me. Instead of answering my thoughts, I lowered the brim of my baseball cap over my eyes to block any view of the city as my tears dropped slowly and melted into the ground below.

I squeezed myself into the trolley pushing someone back to get in. A stale smell of too many sweaty bodies in a tightly enclosed space, on a hot summer day, just made my body feel heavy. I didn't feel like breathing it in. Maybe I was too tired to breathe. I had watched the minutes pass by at work hoping Amy would make it back from her outing with the ambassador in time but she didn't come. As the trolley jerked to a quick start, it caused a few passengers to lose their balance, my cell phone rang. It was *him*. I managed to accept, nudging a few people in the process.

"Hi." Stefanos said curtly, sounding distressed. The sounds of meeting hung in the background.

"How are you?" I asked anxiously.

"I'm all right. Sorry I didn't pick up yesterday. I have not had a free moment."

"Are your guests okay, your staff?"

"No one got hurt, *doksa to Theo*," he responded with the Greek expression for *thank God*. "We're all okay. Damage isn't as bad, but it's bad."

"I won't keep you. I was just worried," I said feeling some relief just speaking to him and hearing his voice.

"I'll call you again when things calm down." A woman's squeaky Greek voice cut him off.

"*Nai*, Cassandra, *tha ertho tora*," Stefanos said, sounding agitated. "Sorry, I have to go, we can talk later." He hung up.

A minute later my cell phone rang again, flashing the 608 dial code from Ithaca. It wasn't my mother's phone. I slid the screen to accept it. All I heard was static. I attempted to call it back, but it was busy. At that moment, the trolley came to a screeching halt. All the passengers turned their attention to a traffic jam on the road, our driver yelled out a slur of profanities from the driver seat; more drama on the Athens trolley. My day wasn't going very well at all.

Before I headed up to my apartment I wanted to see Eleni. A warm feeling of appreciation filled me knowing I could count on her advice and her friendly face.

But that's not what happened. Eleni swung her door open, her forehead creased with worry, her eyes were downturned, appearing somber. Nikos sat on the couch with a similar expression behind his yellow glasses. They glanced at each other. I had walked into something heavy.

"What's wrong?" I asked, my heart in my throat. "Did something happen?"

Eleni glanced at Nikos again then turned her attention back to me. Firmly she said, "Your mom."

I smiled, relieved but still confused. "I just talked to her this morning. She's worried about Molotov cocktails."

"Your neighbor in Ithaca called, Ava *mou*," Nikos interrupted. "Mandy."

"Mindy," I corrected him. I winced. "Mindy called?"

"From a hospital," Eleni added softly.

Before she could explain further I asked, "What hospital?" I remembered the missed call from Ithaca while I was on the trolley.

"Mindy try to call you but she said there was no

signal. I tell her you were on the bus or metro. *Telos panton*, your mom give her my number too."

"I'm confused. Hospital room. Mindy?" I demanded. "Is my mom okay?"

"Ava, she was in a car accident," Nikos blurted out.

"What?" My hands started to shake. "My God, is she okay?"

"She's okay," Nikos said quickly, "but she's had a concussion."

Before he continued, I began to cry. The full brunt of my not being there hit me. I was three thousand miles away from my mother. I was all that she had, and I had abandoned her. My insides knotted up in pain.

"What happened? What did Mindy say?" I reached for my purse thinking about grabbing my cell phone, but my hands shook so uncontrollably I dropped my purse.

"Listen." Nikos placed his hands gently on my shoulders to steady me. "Shhh." He stared at me and began again. "Mindy said that a big truck hit your mom's car. She had a concussion and was out for a while but she woke up and she has some injuries."

I blinked heavily trying to process it all. "Oh, Mom!" I called for her searching Nikos's eyes for comfort.

"Ava, she's okay. Do you hear me?" Nikos lowered his eyes closer to mine.

"Yes," I whispered. She's okay. But I wasn't there to help her. How could I ever forgive myself?

"When she woke up, she say you will be stress about it all," Eleni took over. "She tell Mindy to also call us to help you. She is too weak to call anyone."

I wiped new tears. The fact that my mother's first thought upon waking was to find a way to make things easier on me broke my heart. A wave of guilt washed over me.

"We promised Mindy we'd help you book your flight," Nikos said.

"We looked on the internet. We can try for the one that leaves later tonight," Eleni said. Nikos slid his palm down my back to assure me, but I winced from the light pressure of his touch. I'd almost forgotten about my bruise until that moment.

Nikos pulled back his hand. "What happened? Did I do something?"

All at once, the aches from my heart and from my body wore down on me. I grudgingly found the energy to lift up my shirt to show them my bruised up back.

"It was stupid of me," was all I could say.

They both gasped in unison.

"*Gamoto!*" Eleni cursed. "What is that?"

"From the riots. I kind of got in the middle of things," I explained in a small voice.

"We told you not to go!" scolded Nikos.

"Did someone hit you?" Eleni asked furiously stamping her foot. "I'll kill him!"

"No, I fell on those big marble steps at Syntagma. It's no big deal," I said wearily. I didn't care about the bruise anymore.

"Maybe you should go to the doctor." Nikos bit his lip, looking concerned.

"I'm fine, really. It's just painful to the touch. There's no time anyway. I want to book that flight and see if there is a seat left. I'll manage." My injuries felt so insignificant compared to what my mother had to be going through. "I should've been there. I have to go."

"Don't panic. We'll help you," Nikos assured.

"We go to help pack your bag." Eleni squeezed my hand.

If only teleporting existed, I could have been with Mom immediately. Actually, teleporting would have solved all of my problems. I could have the best of both worlds. Instead I had to pass the ropes to head to passport control at the Athens International Airport. I turned to say a final goodbye to my best friends. Nikos stood there with a furrowed brow and pushed back his yellow framed glasses. Meanwhile, Eleni's arms were crossed as she tapped her heeled sandal. They both waved, half-smiling. Eleni threw me the saddest air-kiss imaginable.

During the ride to the airport, I had called Amy to tell her I was going back to Ithaca to be with my mother. She wished my mom a speedy recovery and asked me to stay in touch. I tried Mom's and Mindy's cell phones, but there was no answer.

I arrived at the gate to find a disorganized line of passengers ready to board, but I felt unsettled. I tried Mindy's cell again and my heart leapt with hope when she answered.

"Ava, how are you, apple pie?" she greeted me. "Are you on your way back?"

"Yes, I am."

"Sorry I missed your call," she went on. "Cell phones need to be off around some parts of the hospital here. Don't panic. I know how you get. Did you book that flight your friends told me about? I can pick you up at the airport tomorrow morning. So don't you even worry your pretty little head off."

I managed to get a word in and interrupt her nervous babbling. "Mindy, how is she?"

"Doing okay, honey. She's too weak right now to talk. She's on a lot of medication for the pain. She has two broken kneecaps, and a broken rib, but she'll pull through, especially once she sees you. Don't you worry, honeycomb," concluded Mindy in her familiar, thick Upstate New York twang.

It was an accent I never managed to pick up. Mom always said it was because I spoke other languages. The announcement for final boarding to New York JFK blared over the loudspeaker. The line shortened quicker than I thought, but at least I would take the flight armed with the update.

"I need to board now," I said hurriedly. "Tell Mom I love her."

"I will, lollipop! Don't you panic now! Have a safe flight."

As the plane took off forty minutes later, and Athens spread out below me, I said a silent goodbye to the city that had become mine. I wondered if I was heading home, or leaving home. I no longer felt moored. I no longer knew where I belonged.

CHAPTER TWENTY-FOUR

TWELVE hours later I'd changed continents and countries, and there I was back in Ithaca, New York scanning a small crowd that gathered in the arrivals lobby of the Tompkins County Regional Airport.

"Cupcake!" Mindy's familiar, high-pitched voice sliced the air as she dug her way in front of the crowd. She walked right up to me, her round, plump body hugging mine. My nose was tickled by the top of her classic beehive like hair-do. She let go, flapping her little arms like an excited baby bird.

"Ava, sweetie, you look doggone tired!" She pressed her plump fingertips together.

Even in my state of tiredness, I had to smile at her sweet gestures that were so familiar to me. She was the only person my mom would trust to watch me when I was a kid.

I kissed her forehead. "Mindy, you're a sight for sore eyes," I said with a slight smile. "How's Mom? Can we go see her now?" The thought of her gave me a bit more energy.

"But, pumpkin pie, maybe you want to go back home and freshen up or change or rest first?" Her eyes glinted with concern. "I mean Greece is so cotton-pickin' far. I'm just worried."

I shook my head. "No. I'm fine. I really need to see her. Please?"

She regarded me for a moment, her lips pursed, before nodding. "Luckily we'll make it in time for visitin' hours if we head out now. Come on, sweet peanut. I should've known a herd of wild turtles wouldn't keep you away now. Your mother is doing okay. She's a real trooper."

During the fifteen-minute drive to Cayuga Hospital, Ithaca swept by as Mindy chattered non-stop. Early dusk began to settle on the town. The familiar rural beauty I grew up with seemed so surreal to me. I couldn't believe I was home. The picturesque oak trees and clean wide streets whizzed by. I half listened to Mindy, as we passed the historic downtown district.

There was a consistent intellectual buzz about the town. With its three universities, there were always college students and professors that elevated the Ithaca's sleepy, rural country charm. Most of the year, sixty thousand students heavily outnumbered the "townies," but I didn't mind. We headed up a road that led to the hospital, the rolling hills rose off the road and there I laid my eyes again on the gorgeous mammoth body of water, Cayuga Lake, which was the center point of my town.

At the hospital, I followed Mindy as she shuffled in front of me, leading me through the white tiled halls. My pulse raced in anticipation, wondering how Mom would be and wondering how I'd feel. We entered a room where I found Mom sleeping. An ache formed in my throat seeing her legs slung in braces that hung from the ceiling. A brace held her torso too. My heart swelled with sympathy.

"Mom!" I blurted out and rushed to her.

She opened her eyes slowly, and her familiar pale

green eyes searched my face, slowly recognizing me and then widening in astonishment. "Oh, dear, I was dreaming about you!" Her voice trembled. "It's been too long." Her short, white, curly hair puffed out like a disheveled bird's nest. She was beautiful despite her paleness. I bounced in place wanting so much to wrap my arms around her, but that wish was clearly impossible in her state.

"I'm so happy to see you, dear." Her mouth parted into a sleepy smile.

"You too, Mom," I choked out. I bent in to kiss her cheek, careful not to fall on her somehow. She squeezed my arm and managed to tap my back just enough for me to wince.

"What's wrong?" she asked.

"Don't worry," I waved off her question hastily. "Just a little bruise from falling." I certainly didn't want to explain anything about that night. "I'm so sorry I wasn't here for you."

"Accidents happen," she said with a slight nod. "Everything's going to be just fine."

"Thank God," I said, feeling most of the day's adrenaline drain out of me at last. I slouched in place. Of course, my mother noticed immediately.

"I know I'm the one in the hospital and all but, honey, you look terribly tired. Mindy, can you take my daughter home, please?"

I began to protest, but Mom cut me off. "You need to get some rest."

Mindy flung a hand on her chubby hip. "I told her!" she squealed. "Greece is too far. I said it's another continent and all. Ain't that so, cookie?"

Her foodie terms of endearment rated high in my

book.

"I just wanted to see you and make sure you're okay. I wanted to let you know that I'm here now," I said firmly.

"I know, little girl. We have a lot to catch up, and we will. Now, go rest."

"So nice to see y'all reunited again!" Mindy clasped her hands together, and her eyes gleamed with genuine excitement. "We best get going, sweet pea. Let's let your mom get her beauty sleep now."

I kissed my mom on the cheek. "See you tomorrow."

A sleepy smile slowly formed on her lips, her eyes half closed. "Glad you're finally home."

My mother's doctor updated me on her condition the next day. She was doing fine, he explained, despite the fact her car was sidelined by a horse carrier truck on a rural mountain highway. She would need a few weeks of therapy before she could get off her crutches. She would be released in a day or two.

After I devoured Mindy's famous steak and mashed potato dinner that night, I settled back into my old house eager to check my Facebook page and e-mail. First, I called Eleni at work where Nikos was probably there for lunch. Mondays were "leftover" days when Eleni's mom brought in her home cooked dishes from the weekend.

"Le Boutique," Eleni chirped.

I cleared my throat. *"E Ava eimai."*

"Ava *mou!*"

"Ava *mou!*" Nikos repeated in the background. I was right. I heard Nikos click on another line.

"How is your mom?" Eleni asked.

"She's going to be okay, thank goodness. I have a lot of physical therapy to take her to, but I'm so happy to see her. I could've lost her," I added more solemnly.

"That's great news that she's going to be okay," Nikos said.

"Tell her we think about her," Eleni said. "*Perastika.*"

"What's it like being back?" Nikos asked.

"It's a blur, really. Nothing's changed, that's for sure."

"That's good, right?" Nikos asked.

"I guess." I shrugged. "How about you two? Add some Athenian excitement to my existence *parakalo!*" I begged. "Any gossip? Did you guys see anyone?"

"Actually, you tell her, Eleni, I know you want to," Nikos started.

I pictured the grin on her face. "So," Eleni piped in, "I bumped into someone, guess who?"

"Stefanos?" I exclaimed hopefully.

"No," she said.

I twisted my lips, I couldn't care who else actually.

"Loucas!" she exclaimed after a pause.

"Really?" I asked. "How?"

"I was at G Club last night, and I saw Clara. Anyway, we start to talk and guess who joins us with his *parea* of friends but the adorable *Loucas*," she said stretching the last word as Greeks do when they tell a story they like. "He remember me from Mykonos and look around the room for you. I think he thought you try to hide from him!"

"Oh, Loukako," I moaned sympathetically then giggled. "So what happened?"

"I told him you went back to New York for a while to take care of your sick mother. I could tell he feel bad. He say he will message you on Facebook, at least."

"He's a nice guy, actually," Nikos chimed in. "Not that you should go for him, but he meant what he said, I think."

"I agree," Eleni said.

"He did nothing wrong, after all," I admitted. "There was just no chemistry on my end, so why would I bother?"

After I hung up, I prepared a mass note to everyone I cared about in Athens, complete with my American cell phone number, my Skype ID, and a few words to let them know that my mom was going to be just fine. I clicked *send* with the hope that Stefanos, whom I included on the list, would call when he saw my e-mail. Within a few minutes, my phone rang with an unfamiliar Greek number. Ah, the power of technology.

"Hello?" I answered excited that my wish came true.

"Hello, *omorfi kinezoula*," he said in his sexy Greek accent.

I sat up straight as surge of happiness ran through my core. "Hi, there," I said as nonchalantly as possible, trying to hide my excitement. "Is this my fisherman boyfriend from Hydra? How sweet of you to call me in America."

Stefanos laughed. "I'm his humble messenger. He sends his regards." In a more serious tone he said, "I just got your e-mail, and I'm so sorry to hear about your mom. *Perastika*. It's good you went back."

"Thanks, it'll be okay. I know that now."

"I'm glad you wrote me, I was thinking about you with everything that happened lately. I was worried when I didn't hear back from you."

Good, he cared. "You called?" I asked in a small voice.

"Of course."

My Greek cell phone was lying in the bottom of my carry on, completely out of battery. "That phone's dead now. Anyway, I'm glad you found me here," I said. "How're you holding up with everything?"

"It's a challenge." He sighed into the phone. "But that's life right? Isn't that what some wise beauty from Upstate New York told me once?"

I smiled and a warm feeling flowed through me hearing his compliment. Could I be falling for him already? We caught up for another few minutes before a woman's voice barked at him in Greek in the background.

"Cassandra?" I guessed.

"She is in crisis management mode. Her specialty, actually. The press wants interviews. So I must leave you, but I want to tell you something first. Do you know what *mou ellipses* means?"

"No," I said softly and very curiously. "What?"

"It's what I feel right now talking to you," he said. "I miss you."

I paused for a moment. My heart felt full. "I miss you too," I said and I really did.

The automatic doors of the supermarket slid open and I followed an employee with a FoodBazaar nametag that said *Bob*, out onto the parking lot on a warm summer day. He pushed my cart happily, continuing to whistle as he unloaded groceries into my rented car.

A month had passed and I had gotten back into the swing of things in Upstate New York. My new routine involved taking care of Mom, who had astonished doctors with her strength and speedy recovery. In between all of my TLC, I had kept in touch with Nikos and Eleni with sporadic Skype calls and exchanging pictures and texts on Whatsapp and Viber. I held a new appreciation for the world of apps. I even steadily kept in touch with Stefanos the same way.

The quiet pace of Ithaca seemed like such a contrast from European city life. FoodBazaar was the size of ten tiny supermarkets in central Athens. There were no happy whistling Greek *Bobs* to help me with my groceries either. I had loaded up on healthy food, except for a few bulk items like anything with peanut butter. I really wanted to drop a few pounds I had earned in Greece. But real American peanut butter, how I had missed it. In any case, things were looking up. After all, Upstate New York certainly wasn't known for Greek food. And there wasn't much in terms of night life since I happily spent every night supporting Mom.

I reached into my purse where I had a stash of Twizzlers. Okay, besides peanut butter it wasn't exactly diet-friendly, but I had missed them too. I popped one in my mouth and munched thoughtfully.

"I hope you have a nice day," Bob the bag boy said cheerfully. I smiled at him. There's nothing like good old American Twizzlers and friendly Upstate New Yorkers.

I drove off. Even after being home for some time, I continued to experience bits of culture shock about the openness of America, the big parking spaces, and the big cars, including the huge rental Ford Taurus I was driving. Legal parking options were endless. People wouldn't dream of *not* picking up after their pooches. Ah, and speaking freely, in American English, without thinking twice.

As for Mom, the pain killers kept her in bed much of the day. When she was up and about she always reminded me, in some form, that she was thrilled I was home.

I'd been catching up on American TV shows, tending Mom's beloved garden, and even sewed the scarves I wanted. I made a gorgeous blue one for Mindy. I also took on a special project and made a few outfits for her precious shih tzu, Chewbacca, as a thank you gift for helping out with my mom. Mindy yelped, clapping her hands when I presented Chewbacca's new yellow velour jogging suit. My blue sailor shorts were next, I just needed the inspiration.

I drove up to the house and sighed. While it was great to be with my mom and see her through her recovery, I couldn't help but miss my friends and the chaotic life that continued on in Athens without me. I walked in with the shopping bags, plunking them on the kitchen table. Mom stumbled in on her crutches.

"How was FoodBazaar?" she asked with a smile.

"Like usual, it's too huge for me now. Is it me or did they double the bulk aisle since I moved?"

She stabilized herself and sat down at the kitchen table. "You always had a thing with that candy isle ever since you were a kid."

"Mom, you need to rest," I said, taking in her tired eyes. "Why don't you head back to your room?"

I busied myself with unloading the groceries, and a moment later, I realized that my mother was still standing there, watching me. Her brow creased with concern.

"What's wrong, Mom?"

"I just want to say something." But clearly she couldn't. Her hands trembled slightly.

"What happened?" I dropped a box of cereal on the counter and stepped toward her. "Do you need your pills? Is it your rib?"

"I'm just so happy you're back," she blurted out in a wobbly voice. "Doesn't it feel good to be here?"

I bent down to kiss her on the cheek and hugged her slightly around her neck, careful not to touch her torso. I took a step back to look into her eyes as they glistened with emotion.

"Sure, Mom," I said softly. "What, what's the matter?"

"Maybe you can stop by the university to see your old colleagues!" She perked up suddenly, surprising me with her change of voice. "You've been taking care of me and all, but you should go reconnect with your old life, Ava."

I had been avoiding doing that, but I kept it to myself. "Okay, I'll go," I stretched out my last words, throwing her a skeptical look.

Her upset face reared itself again and she turned away from me.

"Mom? Is something else wrong?" I sat down at the table.

She inhaled. There was something very wrong. "There's something I want to tell you. Since you're home and you're getting things done slowly, I thought maybe..."

"What?" I asked as if I was scolding Wen or Ru after they misbehaved. I thought for a moment. "Don't you dare tell me you called the university to ask for my job back."

My mom was notorious for interfering with my life.

Whether it was about friends, dates, or test scores, she tended to include herself in my decisions, probably to protect me. Making a call to the university marketing department wouldn't be out of character, even if she was drowsy from painkillers.

"It's your dad," she blurted out.

I froze. I hadn't seen or heard from him in twenty years. *Twenty years*, I repeated in my mind. A shot of grief hit my heart with the mention of that word, *dad*. Did I even have one anymore and what could he possibly have to say?

CHAPTER TWENTY-FIVE

I NARROWED my eyes, feeling my pulse race faster. The tips of my fingers tingled. "What about Dad?" I asked slowly; apprehensively awaiting her response.

My mother looked down at her hands, and I had the feeling that whatever she was about to say was going to change everything.

"He came by," she said quietly.

My stomach flipped in disbelief. "When?"

Mom paused and tapped her fingers on the table. Her eyes searched mine before she gazed out the kitchen window. She couldn't even look at me!

"He came a week before the accident, a week before you came home. I was shocked to see him after so long and, well," she murmured as her eyes turned again to focus on the pleats of her nightgown. "He wanted to see you, but I told him you were living elsewhere."

"He knows I was living in Greece?" I asked anxiously.

"No, I didn't know what to say. I thought that was it. I didn't think I'd hear from him again, but he called today, while you were at FoodBazaar."

"He did?" A sudden numbness took hold of my body. That was the last thing I expected to hear about my father.

"He asked for you again; he said he'd heard you were home."

"Why didn't you tell me?" I demanded quietly. "Why didn't you tell me when he called the first time?" Emotion rose up in my chest practically burning me. I grabbed the corner of the kitchen counter tightly with both hands, my teeth clenched.

"Don't be upset," she cried. "I didn't know if you'd want him to know you live in Greece or what you're doing! I wasn't sure if you'd be coming home and now you're here. He was determined to see you, though, so I figured I'd tell you just in case he happened to drop by against my wishes."

"Stop trying to protect me," I snapped furiously at her. "I'm thirty, now. You don't have to fight my battles for me anymore. I never asked you to." I looked out the window at the trees swaying in the afternoon wind. The sun brightly shone as it did in Greece. Silence fell between us. I swung around and glared at her. "Set it up. I want to see him."

"Are you sure about that?" she asked with doubt in her voice and fear in her eyes.

"This is my one chance. I never had a chance all these years and lately, to tell you the truth, thoughts of Dad have been killing me since Greg left. I don't know why, but I need to see him." I looked straight at her with as much confidence I could muster. "It's my only chance."

She sighed heavily. "Oh, dear," she breathed out placing her fingers to her lips. She looked away from me. "In that case, there's something else you need to know."

She slowly pulled herself up and balanced on her crutches to hop back into her room. I stared blankly at the orange tiles on the wall. What else could she possibly have to tell me?

My mom teetered back in on her crutches. In one hand, she clutched a tattered Reebok shoebox, which she placed on the counter. "These are yours." She lowered her head.

I approached the box and then opened it to find a small bundle of cards secured with a thin, beige rubber band. I pulled out a baby pink envelope, worn with age. My name was printed on the front, addressed to me at my house. I pulled out a birthday card—from my father.

Dear Ava, Happy Birthday. I miss you, Dad.

My heart stopped.

His squiggly, sloppy script came back to me. The date scribbled on the card was fifteen years ago, my fifteenth birthday. I looked up at my mother to find her eyes glistening. My mouth opened but I was completely unable to let out any words. My heart beat furiously and as I snatched the next envelope, my hands started shaking again.

This one had a return address, *José Martin, 555 13ᵗʰ Ave. Long Island City*. I'd always imagined he was living on Long Island where he grew up and I was right. My mind began to fly backward questioning the past and all the times I visited Long Island for weddings, bachelorette parties, and visits with friends.

Was each time a missed opportunity to find him?

I pulled out the card inside the envelope, velvety with a kitten on the front. The date proved it was meant for my eleventh birthday. The same words are printed inside.

Dear Ava, Happy Birthday. I miss you, Dad.

I slammed it down and pick up the next one. A different address, *José Martin, 43 Donovan Lane, Wantagh, NY*. Still, Long Island. I easily read the postmark:

December 28, 1995, just a few days before my fourteenth birthday. I tore it open. The next card took my breath away. There was Snoopy on the cover chasing a butterfly. Underneath it was the same message:

Dear Ava, Happy Birthday. I miss you, Dad.

I threw it back down in the box as if it burned my fingers. I shot another glare at my mother, my heart brimming with confusion. I threw my hands in the air and found myself screaming at the top of my lungs—so loud, my throat scratched from pain. "Mom, these are all from Dad!"

Mom shut her eyes tight in reaction. "Yes."

"You kept them from me?" I demanded, still screaming. I threw the box with all of my strength at the window. My mom cried, lowering her head, as it knocked over a ceramic vase. It crashed to the ground and shattered loudly. "Why?"

"To protect you," she yelled back. She was letting out anger too, but I didn't think she had the right.

"How does hiding something like this," I raised my voice above hers and hastily picked up the box, threw it down, and stamped my foot on it with all of my strength, "protect me?" The cardboard crushed under my sandal.

"He has disappointed us so much," she said hastily. "Ava, you know that. I didn't want you to feel what I felt with him. You deserve more. You deserve better!" Her hand clasped the counter for balance, the other reached out for me.

"But all these years, I thought he'd forgotten about me. I thought I was nothing in his life." My throat ached from my anger. "You know how I felt," I cried. "How could you do this to me?" I gritted my teeth anticipating her answer, my jaw almost in pain from the force.

She remained speechless.

I shook my head in anger. "How could you keep these from me, Mom?" I asked more calmly after a few moments. "He had his goddamn address on these cards, Mom! He wanted *me to know* how to find *him!*"

She leaned heavily on the counter over me. "You can't possibly understand what he did to us, Ava." Her voice was deep and gloomy.

"I understand very well and I understand what it means." Anger and annoyance erupted within me again. I waved my hand in the air to make my point. "You *shouldn't* have kept this from me all these years. Do you have any idea what this did to me? How this made me feel?"

"You are my world, my everything," she stammered. Her eyes were wet with tears. "I just wanted you to be happy, to live without dealing with someone who can only disappoint you."

"You mean *you*. You. You. You!" I pounded my fist on the hard countertop and pulled my hair in frustration. "You weren't protecting me. You were protecting yourself."

"You don't understand." She tried to reach out for me again.

I stepped out of her way and stomped towards the door. I turned around and said in an icy voice, "Make sure he comes. It's the least you can do." I slammed the porch door behind me and marched down the street, and immediately knew where to go.

Within minutes, I sat at my safe place. My oak tree

never really grew as big or tall as other oak trees around her, but when I was a kid, she always had the steadiest stouts of branches. I always came to her when I was distraught, or when I just needed time to think. I even had my own special spot: three branches up, facing the water.

My eyes weighed heavy as I watched the faint clouds change shapes against the blue sky. In front of me, the vast lake sat so calmly. The tree-coated hills gracefully dipped down to the water's fine edge. The sharp hum of locusts interspersed with the cyclic sound of the lapping lake water. Everything was the same as always.

I relaxed into place, realizing how I had missed my old spot. I buried my face in my hands, rubbing my temples. A million questions filled my mind making me wonder how I got to this moment. Could it have been that I was subconsciously waiting for my dad to return home to Ithaca for all these years and that's why I never left? Even without his address, I could have tried. He was on Long Island, after all, just like I'd always suspected. Had I made a conscious choice not to look for him, to disappear into the void he'd created? Did Greg fill that gap in my life?

A flock of ducklings plodded past me and dip one by one in the water. Their mother waited patiently for them, making me wonder if my father had been waiting patiently for me all these years too.

The house was quiet when I returned. I tiptoed past my mom's room knowing she would be taking her afternoon nap.

I had decided to forgive her. How could I blame her for wanting to keep disappointments out of my life? She needed to stop controlling me, that was for sure, but she raised me by herself and tried her best, without any help, to do what she thought was right. I crept into the kitchen and found a note in my mom's neat cursive.

I only meant the best for you. I'm sorry.

Your father will be here in a few hours, at 9.

I stared at the word "hours." All of these years and now, somehow, it had come down to hours. I slouched. I didn't know what to expect but I felt hopeful. My *father* wanted to see me in a matter of *hours*.

I stood at Mom's open bedroom door where the late afternoon casted an eerie blue light through her open window. As I was about to turn away, I heard her stir under the covers.

I stepped in the room. "Sorry to wake you. I was trying to be quiet," I whispered.

"I can't really sleep well anyway," she said, her voice thick with sleep. "Come here, honey."

I sat down next to her and turned on the bedside lamp. She took my hand.

"You were at the lake?" she asked.

I nodded. "I thought about what you said." I placed my other hand on top of hers.

"I understand why you'd be mad at me," she said. "I suppose I always had a selfish part of me not wanting to expose you to him. But I think there was also a part of me that knew I might be doing the wrong thing."

"I remember how it was when he left," I told her. "I remember how it hurt me, and maybe because I'm struggling now from this disappointment with Greg, I understand how much it must have hurt you. Otherwise, I don't think I'd be so calm now saying this to you."

Mom shifted in place.

"I realized, even though he was living in the same state, that he never came by, he never called," I continued. "Letters are one thing, but making the real effort to be with your only child..." I paused and bit my lower lip. "Well, he's the adult. And he didn't make the effort, did he? All those years."

Mom cleared her throat. "He's making the effort now, I suppose." She winced making it seem hard for her to admit that.

"So, you called him?" I asked.

She nodded. "He's going to Rochester tonight and will stop here on the way. He explained that his license has been revoked—too many DUIs, he said—so a friend will drive him and wait for him outside. I won't be in your way. That is, unless you need me."

"I'll be okay," I said quietly. "I can handle this."

"You've been handling a lot of things on your own." She raised her chin slightly. "I see that now."

"More than I thought I could." I gripped my mom's hand tightly this time; I still couldn't hug her like I wanted too. We sat for a moment and looked at each other before I got up. "It's almost five, so I'll start dinner. Actually, I can't believe I'm saying that."

"What do you mean? It's almost dinner time." She threw me a strange look.

"Did I ever tell you Greeks eat dinner at ten?" I asked. "Five o'clock feels like lunch time to me now."

"You've become Greek," she said with a soft smile.

I thought about it for a minute. "No," I said finally. "I think I've just become *me*."

After she devoured my version of *manitaropita* or Greek mushroom pie, Mom retired to her bedroom and promised she'd stay there so that I could have some time alone with my father.

I examined the living room, straightened the pillows on the couch, and readjusted the picture frames so they were all straight. Each photo showed my mom and me together, smiling and laughing. Regardless of what had come and gone, she was my only real family. She was the one who raised me, even if she made mistakes along the way.

My father would knock on my door, the door to his old home, at any minute. I fingered my *mati* necklace thinking that I had been dreaming about this moment, always wondering if our reunion would ever actually happen. *What if he disappointed me again?* It was five after nine. He was already late by five minutes. Then the thought rushed to me. What if he didn't come? What if...

The doorbell chimed and cut off my trail of worries. I walked to the door, took a deep breath, smoothed out my skirt, and inspected myself in the hall mirror. There I was, Ava Martin, about to be divorced, a daughter to Penny, a native of Upstate New York. I was thirty and about to meet the man I've thought about every day for the last two decades.

Perhaps I wasn't so confused about who I was after all.

"You can do this," I whispered to my reflection. I took another deep breath and opened the door.

CHAPTER TWENTY-SIX

I'D remembered him as much larger. I supposed when I was a child, he had loomed over me, larger than life. Yet there he was slight, meek.

Our eyes met as he looked up from the bottom of the steps. He hastily pulled off a dark blue baseball cap and shifted it between his wrinkled, dry, and scabbed hands. He stopped for moment to smooth his thinning black-and-gray hair, which was combed over the top of his head. A thick, worn leather belt held his outfit together, a red plaid workshirt tucked into a pair of dark blue Levi's. The belt also seemed to hold his frail body in place. His deeply tanned skin didn't appear to be the kind one earned by sitting on the beach.

I examined his round face, shaped just like mine. The difference was the wrinkles that drooped down the corners of his eyes, the fine lines on his baked skin. I shot of pity ran through my chest. He had had a rough life, and it was a life I didn't know a thing about.

"Dad," I finally said with a nervous gulp, my hands shook slightly. I mentally told myself to stop shaking.

"Ava," he replied.

I shut my eyes for a second, hearing his voice. I couldn't believe it. He smoothed his graying, small black mustache and glanced down as his eyes started to well with tears.

We both stood there, frozen. I wondered what he

thought of me, how I looked, how he thought my life was over the past twenty years based on the few minutes we had already shared. I somehow picked up the energy from his distress and my pity rose even more.

I moved aside. "Come in," I said softly. "Please."

"Thank you." He timidly walked up the three steps that separated us. He paused at the green plastic grass doormat and scraped his soiled tan construction boots before he stepped inside.

I was locked on his every move, noticing how his eyes were just like my own in color and shape.

He moved slowly around the living room as we entered. "The house is like I remember," he admitted shyly.

"Sit, please." I pointed to the sofa with an open hand. Like my mom always said, I resemble my father. I also inherited his nose and even his lips. A sudden cough from him startled me to snap back to reality.

"Do you want something to drink?" I offered quickly.

"No, no, thank you." His eyes became downcast as he spoke. "I...Ava, I don't know where to start." He looked at me as he placed his cap on the coffee table.

"Me neither," I practically whispered. There was silence.

"You look so pretty, so grown up," he finally said.

I met his gaze but he glanced down to the floor before looking up again.

"You look so much like my parents."

"Really?" I perked up eager to learn something about my heritage.

He straightened his posture a tad, beaming at my positive reaction. "You definitely look like them both. I wish I had pictures to show you but," he glanced down again, and his cheeks became flushed, "I don't."

There was silence again between us. I swallowed hard, not knowing what to say next.

"I know it has been too long," my father began again, cautiously. "I'm glad you finally decided to see me. I wrote you all these years."

"I know," I said. I didn't see a reason to tell him that my mother kept the letters from me. That was between me and her.

"Lately, Ava...Well, I needed to see you."

"Why now?" I asked.

"My life has changed a lot." He placed a hand on his knee and smoothed his thumb repeatedly over his jeans. "I just completed one year of AA. You know AA," he trailed off nervously.

"I know AA."

"One of the steps to sobriety, Ava, is to make amends to the people we've harmed."

I waited, holding my breath.

"I've harmed you, Ava. I, I never meant to, but I did. I don't know how to make it up to you, but I won't rest until you forgive me."

I studied him for a moment, until an answer poured into my heart. "I already do," I said.

He stared in disbelief. "You do?"

I took a deep breath and felt an enormous weight lifted from my shoulders. "It doesn't mean I'll forget what has happened between us, or how much it hurt. But I know I have to forgive you if I ever want to move on. So, I forgive you."

It was as simple as that. But he didn't seem to know what to say. After a moment, he blinked a few times and changed the subject. "So, I have some work now. I paint houses for a friend's family business in Rochester. I'm doing good and maybe I'll move there for the work, you know." He picked up his cap off the coffee table to cup its hard brim. "I might move from the island where I'm living with my third cousin, uh, well, I guess you don't know him. Billo. He's waiting round the corner for me because I can't drive, but he's got work with me too, you know, painting houses."

I nodded as I took it all in. Already, my newfound feeling of peace created an overwhelming feeling of security inside me.

"I'm glad you've been successful with AA," I said with as much encouragement as I could express.

"Yeah, I didn't think, well..." He paused as if he was thinking of what to say next but then settled with, "I'm glad too." He paused again, then said, "And you? I don't know anything about you. What is your life like, Ava?"

I looked down at my hands clasped in my lap. I blinked and prepared myself for a second to dive in. "Well, I had a big, crazychange in my life this past year. And I can't know for sure what's going to happen next." We sat there in silence for a long minute.

"Why?" We asked at the same time. I motioned for him to continue.

"No, you," he said. "Please tell me, why is it crazy? Your life?" His voice was laced with concern.

"Things didn't work out in a relationship I was in," I said.

"Oh, sorry 'bout that," he replied.

I couldn't bear to tell him I was married. It was too much to explain. Being vague was safer. "So, I've been living in Europe."

"Wow, Europe," he exclaimed tightly, his lips

forming a half smile but he looked impressed at the same time. "Where?"

"Greece."

"Really? You were living in Greece?"

"Almost a year," I said, nodding my head.

"You're a free spirit. Your mom and I freaked out when we had to move to Upstate New York from Long Island, before you were born." He let out a tiny chuckle. It seemed like he'd recalled a nice memory of their youth together. I wished I could see it. "You turned out to be a world traveler. How ironic. So you're back in Ithaca now?"

"I'm not sure yet," I said slowly. "I have a lot of decisions to make."

"As long as you're happy." He paused thoughtfully. "Not like I'm so good for advice, but I always wondered if you're happy. You should be happy."

"Thanks."

He opened his mouth slightly and then closed it.

"Did you, uh, want to tell me something?" I asked.

"So this is it," he said with a sigh. Both of his hands squeezed his cap. "I've practiced this in my mind, what I'd say to you. What I'd say," he repeated and his body elevated and deflated as he breathed. "I just don't know why it's so damn hard now," he admitted raising his voice slightly, clearly annoyed he couldn't say what he wanted.

He let go of the cap again and placed it next to him. He rubbed his face before he continued. "What I mean is that I don't know if I'll have this opportunity again, to see you again, especially if you are off to Greece. You have every right not to want to see your old man," he said then let out another deep breath.

He slouched over as if defeated. At that moment, I couldn't imagine my mother and him together today. I thought about the old photos of them, where they smiled and held hands. My mom so fresh and blonde and a whole head taller than my dark haired dad, but they were happy and seemed like a perfect match. As he sat across from me, he seemed so far from those pictures. He was more of a man with a sunken spirit. Their marriage was destined to fail, even without the alcohol. They grew into two different people on two different paths. Just like Greg and I were. Relationships weren't so idyllic like I had thought and dreamed they should be. There was another reality that was okay as long as I was okay with it.

My father glanced up and closed his almond shaped eyes tightly for a quick second.

"I've made mistakes." His voice quivered which sent a tingle of emotion down my spine. "I didn't want to disappoint you with my drinking, and your mom and I...Things are changing now, I'm getting older and I want to be responsible and well, I hope it's not too late."

He stood up and reached in the back pocket of his jeans to pull out a crinkled white envelope with my name scribbled on it in black marker. He looked down at the floor as he handed it to me.

"It's not much, maybe it's almost pathetic, but I'm saving up. I don't know what you're doing with your life, or if you'll want to tell me one day. I'd like that, Ava. But right now, I want to give you something."

I clutched the envelope. "I don't need anything," I said firmly.

He blinked and shook his head. "I want to. I mean, I *have* to," he stuttered. "Making amends and all. It's part of that, all right? It's okay if you don't call me or talk to me again. I've just been working toward this moment for a long time, and I wanted to offer you something."

I opened up the envelope and pulled out a wad of bills. He wanted to give me money.

"I thought it was silly to just hand you five hundred dollars but maybe you can do something with it and it would be from me."

I tucked the flap to close the envelope and laid it down on the table. I didn't expect this. "Thank you," I said. It was not enough to make up for the years that stood behind us, and clearly he knew that. He knew, as I did, that no amount of money could wash the mistakes of the past away. But maybe, I thought, everything that was taking place wasn't about the past. Maybe it was all about the present and the future too.

"I thought of presents and flowers and the things that girls like, jewelry and stuff, but I don't know you," he said after a moment. He started to cry lightly, which took me off guard again. My throat became thick with emotion, not knowing what to do. I didn't know if I should comfort him or just sit there and watch him as his thin, arched back rocked up and down in sorrow and sobs. He buried his head in his hands but I didn't feel comfortableapproaching him, so I didn't. The distance between us was too great. "I'm sorry that I don't know you," he finally said, his voice trembled.

He pulled out a blue handkerchief from his jean pocket and wiped his face. Then, he pushed the envelope toward me. I stared at it thinking how he must have really tried to save to be able to offer me it. My chest ached. I felt sorry for him and sorry for myself. Sorry that our lives became so distant. We sat in front of each other, a father and his daughter who both wished they knew each other, but just didn't. Was it really too late to reconnect? I didn't really know, but I wanted to take my own step to try.

"Okay, then, if you put it that way." I choked back my own tears again as I took the envelope off the table. His face relaxed slightly, his lips turned up so he wasn't frowning any longer.

The motor of an old car that pulled up outside filled the small silence that followed.

"That must be Billo." My dad got up. His voice was strained and unnaturally high pitched. "We need to make it up to Rochester."

"Yeah, you should get going now." I got up too. We stared at each other for a long moment. Neither of us moved.

"We got to go to work real early," my father said, interrupting the silence. He nodded his head slightly, looking proud. He picked up his cap and added, "I got to be on top of things. I'm trying to live better now."

I followed behind him to the door. He turned around as if he wanted to say more.

Instead, I said, "I never expected this. I don't know if we can have a relationship because it hurts," I said holding the envelope. "This is just all so surreal."

"I know," he admitted. "I'm just real glad you didn't mind seeing me. I know this can't make up for all these years." He opened the door and stepped out into the night. "Your mom has my number, and maybe we can talk when you're ready. It's up to you, Ava. I don't want to be a burden in your life. I have no right."

Something inside pushed me to step forward and hug him. He returned the gesture. As his small arms encircled me, I took in an unfamiliar smell of some sharp cheap cologne and cigarette smoke. My cheek brushed against his thinning hair, which was crisp and hard with gel.

"You are beautiful, more so than I imagined," he said shyly as he released me. He walked down the last steps then turned to look up at me, his puffy creased eyes drooped. He got into the passenger seat of the old blue Toyota parked on the street. A Latino-looking man in a baseball cap was driving. My father waved to me, and I waved back. Then, the car pulled away.

I watched the car as it choked some exhaust down the road, but my dad didn't look back.

My mom's crutches dragged on the hardwood floor. "I couldn't sleep," she said.

"Mom," I whispered, barely able to move, barely knowing how to reach out to her with my heavy head and my heavy heart. Mom stumbled toward me, bravely set the crutches against the wall, and hopped over. Then the warmth and comfort of her arms enveloped me. These were the arms that held me all my life no matter what I needed. I couldn't even recall what it was like for my dad to hold me. Was it ever so familiar, so comforting, like this? Did he ever hold me like this at all?

My mother balanced herself against me to keep from falling. She was careful to keep enough space between us as not to put too much pressure on her torso but she managed to hold onto me tighter with a secure grip that also gripped my emotions as tears rolled down my face.

"It's okay," she whispered.

A strange numbness began to sweep over me. I didn't know what to feel about my father.

"Get some sleep, honey," Mom advised gently. "We can talk about it all in the morning."

There was no other choice, no friends to go out with to distract me, no clubs to temporarily house me, and no drinks to buy to drown my tears in. It was just me and Mom, like it had always been. Somehow, though, I felt different. I didn't want distractions; I didn't need to call Nikos and Eleni, and the thought of drowning my sorrow in a mojito seemed so frivolous.

It was ten o'clock, but I eagerly climbed into my nightshirt and slipped quickly under my covers, my mom silently watching my every move. She tucked me in and smoothed the blanket over me as she balanced herself on one crutch. Finally, she brushed my hair aside and tilted her head in adoration.

"You'll always be the number one person in my life," she said. "I wish things could've been different for you growing up. I'm sorry for any choices I made that hurt you."

She didn't wait for my reply. She grabbed her other crutch, shut the lights off, and closed the door. I heard the echo of her movements as she entered her own room and by then I was half asleep.

I settled my head between my hands looking at Eleni and Nikos in my laptop screen.

"How do you feel?" Nikos asked.

"I'm shaking a bit still." I shifted in my seat then

clasped one hand inside the other in my lap. "But it also gave me some closure, you know? He's had problems. That was obvious. We couldn't get specific and it was awkward. I don't know how else to describe it."

"But you see it was not about you?" Eleni asked, pushing Nikos aside to take up more of the screen.

I paused, and then nod in agreement. "It wasn't about me. It was about his shortcomings."

"Like Greg," Eleni said. "We're proud of you. Bravo."

"It's a big step in your life to confront him." Nikos shoved himself squarely back in the Skype shot.

"You guys never quit." I shook my head and grinned. "I didn't actually confront him, but I got answers. I know now that life doesn't work out as you think it will and I'm okay with that."

"Great," Eleni said firmly.

"So you'll see him again?" Nikos asked.

"I'm thinking about it. I don't know what I want to do. I need time to think."

I rested my elbows on my desk again as I peered at my friends through the screen. I wished I was there with them, somewhere in Athens, eating *souvlaki* or drinking a coffee and watching the city go by.

"We're off to *bouzoukia* tonight," Eleni said wearily. "Another name day. It won't be the same without you."

"*Makari*," I said wistfully wishing I was there too.

"Still practicing your Greek means you're coming back," Nikos concluded.

"At some point." I shrugged my shoulders. Whether it'll be to stay or visit, I still wasn't one hundred percent sure.

"Did you hear back from Amy?" asked Eleni.

Amy and I had Skyped last week while she was in

Hong Kong. I said hello to the twins too. I felt terrible letting them down by leaving in such a hurry, but Amy understood perfectly, and for that, I was grateful.

"She says that she and the boys will stay in Hong Kong for the summer, and they probably won't return to Greece. There's some big promotion that Ambassador Wu is in line for, and it won't be in Athens. But she says she'll recommend me to some of the other diplomat moms if they need an English-speaking nanny."

"There are other things you can do too, if that doesn't work out. We'll help you," Nikos offered.

"Take all the time and be close to your mom," Eleni advised with a serious tone.

"How's Stefanos? Did he call you again?" Nikos asked. "I took photos of the repair job at the hotel when I passed by. It's a mess still."

"We Whatsapped the other day," I said. "He's still trying to figure out some things with the hotel. He says I should come back to visit for the summer once my mom is okay."

The truth was I thought about him every day, including details from our date-trip. With everything so uncertain in my life, I had resolved that there was no use to lead him on. I changed the subject easily. "Anyhow, have fun tonight." I glanced at my alarm clock and quickly calculated the time in Athens. "It's eleven thirty! *Piyene tora*, you'll be late!"

"Midnight, late?" Nikos asked. "You forget your Greek culture already."

"What are you going to do tonight?" Eleni asked.

"Staying home with my mom, like usual. We have a doctor's visit tomorrow. She's doing really well. She should be off the crutches soon."

"Send her our regards, Ava *mou*," Eleni said, her red lips kissing the air.

"*Filakia*, we miss you," Nikos added, waving goodbye.

I waved back. "Me too." I signed off and as I got up from my chair to get ready to leave my Skype account rang. I turned, expecting that Eleni would be calling back with another piece of hot gossip. Instead, Greg's name and his smiling Skype photo flashed across the screen. My chest tightened.

Should I ignore it? I wondered. A little green icon showed the truth, that I was indeed online. I made a mental note to switch that thing off. It kept ringing and I continued to stare until it stopped and a text popped up.

Greg Brown: *Are you there? I've been trying to call you but your phone is dead. Did you change numbers?*

I took my seat again. My hands felt strange and heavy as I started to type.

Ava Martin: *I'm not in Athens.*

Greg Brown: *Where are you?*

Ava Martin: *Ithaca.*

Greg Brown: *I'm in Manhattan. We need to talk. I can come up tomorrow after this conference.*

I stopped, and my skin tingled in an icy way. It was the last thing I expected him to say. The darn Skype phone rang again, Greg's smiling photo flashed before me again. I shut my laptop. That was it. I didn't have room for him in my life. No more complications. Whatever he needed to tell me, he could tell me by e-mail.

CHAPTER TWENTY-SEVEN

"I'M crutch-free. Time to celebrate at Teakwood," Mom said later that afternoon, as we returned home from the doctor.

I cringed at her use of the word *celebrate*. I realized she didn't remember that a year ago, I was celebrating something very different. It was my one-year wedding anniversary, a fact I had been keeping to myself. Since I was doing so well there was no need for a discussion with Mom. I did wonder if that was the reason Greg tried to Skype me yesterday, to acknowledge our anniversary. Or maybe he was trying to send me the divorce papers. It was weird to think we were in the same country, same state. I brushed my thoughts aside; I needed to concentrate on the people who care about me, not the people who had walked away.

"Well?" Mom asked, snapping me back to reality.

"Teakwood! Right. But don't you remember? Tonight I'm going out for dinner there with Trina and Kay. They're back from vacation."

Trina and Kay were my two former co-workers at Ithaca State. I was finally ready to do something other than hang out with mom and Mindy and her little dog, Chewbacca.

"Ah, yes, to talk about getting your job back! Yes, go, go!" She shooed me with her hands. "We'll go another time. Just bring me back some chocolate cake," she said excitedly. "I'm so glad that you're home for good, honey."

"Mom," I started, wanting to explain that I hadn't made up my mind but I couldn't bear to. She had just gotten off her crutches and she wanted chocolate cake. "I need to go get ready," I said instead.

"I'm glad your mom's better," Trina said picking up a piece of bread from the basket on our table at Teakwood later that evening. "I always knew she was made of steel."

I had worked with Trina for three years in the university marketing department. She moved to Ithaca after she married a chemistry professor named Bob Dylan. The funny thing was that her husband resembled and even sounded like his namesake folk rocker. Trina hadn't changed her short cropped short hair, and still wore loud, bright colors, which suited her gorgeous dark complexion.

"She must be so glad to see you after that mess with Greg," Kay Smeadley chimed in. "What a complete jerk he was!"

I met Kay when she moved to Ithaca for grad school. She managed the admissions office, which was right next to Trina's and my own. Both women knew about Greg and me from the beginning. They were pretty much my only two friends when I was living here, but I had barely talked to them since I left for Greece. I wondered what that said about our friendship, but they seemed supportive and genuinely interested.

Kay put down her water and nodded, "I agree. I think

that's great that you stayed in Greece, even though Greg left."

"It looks like you made a life for yourself there with your new friends," Trina said. "In so little time too!"

"You guys would love Nikos and Eleni. We go out, there's amazing nightlife, and the islands, and the men." I winked at them. "That's another story."

"It's amazing you live in Greece," Kay said wistfully before stamping her salad fork on the table. "I want to hear about *the man stories!*"

Just then, a waiter stopped to take our drink order.

"Wine, ladies?" Kay asked.

"I'll have a daiquiri," Trina ordered.

"I'll have red wine," Kay said.

I had no desire to drink any alcohol. I wondered if that would change. "A sparkling water."

"You have to tell us more about Greece," Trina said after the waiter departed. "I mean it's so boring here."

"So are you staying there? Or what?" Kay asked.

"I'm sure your mom wants you to be here," Trina suggested.

I nodded. "My mom wants me back for sure. She thinks we're—" I pointed a finger amongst us "—talking about me getting my old job back."

They glanced at each other and smiled. They knew.

"And with the stuff we see on TV, the riots, is it true?" Trina asked.

"The crisis is serious. My best friend's business is going downhill, and my other best friend is out in the riots with a gas mask taking photos and dodging Molotov cocktails. Another friend's hotel caught on fire during a protest, so he's dealing with the damages and other bureaucracy." There was a hollow feeling in my heart when I mentioned Stefanos. "I know the awful sting of tear gas and I don't even protest," I concluded. "But I still love it there."

Trina and Kay glanced at each other then both turned to me.

Kay sighed. "Yep, my life is definitely boring. Did you know they're still cow tipping out by State Route 96?"

"Doesn't sound safe," Trina said. "The riots. Not the cow tipping."

I laughed. "Actually, it isn't so bad. I mean, things happen, but I see it as an honest place. Athens just has this crazy charm. It's like everything is a mess, but once you figure it out, it's your own mess and you love it. Does that make sense?"

"So you can't leave the mess," Kay concluded. "If the mess makes you happy, I'm happy you're in the mess."

"I have to say I love the mess. That's why I think I have to go back."

"Whatever you decide, you should feel good about it. Go with your gut. Your gut is never wrong," Trina said. "If you think a marketing job at the State University of New York at Ithaca is it—make it happen. But if you decide that Athens is your new home, then you need to go back."

"I don't know what to do." I sighed.

I thought I knew where my heart belonged. It was just a matter of getting my brain to agree.

Two hours later, I started my walk home happily swinging my mom's doggy bag of chocolate cake the entire way. Mom was waiting for me outside, and I grinned at her as I approached. "You really want your cake, huh?" I teased her. I bounded up the steps and swung the plastic bag up between our faces, realizing that she wasn't smiling back.

"Ava, he's here," she said bluntly.

"Who?"

I turned around to see a rental car parked across the street behind me. The thought of my father crossed my mind for a second. *Maybe he wanted to tell me something more?*

"Greg," my mom said plainly.

I took a step back, my pulse racing quickly. "Greg?" I asked in disbelief.

"I let him in. He came ten minutes ago, and he said he'd wait. I was just about to call you but he asked me not to. He said you arranged to see him, so I didn't know what to do." She pursed her lips and threw her hands up in the air.

My heart dropped. Greg was in my house. After all of this time, I had no choice but to see him.

"Did you not arrange to meet?" she asked after a moment, narrowing her eyes

"No, Mom, we didn't. What should I do, what did he say?" I started to panic.

"Ava?"

I heard Greg's voice as he stepped out behind my mom.

"I'm okay, Mom," I lied.

"I'm here if you need me," she said and turned back into the house. She peered out of the creak of the door until she shut it, leaving us alone. The whole time I could feel Greg staring at me.

Greg's eyes sagged at the corners and faced me with a downcast expression. He was wearing his hair a little longer so it was a bit wavy. I couldn't help but think he was just as handsome as I remembered him. I took a big step back.

He slid a hand through his hair. "Your mom told me about the accident. I'm sorry you went through that. It must've been a shock." He placed his hands on his hips.

"Thank God she's okay now." I tried not to look at him

"She looks good. *You* look good," he added in.

He looked good too, but I kept that to myself.

"I didn't want to tell you that I was coming because, well, I didn't know how you'd take it. If I'm in New York and you are too, I thought it's now or never."

What did he mean? I perked up trying to understand him. "Now or never, what?" I narrowed my eyes.

"I want to tell you what I've been thinking."

"What have you been thinking?" I gazed at him skeptically. There was a part of me that was dying to hear what he had to say, and another part of me that just wanted him to walk out of my life forever.

"Do you remember what today is?" he asked.

"Of course," I said. *How could he think I'd forget?*

Greg gazed at me for a moment then reached out to touch my shoulder. I stood there.

"I've been thinking about you a lot since I left four months ago, and to be honest I couldn't file the divorce paperwork," he said softly. "I know it was the right decision to have the separation. It made me realize that I *do* want to be alone now. I think I'll feel that way for maybe another year or so. That's just where I am in my life. But maybe we could be together in the future. I want to believe that we have a chance. So what do you say, Ava? Let's commit to that chance on this day: our first anniversary."

My cheeks began to warm up fast. *Was he kidding?* My body tingled with adrenaline. I pulled away from his touch, fuming.

Something snapped in me. I raised a finger at him. "Number one, it was *your* decision for us to separate," I said coldly. "You never asked me. Number two, are you seriously telling me you want to stay married while you live the free, bachelor life for the next year? Third, do you think I'm going to stick around waiting for you to see if *maybe* we have another chance?"

"That's a lot of points," he said, his tone nervous and unsure. He scratched the back of his head, and then stroked his chin with his hand.

"And to say all these things on our wedding anniversary?" I continued. "Are you kidding? What a damned joke!"

"But," he attempted weakly.

"Greg, you're thirty-two, but maybe you're going through some sort of early midlife crisis. I can't see any other explanation for why you'd be standing here saying something so arrogant and delusional. Unless, of course, you're exactly the kind of *malaka* my friends all think you are."

"What's gotten into you?" His mouth fell open, and his eyes widened. "*Malaka?* I don't understand what you're saying, Ava."

"I'm saying that you're ridiculous," I said, feeling a sudden calm settle over me. "I'm saying that in all the months we've been apart, all I've heard from you are wishy-washy, commitment-phobic promises. I'm saying that you've put me down, and you've hurt me. And you know what's worse? The fact that I let you treat me that way, and I let you make me feel that way. But you know what? I was a good wife. I'm a good person. The only problem is that I married a selfish asshole."

Greg jerked his head back, unable to let out a breath.

"I have my issues," I continued. "And I have problems that I'm sure contributed to trouble in our marriage. But I'm wise enough now to know that I'm good enough to leave you. I'm moving on, Greg. You should too."

I felt woozy, but at the same time, my head swam with a kind of delirious high. I hadn't realized I was ready to say all of those things to him yet. Parts of my tirade, I hadn't realized I felt until the words were out of my mouth. But there was not a single thing I wanted to take back. For once, the ball was in my court. And I had decided that we were no longer playing this game.

"But I came up all the way from the city," he finally said. He was still staring at me. "I just figured we'd make up, and you'd come back with me."

"Well, you were wrong," I said. "You've been wrong about a lot. I've changed and so have you. I definitely don't want to be around for the next change you might feel."

"It's in people's nature to change, Ava. Love doesn't change though. I still love you."

They were the words I was dying to hear four months ago, but enough time had passed and the words only made me groan in disgust. "Please, just go and let me know what you want to do with the divorce papers. I suggest you file them." We were both silent long enough to hear crickets chirp in the distance.

"So, I guess you want me to go?" he finally ventured.

"Greg." I looked straight at him this time. "I want you to go. Now." My throat closed up with the finality of it all, but I gulped the sorrow back down.

"You can't mean that," he said raising his arms up in disbelief.

I shook my head. "I mean it, Greg. I want you off my porch and out of my life."

"After all we've been through?" He sounded a tad desperate.

He reached his hand out to touch my arm. I jerked away and started walking down the sidewalk towards his car. He followed me a moment later. He fell into step beside me, and we walked silently side-by-side across the street. When we reached his car, he stood in front of the driver's side door, staring at me. I crossed my arms and realized just how hard my heart was beating. I was doing the right thing.

"I'm sorry it ended this way," he said after a long silence. "Maybe I'll see you again when I come to New York." His tone was apologetic, sad. I kind of expected an arrogant comment or two but he just seemed defeated. He shifted his eyes away from me for a moment. "Like I said, we should be friends."

"Just go, Greg," I said softly, putting my hand up to my forehead and looking away at the road ahead.

But he didn't move. "Should I fight for you?" he asked after a moment. "Is that what you want?"

I tilted my head slightly. "It's too late," I said. "Goodbye, Greg."

He glanced off to the side. I turned around and walked across the street, back toward my mother's house. Behind me, I heard the engine start. I wanted to look back, but I didn't. Instead, I walked into the house and shut the door behind me. My mom was sitting by the open window with a book in her lap.

"Don't tell me you were really reading that." I smirked.

"Of course I wasn't. How could I eavesdrop efficiently while reading a book?"

I laughed and held her flattened doggie bag from the restaurant. "Here's your cake, although it's probably a chocolate pancake by now. You can thank Greg for that. He really pissed me off."

"I heard," she said. "And what I heard made me proud of you."

"Really?"

"I never would've imagined you would want to see your dad and now you just faced Greg unexpectedly after everything he has done to you. Did you mean what you said out there? You really don't want a second chance with him?" Her expression was doubtful as she crinkled her forehead.

I slumped onto the couch. "I'd like to believe he's not the same person I met, but was he always that clueless and I never saw it?"

Mom came to sit next to me, and I rested my head on her shoulder.

"You were in love, my dear." She caressed my cheek. "We do crazy things for love."

I exhaled deeply, concentrating on that thought. The past year was indeed crazy, but I wouldn't change a thing. Things had to be falling into place somehow. Everything would be okay.

"He came on your anniversary too," she said. "I'm sorry I didn't remember."

"I'd like to forget it too." But then I thought about

all I had learned in the last year, and the many ways in which I've changed and grown. "On second thought, no. I can't regret the marriage because it led me to this point in my life."

"That's the right way to think. You'll move on. You'll start over fresh."

I pulled away and searched her eyes with all seriousness. "Wherever I want?"

Mom shifted in place and perked up slightly. "What do you mean, honey?"

"I mean, if I decide to move away from Ithaca."

"You mean go back to Greece?"

"I mean anyplace but here."

She turned away. "To do what?"

"To live, to work, to play, to meet people," I said softly. "You know what a single thirty-year-old newly divorced woman would do anywhere."

"But," she said warily.

I waited for her to continue, but she didn't go on. Finally, I said, "Mom, I'm more secure than you imagined I'd be, right? I'm really okay now. I'm *okay*."

She blinked. "You're saying you don't need me?" Her eyes shone sadly.

"I need you." I hated how I must have been making her feel. "I hope you'll always be there for me."

She rolled her eyes. "What's wrong with Ithaca?"

"Nothing, it's perfect. It's beautiful, quaint, and full of memories. I know the people and the streets. It's a part of who I am. But I want to see what else is out there. I know now that I can do it on my own, and I'm excited about that."

She swallowed hard. "What can I say? It's going to take some getting used to, but how can I argue with you? I'll support you in whatever you do."

She didn't look so sure. "Are you just saying that, Mom?"

Then, she leaned in and said, "You know I'm not happy about you leaving again, but the truth is, I want you to be happy."

"That means the world to me." I wrapped my arms around her neck loosely and came as close to her as I could without placing pressure on her chest, smelling her lavender shampoo.

"The world is yours," she whispered in my ear. "I'm just sorry that I've spent so much time trying to make you forget that."

CHAPTER TWENTY-EIGHT

I REMEMBERED feeling the cool waters of Cayuga Lake enveloping me and surrounding me, the water stinging my eyes as I scanned the murky lake water. Then the crystal-clear blue-green of Greece's Aegean Sea washed in around me, taking over and swirling about me. My heart started to leap in confusion and fear as I struggled to reach the surface of the water. It was all a strange colorful dream that jolted me out of bed—literally. I fell off the side and landed with a thud on my carpet. My arms and legs felt incredibly sore, as if I really had been swimming for hours. I glanced at the red digits on my electronic alarm clock. It was only six o'clock, but I knew I wouldn't be able to fall back asleep. I was conscious, my head was too full of my father, Greg, and the decisions that I needed to confront.

I sat on the floor spotting my old sewing machine in the corner, the one I'd learned on years ago. Suddenly, I knew what I needed to do. I dug through my suitcase to pull out the half-finished sailor shorts I'd started in Athens. I was determined to finish the project.

After a few hours and after a few tries on the inseam, I finally got it right. A sensation I hadn't enjoyed in a long time tickled my fingers. I drummed my feet on the carpet as I hand-sewed the last ivory button onto the front panel of the shorts.

"Perfect." I spread the shorts out on the desk before

me, admiring the contrast of the ivory buttons against the navy twill. I would have to pass the last test. I slipped them on easily; they fit like a glove.

I paired them with a simple white T-shirt and light blue flip-flops. I checked my reflection in my full-length mirror. My curves stood out in a good way. I walked into the kitchen where Mom held a mug of her morning coffee with *The Ithaca Times* spread out on the table. I twirled around.

She lifted up her reading glasses. "So those are the new shorts. I thought I heard you on the machine. Come closer, dear. Those buttons are gorgeous." She examined them with interest. "They're fantastic," she said. "Did you find these at the sewing store downtown?"

"No," I told her. "They're from an Athenian antiques shop. Aren't they unique?"

She put her glasses back on. "You've come far in sewing, Ava. Shorts are pretty hard to do. I think you like challenges more than you know."

I gave her a kiss on the cheek. "I've got to run."

"Where are you off to this morning, honey?"

"Cayuga Lake," I said, recalling the dream I'd had that morning. I grabbed my red rucksack from the counter and placed my iPad inside. On my way out the door, I felt my mom staring at me. She knew that I was going to "my spot" to think. She knew very well that I was determined to make a decision by the time I would come home that night.

Within minutes, I arrived at the tree. I sat there, rested my head on a branch, as the Upstate New York summer heat surrounded me. The lake was purely still, as if it was waiting for me, waiting to hear my decision.

Greg was a thing of the past, I realized. My mom

would be just fine without me. My father would be here if I chose to see him, but that decision was mine. My life was no longer about pleasing other people; it was about pleasing me for once. The bottom line was that I was on my own, and I was okay with that.

I thought for a while, gazing out at the lake and the crystal sky. Finally, I jumped down from the tree and walked to the water's edge to see my reflection. Was I the same girl who left a year ago? Same face, same frame, same smile, but I had changed. Then, in the reflection, a yellow butterfly swooped by. I looked up in time to see her flit across the lake, just out of reach. She headed for the horizon, and I wondered if that was my sign.

I took a long walk through the Ithaca Commons, a square in the middle of downtown Ithaca, where I ordered a big American filter coffee from Starbucks and sat down on a bench to sip it and watch the world go by. My mind wandered to summertime in Greece. August was just around the corner and the entire country would be on vacation. If I went back, I'd be there just in time to join my two best friends. I thought about what amazing adventures we would have and that made me smile. As for Stefanos, he'd be there too. That thought filled me with a strange peace.

For the next few hours, I poked in and out of shops. As I took another break to eat a cheeseburger I chewed my food slowly, slumping my shoulders and longingly gazing out at nothing in particular. Without the bustle of my mom's medical needs, no work, and a pretty much dead college town, I wondered what there was for me to look forward to in my hometown.

I glanced at my watch calculating the seven-hour time difference. It was about the time Eleni would be opening up the shop. If I caught her on Skype, I could show her downtown Ithaca. I walked down to the center of the square, where some teens skateboarded among a few college-aged couples snuggling on benches. I propped myself up on a ledge, logged onto the city's Wi-Fi network and Skype-called Eleni's cell phone.

"Ava, perfect!" she said when she answered. "Nikos is here so we'll log on the video and Skype you back!"

As I waited for their video call, I took in my surroundings. The square was small and quaint, a place where I made so many memories of my life. Right across stood the old fabric shop where I bought fabric to sew the first dresses I ever made for some of my old dolls. My mom used to take me to Miller's Candy Shop after a satisfactory report card. As a teenager, just like the skateboarders, I sat on those benches wasting time with friends, who all eventually moved away. I used to think I'd live here all my life. But I had changed, and maybe my ideas about where I belong had changed too. My Skype rang.

"*Geia sou*," Nikos said brightly as I answered the call. He pushed back red glasses that filled my iPad screen.

"Ava!" Eleni pushed in beside him. "We miss you."

"I miss you guys too!"

"Where are you?" Eleni asked.

"I'm sitting in the famous Ithaca Commons," I said quite proudly, holding my shoulders back. I picked up the iPad and swiveled it around to show them.

"It's nice," Eleni complemented.

"How come people aren't wearing cowboy hats?" Nikos asked seriously.

I frowned for a moment, and then I realized what he meant. "Oh, because I said it's a cow town?" I chortled.

"It's not that kind of a cow town!"

Nikos scratched his head, seeming perplexed, but before I could elaborate, Eleni cut in.

"Something's changed, with you," she said. She peered into the screen closer as if decoding my thoughts through the Internet. "You look different."

"I feel different. A lot has happened since we talked last."

"Did your father return?" Eleni asked.

"No, but Greg did," I said.

"The *malaka*?" Eleni asked and seethed at the same time.

"Why?" Nikos asked.

"He's in New York City on business and he drove all the way up here to tell me that he wants to start over again."

"So, you're back together?" Nikos asked in a cautious way. He glanced briefly at Eleni before looking back at the screen.

"Is that what you think?" I asked with disappointment.

"We both know how heartbroken you are, even though he never treated you right," he said almost apologetically. "So are you together?"

I smiled at them. "No. In fact, in your words, Eleni, I told him to get lost."

They both broke into a smile at the same time, their postures relaxed.

"I think I even called him a *malaka*."

Eleni hooted with laughter and Nikos exclaimed, "*Bravo!*"

"Do you feel good about it?" Eleni asked after a moment.

"I absolutely do. I'm still hurt, of course, but I

can't have him dictating my life on his terms. I'm not going to take anything for granted anymore," I said triumphantly.

They cheered again.

"I learned a great Arab phrase the other day to comfort my friend Leila," Nikos said wistfully. Good old Nikos's words of foreign wisdom.

"This is actually a good one," Eleni chimed in.

"The phrase says that when a cherished person walks out of your life, you shouldn't feel sad, because that only means someone else just as valuable will walk in," he said profoundly.

"Beautiful," I responded. "I love it. Did it work on Leila?"

Nikos adjusted his frames again and threw me a toothy grin. "We have a date Friday."

"*Bravo*," I congratulated him. "I need to feel happy and I think the experiences I've had the past few months with you both and the people I've come to know in Athens helped me see that. I'm going to focus on me for a while. That's what I've decided."

"And so you're coming back to Athens?"

Before I could answer, I heard a deep male voice cloaked in a Greek accent a few yards away. I turned to find someone holding up his cell phone to a confused-looking teenage skateboarder. I started to lose my balance on the concrete ledge.

"Um, did you almost just fall?" Nikos asked.

"Yes," I exclaimed in a high-pitched voice. My pulse quickened and I shook my head for a moment as I gained my composure. My eyes started to feel hot with emotion. "But there's a good reason."

It was him—Stefanos Danos. I blinked a few times

to make sure he wasn't some sort of mirage, but no, it was *him*. His back was turned to me, but I would know that voice, that posture, those gesticulating hands anywhere.

"What is going on?" Eleni asked.

"Guys," I said as I leaned in toward the screen, "you won't believe who is standing here in the middle of Ithaca, New York."

"Show us!" Nikos demanded.

I grinned at them, and then I swiveled my iPad around. A second later, I heard Eleni gasp, so I turned the screen back around.

"Did you see?" I asked.

Eleni bounced up and down in place with a huge smile plastered on her face which elevated my feeling of excitement and made *me* bounce up and down with a huge smile plastered on my face. "You'd better go!" she said.

"*Piyene* but call us back," Nikos said.

"Okay." With my fingertips tingling, I turned off the iPad and hastily placed it in my bag. I swung my hair back and said a little prayer hoping I looked decent. My heart pumped a bit madly. And at that moment, Stefanos turned in my direction, following the pointed finger of the skateboarder and our gazes finally met.

He cocked his head slightly in his classic Greek George Clooney way and looked at me before he called my name, raising his hand. "Ava!"

"What are you doing here?" I stood ready to hug him. Before I could act, he folded me into his arms and pulled back to study my face. I continued to stare in disbelief.

"I'm looking for you," he said with a sweet smile.

"I'm glad you found me."

"You look gorgeous," he whispered in my ear. He placed his hand on my cheek and leaned in to kiss me, slow and sweet. I closed my eyes savoring the moment. Finally, we pulled back and gazed at each other. My Greek world met my American world.

His eyes bored into me. "I've been wanting to do that for weeks."

"I can't believe you're here," I said feeling breathless. "How did you find me?"

"I was actually on a mission."

"Do tell."

"I went to see my son in Toronto. A certain smart and beautiful New Yorker reminded me that it's up to me to make things happen," he said.

"Wonderful." I squeezed his arm. "I'm proud of you. How did it go?"

"It was great. We had a long talk. Even with everything that has happened in Athens, I couldn't make more excuses, plus it was his birthday." He looked down briefly then back at me. "I decided to take a flight down here before I take my flight home to Greece from JFK tonight. It's at midnight, so I don't have much time but I wanted to see you, even for a little bit."

My heart sank, he would leave sooner than I would like. "So you're just here for a few hours?"

"Is it enough time to get a coffee?"

"I think so," I replied. "So your mission is complete?"

"I also wanted to tell you one more thing." He looked at me for a moment. "The thing is I don't know if you are coming back."

"I'm staying." I tilted my head and looked up at the sky for a moment, realizing that I was announcing what was in my heart. My decision was finally crystal clear.

"Oh." He winced.

"No, I mean, I'm staying there." I nodded with a smile.

"Wait. Where?"

I laughed. "Athens," I clarified.

His face brightened considerably. "So you're coming back?"

I nodded confirming further that I was making the right decision—my decision. "I can always come back to the States if it doesn't work out, but I'm going to try it and figure out my life from there."

He beamed. "Ava, that's great news."

"I have this summer to find a job and if I can make it work, why not?" I continued. "I don't know what's in store for me, but my mom is supporting me, I have great friends there, and my heart is there now, above all else. My marriage may have ended there, but it's also where my life is beginning."

We were both silent for a moment. He leaned in to kiss me softly.

"I have good news, then," he said when he pulled away. We sat on a nearby bench. "My friend wants to interview you for a job in Athens."

I gave him a double take. "Really?" I asked. "A nanny position?"

"Actually, it's more in your field. He runs the Olympia Hotel and is looking for a marketing specialist who speaks native English. I recommended you. I don't know if it will lead to anything, but it's a good start."

I beamed at him. "I can't believe you did that for me." It was a sign. My decision was meant to be.

"I want to help you." He squeezed my hand.

"Why?" I asked softly.

He looked at me for a long moment. "Because there's something special here, Ava. With me and you. I want to see what can happen, and I hope you do too."

"I do."

He smiled and the corner of his eyes crinkled. "Come on," he said. "Are you going to show me around your town?"

I laughed as we stood up and began walking toward the shops and restaurants that lined the downtown streets. After a moment, he turned to me and said, "You look gorgeous by the way. *Poly oraia podia.*"

"I have nice legs?" I translated, beaming.

"Are these the shorts you were working on?" He gestured to my newest creation.

"I finally finished them," I said with a nod. "Today."

"Well, then," he said simply, "we have much to celebrate."

An hour and a half later, Stefanos and I sat side by side at the Ithaca Diner, watching our waiter approach us with giant slices of pie and cheesecake. My mouth watered as he placed them next to our coffees.

I glanced at my watch, knowing that Stefanos had to leave in a half hour for New York to make his flight back to Athens. He had suggested going to see my mother while he was here, but we'd both agreed that the limited time was for us. We'd be back in Ithaca again soon if the relationship was real.

"I plan to visit my son in Toronto again in the fall," he said. "Perhaps you'll join me, and we can drop in on your mother too."

I agreed with a smile, liking the sound of planning a future with him—a future that included my mother and his child. Family, I realized, should be at the center of everything.

After we were done with our meal, I called for a taxi to take him back to Ithaca's airport.

As we walked out he took my hand. "I'm glad you've decided to try out Greece for a while."

"It makes sense and it doesn't at the same time," I said. "That's where I am right now, I guess."

"When will you come back?"

"Soon," I promised. "I miss my home."

He smiled. "So, I'll see you there, in Athens. Just in time for August. There are many other things I want to show you in my city."

"I'd be glad to see them."

The cab pulled up much faster than I expected.

"I'll be waiting for you." He kissed me gently on the lips. I closed my eyes. He'd be waiting for me. It was all I needed to know.

He squeezed my hand and got into the cab. I waved as he pulled away.

CHAPTER TWENTY-NINE

"**S**UGAR loaf, do you have room in your bag for this?" Mindy held up a Ziploc bag of her famous pound cake. "I think it'll get squished, but it doesn't matter; it'll still be tasty."

"Definitely." I placed it in my laptop bag. I couldn't say no to Mindy's desserts, although I had eaten my fair share over the summer. I kissed her on both cheeks without thinking. "Thanks for everything."

"Oh, those European kisses, on both cheeks. It's kinda funny, huh, sweet pea?" She giggled enthusiastically, making me grin. "I like it!"

The last time I said goodbye to my Ithaca family was exactly a year ago. Mom and Mindy had come to the airport to see me off. Greg was waiting for me in New York City to take the flight to Athens. At the time, there was no fear of what the future would bring because Greg and I would be a team. Or at least that was what I'd thought. Standing there again, I didn't know where life would take me, and I felt one hundred percent okay with that.

I turned to Mom and examined her carefully. Rather than looking sad, she looked proud. Her eyes gleamed and a knowing smile spread across her lips.

"You know y'all have the same exact smile," Mindy cooed between us.

I laughed. "Do we?" I certainly didn't resemble my

mom, but I was just like her at the same time. Probably more than I knew.

"We do." Mom pulled me into a hug. With the pain mostly gone from the car accident, she finally could.

"I'll leave you two alone," Mindy said. "Safe flight, honey pie!"

Tears started streaming down my mom's face as soon as Mindy walked away. "We are an emotional family, aren't we?" Mom managed to chuckle.

"Thanks for understanding me," I said, beginning to cry too. "Something is telling me that I need to go back to Greece and sort out my life there. It's how I feel. I need to follow how I feel. But I'm sorry I'm leaving you."

She pulled a tissue from her purse. "I know you'll be fine," she said softly as she dabbed the corners of her eyes.

"I will. I'll be back often. I promise."

She placed her hands on my cheeks, her eyes searching me carefully. "This isn't easy," she admitted, gritting her teeth. "I need to let go of you. Again."

"I'm always here for you. I still need you."

A pause lingered between us. She looked away, and then back at me.

"I've been thinking about how I've tried, your whole life, to protect you from things I thought might hurt you, things I've known that hurt me, like your father," she said apprehensively, lowering her gaze for a second. "I'm sorry for that. I realize now that I should've been more honest with you. I should have let you handle things on your own, make your own decisions." She searched my face, her lips pursed downwards. "I worry that by trying to protect you, I hurt you myself."

"Don't worry. I understand why you did it." I took

her hand in mine. "I think seeing Dad this summer was a good thing. But I also understand that maybe he didn't have a place in my childhood. Either way, it's too late to undo the past. We should move on."

Mom wrinkled her brow, throwing me an uneasy look. "I won't hide anything from you anymore. Know that."

"Do you think he'll call about me again?"

"I don't know." She looked down.

"I'm okay either way."

Mom's face softened slightly. I thought it made her feel better to hear that I was prepared for the fact that my father might let me down. She called her attention to my neck and adjusted the chain of my *mati* necklace gently. She then smiled sadly as she lifted her gaze to meet mine. "Promise me you'll be safe."

"I will." I squeezed her hand tight. "Thanks, Mom, I love you." My throat tightened up.

"I love you too." She wrapped her arms around me. "Go," she said through her tears. She patted my back gently as we let go of each other.

As I walked toward the security line, away from her, I knew that there was nothing left to say. I distanced myself knowing she understood why I was leaving. She understood who I had become.

I turned to wave once more, and then I rounded the corner to take the first steps into my new life, and I didn't dare to look back.

FROM THE AUTHOR

If you enjoyed reading *Chasing Athens*, please take a minute to share your thoughts and leave a review on Amazon, B&N, Goodreads or on your favorite book review site. Reviews are essential to a book's success because they are the best way for readers to discover new books. Thanks for your support!

ABOUT THE AUTHOR

Born and raised in New York, Marissa Tejada is an author, freelance journalist and travel writer loving expat life in Europe. You can find out more about Marissa by following her on Twitter, Facebook, Pinterest, Instagram, Goodreads or through her blog and website at http://www.chasingathens.com.

www.ingramcontent.com/pod-product-compliance
Lightning Source LLC
Chambersburg PA
CBHW071231250626
47163CB00001B/126